WAYS TO DISAPPEAR

WAYS TO DISAPPEAR

◉

VICTORIA LANCELOTTA

stories

FOREWORD BY CRISTINA RIVERA GARZA

FC2

TUSCALOOSA

FC2 is an imprint of the University of Alabama Press

Inquiries about reproducing material from this work should be addressed
to the University of Alabama Press

Book Design: Publications Unit, Department of English, Illinois State
    University; Director: Steve Halle, Production Intern: Brooke Lindell
Cover image: Amine M'siouri; unsplash.com
Cover design: Lou Robinson
Typeface: Baskerville URW

Publication of *Ways to Disappear* was made possible in part thanks to the
generous financial support of the Jarvis & Constance Doctorow Family
Foundation.

Library of Congress Cataloging-in-Publication Data is available from
the Library of Congress.

ISBN: 978-1-57366-201-7
E-ISBN: 978-1-57366-903-0

for S., who made sure I'll never find them all

Contents

Foreword

◎

Cristina Rivera Garza

"Here is a Sunday afternoon that will disappear like the rest of them, that will dissolve like sugar in water, like salt," says the narrator of "You Are Here," the short story with which this wondrous book first invites us to share a radical experience with time. Here it is, right before our eyes, this Sunday and a pile of Sundays, just as they were for them, the young couple about to embark on their first adventure. But "they will not remember," the narration states and insists, again and again, less as a reproach and more as statement of a fact, meticulously listing the myriad of details crowding other Sunday afternoons: the first pizza, the condensation on a window, a baby's petal-pink hands, the five inches of April snow. If the young couple coasting the car off their parents' driveway is destined to forget "the beating heart of everything waiting for them," who or what is remembering right now, bringing us to this *here* that is hurtling through time? Who or what is peeking over the shoulders of this young girl and this boy, following them closely as they come together and in love, and later, as they become parents and part ways, perhaps forever? Who or what guards their daughter as she quickens her pace, reporting on the unknowing way in which she wears the face of a father she hardly knew? Writing tells what the state conceals or erases, argued Argentinian writer Ricardo Piglia. Writing, he'd add, is a stateless society. In a fast-paced world marked by the feverish rhythms of a capitalist production prone to crush bodies and territories alike, no one has time to remember. Experience vanishes into thin air. Those who, against all odds, reminisce, run the risk of becoming Lot's wives, suddenly turned into pillars of salt. But in this alternative society which is literature, we can transport ourselves through spirals of time, learning that the past is always about to occur and the future precedes what we became. We can, in this alternative society, conjure memory and restitute the wholeness of time. We can be fully there and fully here, aware at last, although obliquely, of our interconnectedness with both others and with the past. By gifting this concentrated attention on what the state forcibly discards, compelling us to forget and forego, the shimmering stories included in *Ways to Disappear* remind us that experience remains, relentlessly and materially, embedded within ourselves, and without.

The *here* of these stories is many *heres*, all diverse and yet uniquely linked to the landscape of the United States: gravel driveways, dimly lit motel rooms, 24-hour supermarkets, multilane highways, sparsely furnished apartments in precarious neighborhoods where women forcibly learn their place. The dwellers of these *heres* make minimum wage or receive checks from the government. They are withdrawn teenagers, vulnerable brothers and sisters, stray husbands, fearful mothers, girls who barely have a chance to be anything at all. They go through existence with little understanding of what happens to them and around them or through them, but their stories, the stories they are destined to forget, invariably bear the imprint of gender and class injuries.

Coupling and uncoupling, they learn lessons about love and sex that are best forgotten. But do they? In pieces such as "As Though I Have a Right To," a narrator hidden behind the mask of the first-person plural insists on recalling scenes of domestic violence not as an individual but as a collective experience—a methodical imposition of a masculinity mandate so generalized as to become the norm. "We love those unpretty boys . . . . Our mothers didn't care as long as we came home, and as long as when we did we did not carry back into their houses with us some joy or fear or wonder that they had never seen or heard . . . . We fucked the boys to punish them. We made them disappear . . . . We loved the sound of their begging voices, thick with shame every time and every time vowing, swearing, on their mother's life on their grandmother's grave that it would never happen again . . . . We let them lick the bruises they never meant to leave . . . . They broke us like kindling, like matchsticks for the bridges they wished they could burn."

"I say we as though I have a right to," says the community we become as we read ourselves within this we.

Material objects abound in these stories, gloriously described in utmost concreteness. They include features of the landscape, elements of urban design, and a long range of commodities whose brands, flickering in a memory that is transnational, remind us of the reach of US imperialism: Viceroy cigarettes, Wrangler pants, bottles of Jack Daniel's, fast food, mushy white bread. These commodities betray, of course, the class origin of most of the characters, illuminating too their diets, their health, their precariousness.

Textured, enveloped in sinuously sensual sentences, these objects are memory condensed.

Disappearance is a word Latin American literature never takes lightly. Military regimes and authoritarian governments alike have historically disappeared citizens deemed as unruly. During the so-called War on Drugs, hundreds of thousands of poor men and women have disappeared in Mexico only. To be precise: they do not disappear; they are forcibly disappeared. Similarly, the disappearances explored in these stories—intimate, carnal, perfunctory—sprang from a murderous system that relies on the erasure of memory and on compulsory forgetfulness to discipline bodies and break spirits. For as in the world at large, in the United States, "we didn't understand how much so little could cost." Could it be that, in remembering together, we'll place ourselves in the position of reactivating the potency these stories embrace and shelter?

WAYS TO DISAPPEAR

You Are Here

Here is the couple, the girl in the boy's car, three in the morning with the windows open and the headlights off, coasting the full length of her parents' gravel drive, the trees high and close enough above them to black out the blue and moony sky. When the gravel turns to hard-packed dirt the boy throws the car into gear and the girl turns the radio on; when the dirt lane widens at the highway's mouth they swing a wide turn east to follow the moon that is brighter and rounder than any they've seen, that is already lying. The boy pops the tab from a can of beer and the girl peels licorice laces from a sticky cherry wrapper and the pinpoint of road at the horizon is deeper than any galaxy. In two hours they will stop at a Pilot to fill the tank and use the restrooms. They'll buy bags of powdered-sugar doughnut holes and Fritos, Mountain Dews and strawberry Yoo-Hoos and Camel Lights with cash the boy amassed, dollar by five and week by month, from the greasy paper bag on top of the toolbox where his old man keeps the prescription pills he deals at the VFW.

The girl is fifteen years old. She has an angel's lips and a snake's tongue and a baby who moves like a moth inside her. The boy is seventeen. That is all he is, so far.

Here is the town that is smaller than their desire but big enough for a motel overlooking the exit ramp, U-shaped with a railed walkway outside their second-floor room. To the left is the highway that flows like black water, to the right is the traffic light that marks the line of town, beneath is the rusting roof of their car, above is velvet sky. They are closer to it, here.

The motel rents by the week at a reduced rate, rooms with kitchenettes and salvaged café tables in them, linoleum floors that curl at the seams. The bedside tables are gouged and scarred; the carpeting smells of mildew. They prop the door open with a chair and ferry their belongings up from the car: two duffel bags, a backpack, a cardboard box with softening edges, the top flaps tucked secure. This pile in the middle of the floor is a bigger wonder to them than a pyramid, and they fall on the bed, legs twined, breathless, until the girl nudges the boy up to close and bolt the door.

Here are the rough sheets, and the blanket, thin and too narrow for the bed, the pillows they fold and wedge under shoulders and hips; her legs smooth and his covered in soft dark hair, her rounding belly pressed to the slick concavity between his hip bones, their puppy breath. Here is the jut and dip, here is the imperative. They sleep in the starry glow of highway lights and wake to a candy sun that burns lemony through the thin curtains, and the blurry words they whisper back and forth are halfway between plans and promises.

The girl stocks the cabinets with boxes of cereal and cans of soup, crackling packages of noodles, bags of discount candy. The boy walks to the convenience store for soda and beer, and the amputee who works the register does not ask for ID. His left arm is furled and delicate and peters into a slender and fingerless tip below what passes for an elbow. He bags efficiently, and with grace. His own son is a titan, a potentate, a captain of industry; broad of shoulder and smooth of jaw and despairing of ever touching his lips to the beautiful skin of his wife's twenty-five-year-old brother. When he can, the amputee slips packages of peanut butter crackers into the boy's bag before handing it over to him.

At night the boy smokes cigarettes on the motel walkway, shirtless, pale as the crescent moon above him, and the girl sits in the open doorway, legs like ribbons stretched across it, and the highway that delivered them to where they are snakes dark and almost silent to the places they still dream of. The traffic light at the intersection flashes yellow and the spindly pines stab black at the resting sky and where they are is the beating heart of everything waiting for them.

They believe this. They are too young not to.

◎ ◎ ◎

Here are the weeks and months, the mornings breaking grayer and the rain falling colder and the clouds sinking thick, the ground crusting over with rime; here is the screaming baby, her eyes hot slits and her balled fists plums, her mouth wide and wet and livid; here are the baby's grandparents who are no longer looking for their son and daughter, who refuse to speak their names, who are careful not to sit in the same pew at church on Sundays, but who cannot help but jump when they see a car that looks like the one in which their children drove away, unseen, unheard, unimaginable.

Here are the children and their sleeping baby, the three of them in bed in that room between the interstate and intersection while the snow feathers the black sky. They share a set of men's flannel pajamas, the bottoms on the boy and the top on the girl, the legs and sleeves almost wide enough for both of them to burrow into at once, plaid like Christmas paper, brand new. The girl waits tables at a chicken-and-rib shack and the boy loads pallets at a garden supply center; they keep a neat list of expenses in a spiral notebook held closed with rubber bands in the utensil drawer. The girl's handwriting is buoyant, round and looping; the boy's tilts headlong for the paper's edge.

This indicates everything, and nothing.

The door is locked three ways, knob-turn and deadbolt and chain. The girl curls her legs up under the flannel and the boy flings an arm over the side of the bed and between them the baby wakes. Her fingers wave like anemones and her eyes are riptide blue and in the silence before her cry the wind readies itself; the snow spins itself up into a silver plume. The world knows she is in it.

◎ ◎ ◎

Here is the slow thaw, and the fox that creeps through the sweet new green; wet teeth, wet fur, sharp ears and snout, so pretty in its stealth, its silence. Here is the lullaby, cicada hum and truck horn, water dripping on cracked tile and the buzz of walkway lights, the fade and crackling swell at the bottom of the radio dial: voice and static and the tin roar of applause from the stands of a dusty arena inside that metal box on the stained and listing dresser.

The girl has had enough of every station and the boy is quick to turn the volume down when she asks, if she asks. They have traded the notebook for an actual ledger, three-columned green pages bound in stamped faux leather, two debit cards and a neat stack of cash in a manila envelope tucked inside. They pay the rent on time, or early. They lean together over the classifieds and circle ads for one-bedroom apartments in neighborhoods they have driven through, yards dusty and sidewalks cracked, but yards and sidewalks all the same. On Sundays the girl holds the baby in her lap while the boy slows the car to peer at red-and-white *For Rent* flags staked in scrubby grass.

Shotgun porch fronts, brick-faced quadruplexes, signs taped to windows or balloons tied to mailboxes or creased poster boards with phone numbers markered at a slant across them. They drive up one street and down the next, slow and squinting, nothing like that first dizzy streak through the soft and rushing night, like that dark fizzing gallop into everything.

Vinyl-sided duplexes; a row of bungalows, porches sagging and paint chipping, set along a fresh-poured drive. Door after door and the rooms behind them sealed and empty; drop ceilings or dusty carpet or transom windows but each room the same in its emptiness, in its waiting for the first boxes to be set down and slit open, the first bowls put on shelves, the first coats in closets.

A rusting push-mower in a yard, a blue plastic pony tipped sideways and rigid on a walkway, eye and ear open to the quiet sky. A sandwich board by a rental office doorway: *If You Lived Here You'd Be Home Already*.

The first pizza delivered and eaten by candlelight, the first wax drippings and red wine stains on the kitchen counter; the first breakfast in bed, the bed an open sleeping bag piled with quilts on the floor and the breakfast burnt coffee from the convenience store down the street and slices of cold pizza.

The baby smacks the flats of her tiny hands on the car window and the Sunday houses float past in the pale April sun. The boy thinks about what it would be like to have a lawn to water, gutters to clean and leaves to rake; to come in from shoveling snow and drink hot chocolate with his daughter, her hair in red ribbons, her cheeks sticky with marshmallow. The girl dozes. She dreams of slipping fully dressed from bed and floating to the chipped dish on the table in their rented kitchenette, of hooking the key ring with one ghostly finger and passing like sweet pale smoke through the scuffed and dented door, of aiming the car into everything.

The first drink poured after the first caught lie, tongue and throat on fire and the sun going cold, windows clean and glittering; the first glass thrown, the door slamming and the moon going black above the howl and chain-rattle of the dog across the alley; the first fuck that hurts and the last one that doesn't.

She dreams of tires on smooth asphalt, the dark cool smell of it under stars and the fog tipping the tall grass silver; of windows open to a silence deep as the velvet sky and every bounce and jerk of the wheel beneath her fingers; of the song she can sing without knowing the words.

They pull into the motel lot and the boy takes the baby; the girl blinks and stands and stretches. It is just past noon but already the sun is giving up, going white behind the blowing clouds, a bright diffuse circle in a graying sky. The trees are bare and indifferent. They climb the metal stairs, the boy in front with the baby wrapped inside his jacket and the girl a few steps behind, one hand trailing along the rail and the other deep in an empty pocket, eyes half-closed as she drifts up after them. The boy unlocks the door and shoulders it open for the girl and the three of them close themselves inside.

Here is a Sunday afternoon that will disappear like the rest of them, that will dissolve like sugar in water, like salt. They will not remember the black-and-white movie muted on the television, the condensation on the window and the hiss of the heat pump below it, the sleeve of saltines and sticky jar of grape jelly, the peanut butter and apple slices on a plate by the bed. It is possible they will not even remember the bed.

The girl clicks the television remote until she finds a football game for the boy to watch but he turns to kiss her instead: even now he cannot concentrate on anything but her when she is this close, when he can smell her sweat mixed with the pink perfume she sprays inside her shirt every morning. The baby is sleeping just next to them and still he cannot think of anything but sinking himself into the tight soft heat of her until the room goes white and the blood roars tidal in his ears.

She shimmies out of her pants and underwear, because on this Sunday that will be forgotten she still believes she loves him— he is, after all, the one who brought her here, and if *here* is not enough—not yet, not quite, not ever—she does not yet doubt that he will bring her to another *here*, a different and better one, one she will never want to leave.

The bed squeaks as he moves on top of her. She closes her eyes and tries to conjure the glimmer and sigh of midnight in June, Libra balanced above her and new grass pressed below and every-where else his skin, warm and wet and salty on hers.

She tries but she is no magician. She opens her eyes to thin brown curtains, flattened shag carpet and walls scuffed at the floorboards. She looks at the baby struggling to free her arms from the blanket as the heater clanks and whooshes and understands, for the first time, the end in every beginning, hidden like a seed in fruit. It is still tiny but it is dense as iridium, it is already too heavy to bear, and love will never be enough to lift it.

She would split the sky if she had the breath.

Here is this Sunday in this room before the years of Sundays pile white and light and hollow, before they crumble like chalk and blow into talc-white clouds. Here are the baby's petal-pink hands, tiny flags waving semaphore to the sky she does not know yet. Here is the girl's wet cheek under the boy's warm hand and when he asks *Why are you crying?* and she says *I'm not* he does not argue because to argue is to admit and to admit is to accept: responsibility, defeat, the cold and waiting silence.

They will disappear from this room like everyone before and after them has done; they will leave less than some and more than others and none of it will matter. They will think now and then of the baseball cap with a tear in the brim or the stuffed green giraffe until they don't, and when the room itself disappears in an explosion of brick and glass and molding plaster they will have no idea of its obliteration, the girl by then in a small office strewn with schedules and order forms and mailers and the boy in the waiting room of a free clinic with a pain in his chest that he has been ignoring for days and the baby in lemon-yellow corduroy pants and a paint-smeared smock at a low sturdy table strewn with crayons and watercolors and clay in the preschool she hates to leave.

When the motel is razed they will be miles away, from it and one another. The baby will attend the preschool from eight until two. The girl will be responsible for scheduling sixty employees among four warehouses. The boy's blood pressure will be two hundred over one hundred fifteen.

Here are the numbers they will not remember: of the highway, the exit, the room; the street address of the garden center or chicken shack or bank, the three times that Sunday the girl wrapped herself around the boy while the television droned, the five inches of April snow that fell that day, or the seven hours it took to melt.

◎ ◎ ◎

Interstate, intersection, interlude.

The boy leaves because he can, and the girl is left because she is. He leaves while she sleeps and she sleeps while he drives. The baby watches: the dark and the lights sliding through it, the rise and fall of her mother's bare shoulder, the cooling expanse of her father's pillow, the breath and tick of this night. She bats her wrapped feet, and her hands, pink as empty conch shells, come furled to rest on the blanket.

Interstice, interval, interdiction.

The stars burn toward extinction above all the idiot flesh below them.

Here is the on-ramp and mile marker and exit sign; here is the fork in the road and the fork in the tongue. The regret the boy feels is bright and buoyant; he rides it like a salt swell over the crests of hills he anticipates before the tires meet them.

Here is the cold bed in the dark room, the silver windows and turned milk. Here is the wet body waking, tears and sweat, cheeks and legs, pupils wide and black and searching. Here is the mother, her acid panic and radiant fury, her howl. Here is her impulse: to throw the damp sheet off and run barefoot out into the late snow, hair snaking behind, catching nothing and leaving everything, Medusa, empty and ravenous and pure.

Here is the unburied daughter, the dead star, the white dwarf.

◎ ◎ ◎

The years unfold, bear up, become: a box, a house, open to the sky. The walls fall open and flat, roads snaking across them. A red arrow: *you are here*. But not for long. Longitude, latitude, the curve of rivers, of breathing paths. Fold it again, smooth it to fit into a pocket. Shake it open and watch the rooms as they scatter and fall, the moons in them.

◎ ◎ ◎

Here is the woman who was the girl and the girl who was the baby; here is the breathing ghost. They live in a one-bedroom apartment in a complex with an overgrown courtyard and an in-ground pool that is filled with dead leaves in the winter and mossy green water in the summer. They have wall-to-wall carpeting and a ceiling fan in the narrow kitchen and a TrimLine phone mounted on the wall of the pass-through. They have a pass-through. They eat dinner sitting cross-legged on the floor in front of the television set, English muffin pizzas and Tang, popcorn hot from the handled foil pan, sleeves of chocolate-covered graham crackers and tart green apples slivered.

The girl wears her father's face without knowing it. She doesn't remember him; she has no idea that she squints against sunshine with his eyes, that her forehead knots itself into the same crabbed furrow as his did. At night, in the mint-green bathtub, with the tiny window near the ceiling open to let the summer in, her mother scrubs that furrow smooth with a kitten-shaped sponge soaked in shampoo the color of marigolds. *Lather, rinse, repeat*, say the instructions on the bottle, but the furrow won't stay gone.

She lifts her daughter from the water and sets her dripping on the bath mat, a slick and wriggling seal, then wraps her in a towel, rubs at her shoulders and legs in the sweet close air, the freckled forearms and scabbed knees, the rose-petal heels she cups in her palms in sleep. She will never be rid of him.

From the open window, crickets, a shout and chlorinated splash, keening guitar swallowed by the spin of a radio dial. She leans to whisper into her daughter's warm ear, lifts and carries her out to the sliver of balcony that overlooks the pool and the fence and the woods beyond.

Here is the broken earth and gutted tree, here is the gypsy moth. Here is the black leaf, the soil that remembers nothing and the skin that remembers everything, the spit and mud and waking dream. Here is the cool ground, tooth and root and bones exposed, scraped clean and waiting.

◎ ◎ ◎

She is twenty, twenty-one, twenty-two, five feet four inches and one hundred pounds. Her hair is strawberry-gold, her hair is copper, her hair is banged and blunt as a Dutch boy's, her hair falls in skeins to her waist. Her hands are seashells and her eyes are winter surf and her untouched skin is cool and smooth as limestone.

She dissolves Benadryl into her tea at night and No-Doz in her coffee in the mornings and in between she stretches wide across her empty bed, in between she prowls the dusty floors with a cigarette in one hand and a tumbler of wine in the other, in between she dreams that when he finds her he doesn't recognize her, when he touches her he can't feel her, when he fucks her he tears her in two.

He is twenty-two, twenty-three, twenty-four, he is sleeping sunburned in a hayloft, he is kneeling at Easter Mass, he is huddled in a thrift-store parka in the doorway of a truck stop. The air is frozen, crackling black, full of gasoline and burnt coffee and the perfume of a girl whose name is Shelly or Shelby or Beth, whose nails are purple, whose lips are silver, whose hair glows blue beneath the diesel sky as she leads him across the cracked and rumbling lot.

In the back seat of her car Shelly or Shelby or Beth pulls an unzipped sleeping bag around them and a blanket over that, tugs her mittens from her hands with her teeth and his shirt from his pants with her cold fingers. He feels something hard and smooth beneath his hip and she kicks a textbook to the footwell. *I'm studying to be an agronomist*, she tells him, and pulls a neat leather case from between the seat and the door, opens it to clean works shining on fawn-colored felt. *I made dean's list last semester*, she says, then ties him off and lowers her heart-shaped face to his arm, sucks at a vein until it throbs fat and green, and slides the sunshine home.

In an hour or a year he staggers back across the oil stains through the lines of idling trucks, through the pop and fizz of cold sparks. He shoulders the glass door open, steps slow and careful past the displays of cassette tapes and magazines, the metal racks of sunglasses and fringed neon T-shirts and shelves of insulated plastic cups, the bright and throbbing abundance, the screaming promise of diversion, of fulfillment, of the God-given right to stupor.

He collapses in a bathroom stall, works his hands into the pockets of his jeans and pinches out torn bus schedules, water-stained receipts, a bent prayer card from a congregation in Missouri.

Green hills and a pulled-sugar sky, a steeple rising into it. *Beloved, now we are children of God.*

The metal door to the stall rattles and he shrinks back against the wet tile, works another slip of paper that is not cash from his pocket. *100% cotton. Made in the USA.* He can see heavy work boots and jeans soaked at the hems on the other side of the door. He watches, fascinated, waiting to see if they decide to stay or leave. Nubs of ice cling to the laces, to the frayed tongues. In this bright metal box he could wait forever.

◎ ◎ ◎

Shake well before using, toxic if swallowed, fragile.

May cause drowsiness.

Heavy object, lift with care.

◎ ◎ ◎

The daughter who was the baby is a comet, is an eclipse, is a tidal wind. She drags the sky behind her. She is one thousand days old she is ten years old she is one hundred fifty months old and still the sky snaps and billows at her bare brown shoulders.

She trails eggshell and feathers, thistle and gingersnap, tooth and bone and petals. She dives into ash and swims through lava and climbs out ice-blue and shining. She has her father's brow and her mother's chin but in between her face is some new planet's moon.

Except she isn't and she doesn't because she is nothing but a twelve-year-old girl, knots in her hair and scrapes on her knees, pierced ears and bitten nails and a stutter when she's nervous. She is not perfect and she is not magic and she will never belong to more of the world than she did before she entered it; she will never travel farther than she already has. She will be lucky if she is precious to someone; if hers is the face that appears in someone else's wakeful darkness; if she is someone's only prize. She drags nothing but the years behind her.

◎ ◎ ◎

Here is the world before her, the car on the dark road and the boy and girl who will be her parents inside it, arms stretched long out the open windows and fingers spread to catch the dusk, hands bouncing and skimming the warm rush of it. Here is the cracked leather hot beneath their thighs and the tires' bump and lurch as they turn onto dirt, the kick of dust behind them and the high grass flattening.

She is older now than her mother was then and she is colder than her father. She carries his picture in her backpack, his stranger's face creased and faded, tucked into a deck of cards she lifted from a gas station. Her fingers are quick and her step is fast, her eyes are needle sharp.

The deck of cards from a greasy shelf in an Amoco; agate earrings and knitted mittens and crystal-beaded key chains from drugstores and arcades; a turquoise bracelet, rusted Hot Wheels Camaro and a torn and penciled map from her mother's chest of drawers. She takes only what won't be missed, which she already understands is most of everything. She keeps what she takes in a shoebox on her closet shelf. She keeps her own counsel. She keeps her guard up.

Here is the only end to every story: everything disappears, and everyone. She knows this. She sleeps peacefully next to it, she breathes its regardless chill and does not dream of warmth, does not dream of where her father might be or what her mother might do if she found him.

She is the well they meant and the harm they didn't, that boy and girl, immortal for as long as it took to make her and no longer than that. She is what is left, and the world after her will be no different for her presence in it.

Supplication, expiation, absolution.

A water-stained address book from a table in a sub shop, a birthday card from a purse left open on a bowling alley snack bar. A waiting heart, an empty house, a dark and silvered mirror. She takes only what's already been forgotten. She takes all the time in the world.

Here is the ghostless machine and the hatless magician; here is the snake that does not rattle; its pretty slither and flick. Here is the fallen apple, and the poisoned tree. Here is the long box and the turned earth, cooling. It is all, and it is enough.

So Happy

In the days before Frank came home, Isabel and her sisters scrubbed the house from the cellar up, from the kitchen and the wood-paneled den to the front room above, formal and narrow behind the silent front door, and then to the bedrooms, two airless boxes with a black and white tiled bathroom between them. They sloshed hot water and vinegar over the kitchen floor and polished the windows with newspapers. When they grew tired or bored they unwrapped sticks of Beech-Nut and lit cigarettes from a communal pack of Viceroys, drank the leftover beer they'd taken from the church supper the previous week. They strung the basement with crepe paper and streamers that Ollie from the five-and-dime had donated, moldy and faded and torn; vacuumed carpets and cushions with the Eureka they'd borrowed from the rectory. When they finished Isabel's sister Lina took the vacuum back along with a covered plate of homemade fudge.

Her sister Anna fried up scrapple for sandwiches and mixed a pitcher of their father's dandelion wine and 7-Up, sliced the last of the peaches into it and put it in the icebox with the bowls of potato salad and macaroni the neighbors had already started to bring.

They did these things and Isabel could not keep from glancing at the calendar, the clocks, as though in them she could see his way: from France to London to Southampton; New York to Fort Meade to Baltimore. Helicopters and ships, his thumb, his two feet. She had not seen him for two years and she had come to believe, without ever quite admitting it to herself, that she was not married at all. The night before the party she lay in bed and drifted to the sounds of the radio, the trucks on the street below, empty bottles rolling and bouncing down the alley. The wind. She could not picture his face; their wedding photo was tucked under his folded clothes in a drawer she never opened. She was twenty-two years old and her husband was coming home and her husband was someone she had never met.

In the morning she unboxed the dress she'd been saving, shook it out and stepped into it. She tied her sandals on. The tops of her feet were tanned, her toes painted coral. She powdered and lipsticked herself and caught her hair back in mother-of-pearl clips and the neighbors, as they came, hugged her; held her out to admire her, to tell her what a lucky man Frank was.

Who's Frank? she thought, but only for a moment. The house filled and Lina brought her a whiskey-and-soda in a coffee cup—Shh, she said, don't let on, it's from Anna's bottle—and two aspirin. She smoothed her hair and touched the tip of her pinky finger to the corner of Isabel's mouth—Just a little lipstick smear. All gone.

Isabel's mother had the telegram and the bus schedule and when it was time she shooed Isabel up the stairs. She stood at the front door, watching. Below her Perry Como finished singing and Johnny Mercer started and Anna yelled Hey Vi, where's Clyde been these days? and her cousin Vi shrieked with laughter.

He was swinging open the metal gate before she realized who he was. He climbed the steps to the doorway and dropped his bags and his hat on top of them.

Hey, doll, he said, and she saw that his front tooth was broken. His uniform was wrinkled but clean and she was surprised to see that he carried no gun or canteen, that no grenade hung heavy from his belt. He reached for her hand and she let him take it; she tried to remember if that tooth had always been broken. Her mother would know, or one of her sisters.

They're all waiting for you, she said, and pulled him in behind her.

Back in the kitchen Isabel wedged cans of beer into a tub of ice. She wiped her hands on the front of her skirt and swung through the crowd with pitchers of spiked lemonade, passed trays of crackers spread with pimento cheese. She kept moving, moving; Anna's bottle was hidden in the cabinet beneath the sink and Isabel washed her hands every chance she got, tipped out more whiskey into the cup she'd left behind the hanging dish towel. There's my girl! Frank shouted, whenever she slipped past. Lina and Anna served chicken cutlets and fried smelt and stewed tomatoes and Frank balanced the neighbors' children on his lap, on the stiff new trousers he'd changed into—My civvies, he said, Looky here! He held a giggling boy on one knee and a bottle of beer on the other and his face went damp and blotched. My my Vi Vi, he said, eyes frantic with glee, I remember that smile! and Vi blushed and took his empty bottle and brought him a new one.

Isabel lit one cigarette off the end of the last. When Father Sal finished eating she took his plate and brought him a cup of coffee and a slice of her mother's nectarine cake. Your lipstick, her mother whispered in her ear, You need to put more on, but Isabel wiped down the bar by the record player and pretended not to hear.

Vi's about ready to keel over, Lina said, suddenly next to her, plucking the cigarette from Isabel's fingers. She smelled yeasty and sweet. And Ollie just told me Clyde's coming after—Bel? she said. You okay?

Isabel looked out over the den and the hallway filled with the people she'd known her whole life, all of them overheated, giddy with happiness and relief, drunk and blazing with hope. Like children, she thought, like strangers.

Back in the kitchen at the sink her father took her by the arm and squeezed—That's enough, he said. Go take care of your husband.

I'm A-OK, Frank sang out, to no one, Nothing to it, he said, his knee bouncing, and around him everyone danced, and outside the sun burned white then orange over the August street, the plastic chairs Isabel and her sisters liked to sit in after dinner, smoking cigarettes and listening for the ice-cream man, the bell; the slamming doors and shouting children.

When the last guests climbed the back stairs to the alley Isabel untied her sandals and slid out of them, wrapped them into a neat bundle with their laces and let them fall to a chair. The room was hot, swollen with sudden quiet and the night that had dropped when she wasn't looking. There was a high whine and buzz in her ears and she swatted the empty air around her and imagined her sisters in the bedroom they shared, tuning the radio to the baseball game, separating out ropes of thin black licorice.

Well then, she said, and began to collect the dishes and ashtrays and empty glasses, I should get things straightened away, and as she reached across him Frank caught her around the waist and hoisted her into his arms, his mouth hot on her throat.

That's my pretty doll, he said, that's my slice of pie. Her neck smelled of sweat and talc and Emeraude. The combs were loose and her hair feathered across his cheek, his brow, and her thin arms were tight around his neck.

He carried her up and into the bedroom he had not seen for years and almost wept at the double bed, the mint green chenille spread and white cotton shams, her nightgown folded at the foot. He'd been gone for years and this room had been here all along, exactly this small and square and neat.

He opened the closet door and threw her inside, slammed the door and dragged her vanity table in front of it, exactly like their wedding night and nothing like it, when she had locked herself in the bathroom before they'd even got near the bed; when she had not come out until she heard him collect his wallet and cigarettes and slam the motel-room door behind him.

But Frank was not thinking of that, not at the perfect end of such a day. He stood swaying in the center of the braided rug, breathing in the wonder of such a room existing while he'd sloughed through piss and cut through bone.

He wandered the house, drinking through the bottles the guests had left behind, picking at slices of cake on paper plates, the frosting gone gritty and dry. He marveled at everything he'd come back to: the shining linoleum floor in the basement kitchen and the crepe-paper streamers over the table, the worn runner up the stairs to the front room, doilies on the sofa arms and a telephone table with a pad and pen, a china shepherdess in the window. His kitchen, his stairs and sofa, his pen: all of it, waiting for him. In the morning there would be the hiss of hot coffee; the rattle and clank of the milkman's bottles. For now there were his wife's ragged screams, her hammering fists on the door of the closet where he would hang his clothes. He was so happy. In the kitchen he found Anna's bottle of whiskey and took it back up to the bedroom with him, set it on the shaking vanity and lifted the nightgown from the bed. It was the palest yellow, edged with white eyelet. He sat on the floor in front of the closet, watched the door jump as she pounded it. His girl who'd waited for him, who slept wrapped in daffodils: her fists were no bigger than acorns, her mouth was salty and smooth.

When he took her out to fuck her he sang her the most beautiful songs he knew, volkslieder and chansons in those bloody tongues he had never learned to understand. The words tasted of dirt and rot but he sang them for her anyway, he sang them into her wet open mouth. He poured whiskey into it and rocked her when she sputtered and hacked, kissed her sparrow shoulders. Are you ready now? he said, unzipping her dress, his pants, pulling her onto his lap like a doll. His wife, his life. He had never felt anyone more clean. It would take the rest of his days to earn her.

When he finished he slipped the nightgown over her head, coaxed her arms through and smoothed her hair. He set the mother-of-pearl clips on the table by the bed, splinters of moon.

Bedtime, he said, and lifted her up onto the mattress and watched her curl onto her side, a closing flower.

They woke the next morning to a tangerine sun, a sky egg-pale and blue; to the rattle of the milk truck and the slap of newspapers against each door on the block. They woke to damp skin and wrinkled pillows, to sheets pushed down and heaped at their bare dusty feet, to their clothes that smelled of smoke and whiskey in piles on the floor. They woke to the parched Friday morning and the stretch of years beyond it, too long and bright to see.

◎ ◎ ◎

Isabel tells the story, breathless, to anyone who will listen—to Marie at the bakery and Betty at the hairdresser's, to the girl from St. Casmir's whose name she does not know, who does the priests' laundry in scalding water, eyes averted, hands cracked and weeping.

The day he came home?—you couldn't *peel* me away from that window—I was so excited to have him back, I had that bus schedule *memorized.*

The girl's hands are raw meat but Isabel takes them in her own and squeezes, there on the sidewalk outside of St. Casmir's under a crackling fine fall sky: I didn't know what happiness *was* until I saw him walking up those stairs.

She tells the story and it begins to be true and she finds she cannot stop: she spins the day like cotton candy on a paper cone, as insubstantial as that and just as irresistible. There are versions, variations; embellished and enhanced, tricked and shined to suit, to order. Sometimes he comes with flowers, sometimes with a bandaged cheek. Sometimes she falls to her knees, or weeps, or throws herself into his arms and he catches her, kisses her, harbors her.

She is not confused and she is not dishonest and if she does not know exactly how to love him she knows, indubitably, how to love the day she is building from long summer shadow, from hot brick and humid dusk and Saturday matinees.

He is Gene Kelly and Robert Walker and Spencer Tracy and he appears on the walk in late August light, soft as honey and warmer. His eyes are clear and his hands are soft and where he's been is a dream and if not a dream then forgotten and if not forgotten then not real.

His hands so soft she can't feel them.

Her lips are sugar-pink and her eyes are blazing and on Sunday mornings she kneels at Mass between her sisters while he sleeps, strung across the bed she's left; he dreams of burning fields and burning flesh and the women who scrabbled at his feet. He dreams of singed hair and gaping mouths, powdery gray skin and satin ashy bones.

Isabel genuflects and outside the church she tugs her gloves off and leans in with her sisters, three on a match. To Lina, to Anna: When I saw him I thought my heart would *explode.*

The more she says the more she believes until the day becomes what it was supposed to be all along, and she lets it, and it does.

At night after dinner she brews coffee and he sloshes whiskey into the cups, holds the kitchen door open for her. They climb the stairs into the dusk. Their cigarettes wink and flicker and when the wind comes up she shivers.

In the winter Frank puts the storm windows up and Isabel takes the comforters down from the high closet shelves, shakes them out and hangs them to air on the clothesline in the thin December sun. In the spring he plants rosebushes in the scratch of soil outside the kitchen steps, their branches dry and gnarled. The blooms sigh open and the petals fall; even the thorns are dull. In the summer she draws a cool bath and sinks into it, holds a beer bottle to her forehead.

And each night he comes on his knees to her, naked and wet as a bird, pink eyelids and ruffled hair and scraped knuckles, an abyss behind his eyes. He crawls to her through broken glass and rusty wire that disappear behind him. He lays his head on her lap and breathes her powdered silence and his fingertips on her arms are like feathers; he has bitten the nails away.

He sucks at the glass necks of bottles, an orphan, a beggar; he scrubs himself raw in the shower, and still he cannot stop remembering. She washes his clothes and combs his hair and is shocked, shamed, at how easy it is to love him like this, stripped and licked by flame, broken and ragged and hers.

◎ ◎ ◎

Their daughter cannot stand to be held. In the crib her eyes flutter and her fingers wave, her lips pucker and suck at the air. She will roll and coo for hours. In her mother's arms she stiffens and heaves; in her father's she shrieks herself limp. But when they dress her and stow her in the carriage, push her up the street to the park or the playground, she smiles up at the wavering sky, at the faces that lean and shade her. Lina and Anna, Clyde at the newsstand and Grady on the corner—they cannot get enough of her on these afternoon walks, her potato softness, her curling hands. She is what Frank and Isabel were meant to do and they've done it: the neighborhood is pleased.

Frank tucks the blanket around her and slips a pacifier between her lips, deft and quick. He loves her with a ferocity he has no hope of understanding: when he looks at her the rest of the world is eradicated, annihilated, and so he cannot stop looking.

Isabel drifts back, squints against the sun. The baby is tolerant of the neighbors' attention, affable and sweet. She reaches for their faces with her dumpling hands and Isabel watches, curious.

She cannot decide which she is more surprised by, her daughter's sudden presence in the world or her inevitability; the warm shock of her solid flesh or the eyes she has known forever.

In them is a waiting storm. They watch her for signs.

◎ ◎ ◎

Isabel stays home with the baby and Frank works extra hours at the lumberyard and when he's finally promoted to a desk job she buys a London broil and a bottle of Cook's Champagne and a blouse she's been eyeing for months, a deep-brown satin that buttons with ebony roses. She puts the meat in the oven and the champagne on ice and their daughter in bed; she lines her eyes and rouges her cheeks and dabs Emeraude on the insides of her elbows, her wrists and thighs.

Thank you, Frank says after dinner, and rubs a hand over his quiet face. You didn't have to do all this. The bottle is empty; there are ashes and melted wax on the tablecloth where the candles have guttered. Frank pulls himself up from the table and she sees, for the first time, the old man he will be unable or unwilling to avoid becoming. When he kisses the top of her head and disappears to the sofa she does not follow him. She closes her eyes and imagines her lap full of flowers, sticky and strange and delicious, that her daughter and husband will never see.

They go to Philadelphia, to New York; they stand ten deep on the sidewalks for Columbus Day parades. They wave plastic flags and raise plastic cups and their daughter's hair grows long and brown, it waves and fades to gold at the wispy ends. They send her to the parish school and her lips without lipstick are fleshy and red; she gobbles her books like a prisoner. Her hips flare, impatient. She does not study because she does not have to; she is incapable of mediocrity or failure. There is nothing for Isabel to do for her.

To the new priest who comes after Father Sal's heart attack: I wish you could've seen it—all that work my sisters did and I didn't care about *anything* but him coming home. Oh Father, I couldn't think of anything but him.

To her seatmates on bus trips to Atlantic City and Virginia Beach: He was so *handsome* in his uniform, coming off that bus—he took my breath away!

They do not go to Paris or Rome or London. They do not go anywhere that would require them to set their watches to a different time, to read street signs or menus in a different language— There's nothing out there, Frank says to her—Well, nothing good. Nothing better than here.

And Isabel does not argue because all she knows is *here*.

Sometimes, at work in the lumberyard on a warm Monday morning, Frank stops and pictures his wife in their bright quiet bedroom, smoothing the blanket across their bed, and his daughter at school at her desk, drowsy, drifting. The kitchen window that sticks and the curtains, the bottles of dandelion wine, the glass vase of plastic peonies and the saucer of greening pennies beneath it—such grace that he touches, day by month by blurring year. And he weeps without knowing why.

Frank's eyes grow dry and tired. He buys a porcelain lamb for the shepherdess in the window and when he gives the box to Isabel she struggles with the paper, the ribbon and lid; her hands are stiff and clumsy and she curses them, impatient for the shepherdess to have her charge.

The mother-of-pearl combs become lost in the gray of Isabel's hair and so she cuts it and offers the combs to her daughter but her daughter shrugs them away, braids her hair and ties it with a ragged strip of leather. She is almost pretty, or would be.

Isabel tucks the combs away and Frank buys her fox-trimmed gloves, presents them in a crinkling nest of tissue. Their daughter floats from room to room, dreaming serious dreams. She loves her parents, whoever they are; she bides her time.

On Sundays Isabel makes a batch of sauce with sausage and braciola and carries the pot, still warm, five blocks to Anna's house. She balances it on the stoop and lets herself in with her key and crosses herself at the threshold. The house is always dark, too warm; it smells of tea and camphor. She calls out to her sister and her sister's husband who can no longer speak, whose eye and cheek and mouth have been pulled and stilled by stroke, useless as the rest of him. She says a prayer, vague and pallid; for him to choke and drown in his own saliva would be a horror and a mercy.

Frank puts up the storm windows and checks all the sinks, the spigots and pipes for looseness, for leaks, for drips. He leaves the lumberyard early and on his way home he stops at Marty the Czech's place for a beer or a shot of homemade cinnamon liqueur if Marty's wife is in. If a card game is up in the back room he stays for a hand or two, and if Marty's cousin Cilka is there he stays for longer. Cilka's eyes are gray as the winter sky, and colder. She wears clothes from Marty's wife that are too big for her, pinned waistbands and rolled cuffs, and Frank remembers his daughter on the floor of their bedroom, surrounded by a riot of Isabel's sweaters and scarves and wrapped like a mermaid in strands of beads. Cilka reaches across him for a shot of vodka and rests a hand on his shoulder, strong and small and bent, gripping with pinky and pointer and thumb. Her missing fingers are in the char of a strafed and flattened house in a village outside of Brno—I did not lose them, she likes to joke, her voice full of vodka and gravel, I know exactly where they are. When Frank stands to leave Cilka slips into his chair, flips her skirt out behind her and straddles the seat with her legs, bare and American-strong. Still warm, she says, laughing, waving him goodbye with her funhouse hand.

When their daughter disappears Frank and Isabel are on a charter bus on their way back from a trip to New York, aching from a day of sightseeing and coffee shops, cafeteria and cashier lines, from the sprung and tilting seats in a damp theater far from Broadway.

It is a Sunday night in November, kissed by smoke and frost, and while their bus is heaving through New Jersey their daughter rolls her clothes and tucks them into an oversize duffel. She packs a knapsack with her hairbrush and toothbrush, her glasses; her journal and address book and a stack of used paperbacks from the community-college bookstore for the classes she has not attended in weeks—philosophy and modern poetry, social justice, western civ.

Frank's head is resting on Isabel's shoulder, his eyes half-closed then floating open to the rhythm of the tires on the seamed concrete. It has been a fine day: the fifty dollars he won playing cards with Marty on the ride up, the prime rib for dinner, the potatoes mashed with sour cream and sprinkled with a green lace of parsley and chives. Isabel rustles through the shopping bag beside her and he lifts his head, blinks at the lights swooping past.

I hope she likes it, Isabel says, flipping the pages of the organizer she bought, bound with faux leather and edged in lustrous red. She's so particular, she sighs, it's hard to tell.

She would not have bought the organizer if Frank had not insisted, had not stopped at the window of the luggage store when he saw it.

He is so proud of her, of the college and the books; the strange classes that meet every other day, or at night.

But it's for men, Isabel said as they stood on the sidewalk, see? She pointed at the display, the briefcase propped next to it, the desk blotter.

New Jersey unspools behind them and their daughter bounces the duffel down the stairs. She stops in the kitchen, opens a can of beer and pokes through the refrigerator, the flat wrapped packages of meat and cheese, the plastic containers of sauce, of pasta, of blanched and dressed greens. She uncovers a bowl of spinach, pinches the slippery leaves up with her fingers. If she stayed away for twenty years she'd come back to find the same jars and dishes, the same potholder hanging next to the stove, the same prayer card taped to the kitchen door.

There is no boy waiting for her outside it, there is only the heaving world.

You don't worry about her like I do, Isabel says—When I was her age I already knew I would marry you. Frank takes her hand, holds it in both of his own. He knows better than to correct her.

After dinner they shared a slice of coconut crème pie even though it would make them late, make them have to hurry to meet the bus.

When I was her age all I could think about was you.

Their daughter has money, maps and bus schedules and the addresses of people she does not yet know, spread across the mid-Atlantic like beacons. They are not waiting for her but they'll be ready when she comes.

She drains her beer and sets the empty can on the table at her father's place, the empty bowl of spinach at her mother's. She has paper in her knapsack, and envelopes already stamped and addressed, already trained for home.

If she would only make an effort, Isabel thinks, put on some perfume and lipstick, a pretty ironed skirt.

To her daughter when she was a little girl: I missed the whole party, she said, eyes closed, smiling, just watching for your father to come home. And when he came!—I just wanted everyone to leave. And your aunts were so angry with me, after all that work, how I shooed everyone out.

It has taken her half a life, more, but she has polished that day into something perfect, made it a smooth shining orb of a day, warm and gold as the August sun. Like blown glass.

Frank drifts, close to sleep. He thinks that he will make a point to stop at the bakery this week and ask Marie for a coconut crème pie, surprise Isabel with it.

Their daughter makes a last sweep through the house. Her bed is neat and made, the bathroom light off. She finds a half-empty pack of cigarettes on her father's night stand and pockets it. She leaves his dog tags, his spearmint Life Savers. Her mother's dresser is crowded with jars of cream and bottles of perfume, her rosary in its porcelain dish. She slips a lipstick into her pocket, red and bright as thirst.

Frank rouses himself and stretches and Isabel begins to straighten her bags and their daughter checks to make sure the porch light is on for them before she slips out into the early smoke of another war, another world; into the floating curling incense, the exuberant fury. She does not leave a note—her note is in the papers, on the radio and the news at night. Her father will know how to read it.

All I want, Isabel says, is for her to be as happy as I am.

Are you? Frank says, but she has turned to look out the window at the silvery dark, vaporous and cold and ghostly, slipping behind them so fast. The skin of her cheek is etched and fine. He knows that skin, the flesh beneath it, he knows her muscle and bone. Only her heart is strange.

Their daughter is already at the bus station. She unwraps the scarf from her throat and buys a paper cup of coffee, sugars it and presses toward the departures board, looks for the next bus leaving.

I think I'll try to make that pie, Isabel says. She turns back from the window. What do you think? Would you like that?

His face is so close to hers, his creased chin, the gray scratch of whiskers. She has seen it in every weather and still she wonders who lives behind it.

◎ ◎ ◎

By the time they arrive at the station their daughter will be gone, her coffee cup crushed and tossed light in a basket, her duffel in the hold of a different bus and her knapsack on the seat beside her. But right now they are thinking of their waiting house and she is watching the schedule board, her heart thrumming strong in her ears.

Did you take the extra blankets down? Isabel says, and Frank nods, and their daughter presses closer to the board, to wherever it is she's going. Her heart is a hammer, rhythmic and sure, and there is just enough time for her parents to close their eyes, to sleep away the last few miles, while Akron becomes Albany becomes Atlanta, while the world spins hot and the world catches fire. She watches the letters flip and waits for the cities to come to rest.

Like We Did

We were waiting for my brother to die and pretending not to. We were doing an okay job of it, Libby and Spencer and my brother and me. It was June and then it was July. We went to the pool or the movies while we waited, or the state park if the weather was good. It was almost easy, or it seems that way now.

We waited sometimes parked at the mall after closing in Spencer's mother's car and sometimes in Libby's basement. We spent my brother's time together, but Libby spent the most of it, hand over fist, head over heels. We waited while the moon slid from Gemini to Leo and my brother's pants slid low over his hips, only a little lower than everyone else's, at first.

We did what you do. We got as drunk as we could as much as we could, and then we'd hold hands in a loopy chain and trip through backyards and across the two-lane to the 7-Eleven. It was bright inside, too bright for my brother—he had to wait outside sometimes while the rest of us squinted in front of the Slurpee machine. We got Slim Jims and Twinkies and Pringles just like everyone else in the normal world, just like you.

He didn't look sick until it didn't matter anymore, which was good for him, because he was used to girls. Of the two of us, he was the one with the looks. But what I looked like didn't matter that summer because Spencer liked smart chicks—that's what he'd said one Friday in March, the day before the last snowstorm of the year. He parked himself in front of my locker so I couldn't open it and he said, apropos of exactly nothing, *I like smart chicks.* Libby heard; her locker was next to mine.

If my daughter fell for a line like that.

◎ ◎ ◎

Libby hated her freckles but I wanted them. All I had was a birthmark on my shoulder. I had hair that was straight as a ruler and Libby wanted that. In eighth grade she wanted my sophomore brother but he teased her almost as much as he teased me. When she decided she'd had enough, she found a junior swimmer, but my brother didn't care. I don't think he noticed.

It was common and universal wisdom then that boys teased because they liked you—every mother said so, from kindergarten on, through hair-pulling and spider-dangling right up to name-calling and worse. But I told my Greta from go: they tease because they're assholes. They tease because they think they can get away with it. Don't be flattered and don't ignore them and don't let anyone tell you it's okay. Don't let them get away with it.

What do you expect her to do? my husband Charlie would ask, patient but perplexed, when she was five and seven and ten, and I had no response. She's thirteen now and if he asked again I'd have an answer, but he hasn't.

◎ ◎ ◎

Spencer shows up on the local news every now and again, handsome enough, thick salt-and-pepper hair and nice skin. He looks like he's still too smooth with the ladies. He looks like he might in fact call them *ladies*. His suits are nicer than lawyers usually wear, and they fit better. If I'm in the kitchen reheating leftovers or carrying a basket of clean laundry upstairs and hear his voice coming from the TV, it's as though a fickle wind has just blown me fifteen years back.

It's resonant and authoritative, his voice: it swings easily between grievously dismissive and dismissively aggrieved, depending. You'd think a jury would find either tone insulting.

That's why you've never been put on a jury, Charlie says.

Sometimes on weekends Charlie ambushes my clean laundry route. He'll appear at the top of the basement stairs or in the bedroom doorway and take the basket from me, slide his tongue in my mouth and his hands in my pants. He's a quick one, and more graceful than he looks; he can kick the basket out of the way and walk me over to the couch or bed before I can even think about arguing.

Not arguing is something I'm working on.

What did you do to deserve him? Libby will say, while we finish our wine and he clears the table and warms the caramel sauce for the ice cream, and she'll be joking, but not really.

What I did was stay alive long enough to meet him.

◎ ◎ ◎

We didn't spend much time at our house—my brother and I didn't offer and Spencer and Libby never suggested it. There was an oversize calendar on the side of the refrigerator, a magnetic dry-erase with doctor appointments in green and medication side effects in red and a list of phone numbers in blue that kept growing like a stalactite toward the floor. The vanity in the guest bathroom was covered in prescription bottles and our parents smiled like hostages. There was too much to ignore in our house.

My brother and I went through the liquor cabinet. We pulled dusty Christmas-gift bottles of Johnnie Walker and Rémy Martin from behind the cocktail forks and napkin rings our parents hadn't used for months and wedged them down into our backpacks, sweatshirts and beach towels wrapped around them to muffle the slosh and clink.

I put on the makeup my mother didn't bother to wear anymore and if she noticed she didn't say anything, so I sprayed on her perfume too. My brother didn't even try to be slick, he just opened the master-bedroom door and went straight for the wallet on our father's nightstand. He would pocket forty dollars and toss the wallet back on the table, not bothering to make sure it landed in the same spot.

Fancy, Libby said, when I waved my wrist in front of her face. We were in the park, drinking Johnnie Walker and Mountain Dew out of paper cups at a picnic table. This was fucking July already, purple sky and dusty leaves and the hot buzz of cicadas. Little League was over for the season and the baseball diamond behind us was empty except for my brother running tagging drills to prove he still could. Spencer watched from home plate, holding Johnnie by the neck.

Spencer didn't have to prove anything. If Spencer got short of breath it was because he'd been doing wind sprints, if he ran a fever it was because he had the flu, if he threw up it was because he drank too much. If he got tired of watching my brother on the base path and ambled over to the picnic table where Libby and I were sitting it was because he was seventeen years old, not because he was a bad human being or a worse friend. I hated him anyway, and when he kissed me I hated myself for letting him. I hated myself more for liking it.

Truth: I more than liked it. If my brother had collapsed in the dirt I would've pretended not to notice, just so Spencer would keep kissing me.

You smell good, he said, when he came up for breath, and behind him Libby rolled her eyes, swung her legs free of the bench, and picked up one of the plastic cups.

Gonna go see what Wade Boggs over there is up to, she said to no one. Her legs were long, pale for August. She wore sunscreen when everyone else basted themselves with Hawaiian Tropic oil.

Spencer went for my mouth again, his tongue hot with Johnnie Walker and cinnamon gum and his hands in a hurry, on my neck then my shoulders then down my back—as soon as they landed in one place they wanted to move on to another. I understood this. I was inexperienced, not stupid. And while I was not opposed to their intention I was also in no rush: I'd hardly had a chance to consider the feel of his fingers at my hairline, behind my ears, on my jaw before he took them away. I anchored my hands over his on my waist to still them and opened my mouth wider.

I would think of him in a tourist bar decades later, on an island in the Caribbean with Charlie, sunburnt and already drunk when the bartender poured shots of Fireball whiskey for everyone there. I threw it back and when the cinnamon burn hit my throat I almost dropped to my knees, that night in the park a hurricane roaring through me, frogs and crickets underfoot and the silvery blur of stars overhead, Spencer's hands, my skin sweaty under them, Libby's long white legs flashing on the base path and my brother close behind, T-shirt stuck damp to his skinny chest, sneakers kicking dust, running like the devil himself was after him.

◉ ◉ ◉

Everyone says Greta looks like me. She doesn't, but I don't bother disagreeing or explaining.

She's dressed and ready in a flowered skirt and slouchy sweater and clean shiny face, her two best friends on either side of her with their halter tops, their skinny jeans on skinny legs, their glossy lips and glittery eyelids. Charlie has the camera—we broke out the actual non-phone device for the occasion—and Greta's friends find this amusing. Their parents click away on their phones.

The occasion is a dance at school, the kind of semiregular not-important dance that we used to call a mixer. No dates, no stress, just a DJ and some strobe lights in the gym. A few of the kids even dance, Greta says.

We have it down, these other couples and Charlie and me: we rotate dropping off and picking up, the girls in the back seat of one of our cars, texting from the minute they pile in to the minute they spill out onto the lawn in front of the school, the metal doors propped open and the hallway inside glowing the same urinous yellow it always has. While they're gone we rotate hosting duties, which generally involve nothing more than decent wine and trashy snacks and Netflix. Tonight, for example, we'll be enjoying the finest Cool Ranch Doritos and Ring Dings and pizza rolls, *Sharknado* on the wide screen.

I know how insufferable this sounds, how self-satisfied and clever. But that's not what we're after, these nights we spend whistling past the graveyard of our girls' childhoods with high-fructose corn syrup and hydrogenated fat, sodium and stupidity. We are not trying to be clever. We are trying to be numb.

Dad, Greta says.

One more, he says, and the girls oblige, Greta staring into the camera straight on while her friends pout and pose and cock nonexistent hips, giving him exaggerated winks. Their mothers roll their eyes but I can hear their hearts hammering panicky up into their mouths, beating *not yet not yet not yet*.

And then the girls are shrugging into their coats, slinging purses over their shoulders and checking their phones for last-minute intel while one of the other fathers opens our front door with an exaggerated footman's flourish.

Ladies, he says, with just enough Jerry Lewis to make the rest of us old people cringe, and the girls are out the door and bounding down the driveway.

Have a vodka tonic waiting for me, he says, and his wife salutes, and then he's gone. Headlights bloom in the front window and the men go to the kitchen to uncork wine while the three of us sink into the sofa, into the buzzing pink silence our girls have left behind, into their cotton-candy air, its melting sweetness.

◎ ◎ ◎

Here's something: after a while we wouldn't let him drive. In the spring he'd taken turns with Spencer but that stopped by July. At first it was just little things—taking turns too fast, or slamming the brakes so we'd all fly forward. Then bigger: no headlights at ten p.m., then the wrong way down a one-way street, Libby begging him to quit and Spencer yelling For Christ's sake stop and me frozen in the seat behind him watching his hands, white-knuckled on the wheel like he was going to pull the steering column right out of the dash. I didn't move until Spencer lunged over the seat back to grab for the wheel and my brother finally eased off the accelerator, turned the car into someone's driveway, and cut the engine.

Fuck all of you, he said, calm, staring straight ahead into the dark, into the front windows of whosever house it was, bluish curtains drawn back and a bright lamp on a side table, an empty sofa, some stairs we could just see in the shadows. No one answered him. We all sat breathing until we saw someone moving in the house and the porch light came on. Spencer opened his door and got out and then the rest of us did, still silent. We all got back in, my brother and Libby in the back this time and Spencer behind the wheel. He reversed down the driveway, stopped and signaled and waited until the road was clear in both directions before backing out onto it. He didn't turn the radio on or lift his arm for me to scoot under and I didn't slide up next to him. Libby whispered something to my brother and he made a noise that would've sounded like laughter if I hadn't known better.

◎ ◎ ◎

Charlie goes upstairs to say good night to Greta while I collect crumpled cocktail napkins and candy wrappers, load the dishwasher with glasses and the little blue-and-white plates we got in Portugal. I drink the rest of someone's wine while I tip bowls of leftover chips into bags and tuck plastic-wrapped cupcakes back into the family-size box.

Libby used to peel the frosting from cupcakes in one careful piece, set it on the cellophane, and then work the cream filling out of the cake with the tip of a finger. Filling, cake, frosting, in that order, every time. When Greta was just a little thing Libby tried to teach her the method and was horrified when Greta told her she didn't like frosting.

My girl is nothing like we were. She reads labels on cereal boxes and keeps track of when the filter on the water pitcher needs replacing. She won't eat fast food or drink soda or put plastic containers in the microwave.

Where did this kid come from? Libby says sometimes, pretending despair.

Charlie, I tell her, pretending shame.

I pour myself more wine and set aside a few cupcakes for the next time Libby and I get together. I don't invite her to these movie nights and she doesn't make me feel guilty for it and if there's ever a reason to bring them up we're careful to be jokey, both of us with our good reasons.

When she looks at Greta she sees who I see. We don't joke about that.

◎ ◎ ◎

My brother went on a new drug protocol in August and we started going to the pool again, to the club where Spencer's parents belonged. We dragged chairs together at the deep end, we lotioned each other's backs, we took turns doing snack-bar runs. My brother with his shirt off was just regular-skinny, not sick-skinny, and no paler than Libby, and if you didn't look too closely you wouldn't notice how his nails and lips blued if he stayed in the water too long.

We set Libby's boom box at the head of the chairs and fished loose cassettes from the bottom of her backpack, wound the tape with ballpoint pens. We turned the volume up—Spencer knew the lifeguards. The lawnmowers by the tennis courts were louder, and the little kids playing Marco Polo.

Spencer did my back and the hot wind smelled of coconut, cut grass, and pizza. Libby's curls were chlorinated, bright gold and frizzed at the tips. She flipped them over a pretty, freckled shoulder and my brother reached across the chairs to grab a handful and tug, just hard enough for her to sigh and stretch a foot to touch his leg.

The pool deck was hot white concrete, reflective, rough. I walked behind Spencer on my toes, the balls of my feet. It felt ten degrees cooler in the trees behind the clubhouse and my skin marbled up beneath the damp of my bikini. Spencer slid his warm hands under the bottom of it and my ass was a perfect fit, his thumbs on my hip bones and his fingers at the crease of my thighs, some new kind of warm. I pressed into him, I slid my tongue into his mouth, I felt him breathing into me, felt him speaking into me, so much *into* but not everything, not yet. I felt him whispering Please please, felt the sun between the leaves pricking my burned shoulders, felt his fingers circling and tugging at the cold fabric of my suit, felt the sky begin to come undone. That was the entirety of the two o'clock world, sun and shadow, grass and dandelions under our pruney feet and the lifeguard's whistle, splashing, kids crying, adult swim, the smell of the fryer and hot parking-lot tar and our own bleachy sweat, everything breathing, everything *vibrating*, all of it so fucking alive.

We didn't stop because we wanted it to end. We stopped because we wanted it to last.

I'm awake in the slowest hour, kneeling by Greta's bed. She's on her back, arms splayed over twisted sheets, mouth just open, breathing.

She can sleep through anything, same as her father. Whatever benevolent gene they have, I want. What's a fair exchange for eight uninterrupted, unconscious hours, five times a week? Or even six, three times a week? I'm not greedy.

Whenever I complain about not sleeping, Charlie points out that most people waste a third of their lives asleep—this is exactly how he puts it, *waste*—and tells me I'm lucky.

You get extra time, he says, as though extra time is only and ever a good thing, as though it is a thing at all.

Greta would sleep half her life if she could. I know it's irrational but it makes me crazy, the way her eyes flutter closed on a ten-minute car ride or during the noisiest scene of an action movie; it makes me want to poke her shoulder or flick the bottom of a bare foot.

It's normal, Charlie will say, shaking his head at my gross impatience, at my behavior unbecoming a mother, *It's hormones, she's thirteen, they're all like that, they sleep all the time.*

It's not hormones, I want to say to my tolerant husband: I want to yell, *It's that thirteen-year-olds are by definition fools, it's that thirteen-year-olds don't get how time works.*

I want to say *there's no such thing as extra time.*

I brush the hair from her face, smooth it across the pillow. My sweet stupid beauty, it's all I can do to keep from shaking her awake and yelling *Don't wait. Do it all, do it now, do it over and over until someone or something stops you and even then. Even then.*

Do what? she'd say, blinking. My good girl, my little mouse.

Everything. Anything.

The party clothes she hates are strewn over the floor, skirt panels crushed like petals, tights a shimmery snake. Her closet is filled with flounces and pinks, neat buttons and cuffs and clean canvas sneakers, no wrinkled flannel or frayed denim or too-short cutoffs.

Every article of clothing is a reproach.

She's slept in this room for thirteen years, her dreams floating invisible up to bump and drift along the ceiling.

A sweater stitched with snowflakes, a scatter of daisies on a dress: the truth is I don't know the girl who would choose such things, who would take the time to match shirt and socks, to braid her hair before sleep so it doesn't tangle.

I don't know her but she's mine all the same, this meticulous stranger, this crosser of t's and dotter of i's, this list-maker and pile-straightener.

I have, on occasion, rearranged her desk when I come in to drop off clean laundry: turned a pen wrong side up in the cup, nudged a stack of index cards out of true. By the time I kiss her good night, order has been restored. I check every time.

Sleeping, now, in her soccer shirt, with her quivering fingers and dead boy's face, her butterfly breath.

I have mismatched socks deliberately, blue stripe with green. I have tucked a pink shirt in with the whites. I have come into this room on slumber-party nights when she's safely locked away in another frilly bedroom, put my iPod into her dock and my wine-glass on her desk and made myself comfortable on the floor in front of her dresser while my music shakes her windows, while my fingers find their way into pants pockets and jewelry boxes and sweater sleeves, while they brush and tap along the back edges and corners of sacheted drawers. I have not even bothered to pretend I'm not looking for something, or that I'm not disappointed when I don't find it.

◎ ◎ ◎

An incomplete list of the things we didn't talk about: college, internships, what we wanted to be when we grew up. Turning eighteen. We didn't make a big deal of it. It wasn't exactly conscious and it wasn't much of a hardship—it was a luxury for at least three of us, to be able to live so completely in the buzzing heat and itch of that summer, even if we didn't realize it then.

We talked about how tired we were of the music that was piped through the arcade at the mall and whether or not there were really security cameras in the ceiling of department-store dressing rooms. We talked about who'd disappeared together at the last party, who'd fought and not made up.

We didn't talk about lymphocytes or Methotrexate or what we thought we'd major in. We went to the movies and we went to the mall and we didn't talk about the flannel shirt my brother wore in the air conditioning or the hot rash that snaked from his wrists to the hairless white flesh of his armpits. We talked about the beginning of school, senior year for the boys and sophomore for Libby and me, but not Thanksgiving break. We talked about getting tickets for an all-ages show on Labor Day but not for a festival the weekend before Halloween. We talked about who'd been busted for drinking at a party in an abandoned house the next town over but not about who'd snuck through the back door, ran a stop sign in their mother's Camry, and got broadsided by a pickup; who bled out in a ditch before the ambulance got there.

◎ ◎ ◎

Libby got married at twenty-two and divorced at twenty-five and in between she lived in Austin and San Francisco and tour buses. She didn't fly first class or stay in penthouse suites or ride in limousines—all that happened after, and anyway it didn't last.

I saw her ex-husband in an airport bar once—it took me a minute to recognize him without the hair and the leather and the entourage. He was sitting at a table by himself with his guitar case across the empty seats, a beer and a shot and a fat book open in front of him. I couldn't tell what it was. He used to quote Oscar Wilde all the time and drive Libby crazy, though that wasn't why she left him. My flight was delayed and I was ready to go over to talk to him when I saw two girls, giggling and whispering behind their hands, already blushing just looking at him. They were trying to be casual with their phones, trying to get a picture without his noticing, and doing a shitty job of it. They saw me watching them, and instead of putting the phones away or otherwise composing themselves, they flipped me the finger—these two pretty things who didn't look old enough to even know who he was. The Oscar Wilde thing had made me nuts too, but still. He was a better husband than anyone expected him to be, or would have believed.

◎ ◎ ◎

I remember when they recorded this, Libby says—I think I lived on ramen and Skittles for the better part of a year. It's a Thursday night. Charlie's picking Greta up from her environmentalist club and Libby and I are drinking wine on my back deck even though it's not exactly warm. No crickets yet, just the speakers turned out the open kitchen window, her ex-husband's ex-band on the radio. The DJ talks over the opening chords.

I hate it when they do that, I say. You should've stuck it out long enough for the caviar and champagne.

She lights a cigarette. Right, except by that point you have to fight your way through the groupies to get any. *Caviar*, I mean. Get your mind out of the gutter.

At her wedding reception I'd gotten high with the best man, lights strung above the planked wooden stage on the damp lawn of someone's farmhouse, metal tubs of melting ice and beer cans, cupcakes and doughnuts and peanut butter cookies on long tables covered with crinkly white paper. We bobbed spiraling Krazy Straws in bottles of sparkling wine, licked strawberry jelly and marshmallow crème from our fingers. Onstage Libby's beautiful groom tapped the mic and the best man tuned his guitar while the drummer brushed the snare, and when they began to play I danced with Libby, both of us drunk and barefoot in our lacy vintage dresses, the other guests circling us in a pinwheel of joy.

The song ends and Libby crushes her cigarette out into the ashtray I keep for her. She half smiles in my direction. Admit it, she says, it's a pretty bad song, am I right?

Well, I say, it hasn't aged very well, and she laughs, lets her head fall back and gazes into the sky, this person whom I've loved longer than anyone still alive.

Unlike us, she says, stretching her arms as though she expects them to fill with stars.

◎ ◎ ◎

He hated country music, high-top sneakers, Thousand Island dressing. He hated being kissed on the neck—I know this because Libby told me, one day when we were treading water at the deep end of the pool, Spencer and my brother at the snack bar getting pizza.

Oh God I don't want to *know*! I cried, coughing out water, squeezing my eyes closed, only half pretending to be disgusted, and she grabbed me by the wrist and paddled us both to the edge so we could hang onto the smooth concrete lip.

Yes you do, she said, her eyes wide and bloodshot but steady on mine, you do want to know. You want to know everything so when you forget some of it, there's more.

◎ ◎ ◎

He did turn eighteen, and he turned nineteen. He was nineteen when I was seventeen, when our parents left his hospital room just long enough to see me walk the stage for my diploma.

He was nineteen when I was twenty-four, when Spencer graduated from law school and threw a party at his parents' house and we fucked in the master bath, his shiny imported girlfriend explaining torts to Libby in the backyard just below us.

Why did we never do this? Spencer said into my ear, his legs behind mine, bracing them, his belly and chest against my back, my arms and forehead on the cool sill of the open window. I could hear her bracelets jangle, twenty feet down.

If she had looked up. But she didn't.

His lips in my hair, his arms wrapping me from behind, his hands where they'd been before and where they hadn't. The bathroom still smelled of fabric softener and the pink soap rosettes in a dish by the sink, just as it had when we were fifteen and seventeen, when some of us were nineteen.

Why did we wait? he said and said and said, pounding the words into me, laughter and cigar smoke floating up from the lawn below us and through the open window, the sound of car doors slamming and corks popping, and I had no good answer, not then, not while I was finally doing what I thought I'd wanted to do for years. I still don't. I don't know why anyone waits for anything.

◎ ◎ ◎

I didn't talk to Libby's ex-husband in the airport that day. You have to put down the years you carry for a conversation like that, and you don't realize how heavy they are until you try to pick them up again. I left him to his drinks and his book and his current level of fame, which, from what I could gather, was manageable and dignified and maybe even enjoyable. The giggling girls scuttled off and the people our age walking by who noticed him slowed just enough or turned to look over their shoulders or nudged one another, smiling in happy surprise.

I can't imagine what it would feel like, to make strangers happy just by existing in the world.

◎ ◎ ◎

At night I woke to my brother slipping under the sheet next to me, his arms stringing my waist, his metallic breath.

Please don't tell anyone, he said into my shoulder. I could feel the blink of his lashes through my nightgown. I shook my head—I won't, I promise.

When I was eight and he was ten we liked to camp on the

carpeted basement floor, our sleeping bags crowded into a too-small tent. On Friday and Saturday nights we were fabulous famous people and we took turns interviewing each other: I was a gymnast, a jockey, a model; he was a race car driver, a pilot.

Do you remember that tent we used to have? I said. The cassette recorder?

He was silent. His skin on mine was damp and too cool, his flesh insufficient cushioning for the knobs of his bones.

Do you remember the tapes we—

He stiffened. I don't, he said. He turned to face the window, folded himself into an origami boy. It's a waste of time, he said, thinking about all that.

I wrapped myself around him, I could feel time burning through him, too fast for his breath to catch up. We watched the night stretch and settle, licorice sky and Necco moon on the other side of the window, our parents unconscious in the master bedroom that had been pristine but was now stale with our mother's unwashed laundry and the towels our father cried into when he thought no one could hear him.

Don't let me fall asleep, my brother said.

He was nineteen when I was twenty-nine and thirty-five and forty-two. He was nineteen when my daughter was born and he'll be nineteen when she dies.

⊚ ⊚ ⊚

Greta has what she refuses to call a date. It's just Mark from the history research group, she tells me, as though that explains the categorical resistance. Plus we might be meeting some other people, she says, so.

She brushes out her hair and smooths it back into a low pony-tail. She's wearing cropped gray jeans and a purple sweater, no makeup that I can see.

So, I echo, like an idiot. Where is this non-date happening?

Carson's at the Plaza. His mom's taking us and Dad's picking up. I already asked him. She slips her feet into canvas flats, collects her purse and phone and keys from the bed. She has ankles like a fawn, wrists I can circle with finger to spare.

Did you want to put on any perfume? I say, because I got this sample I think you'd—

Mom, she says, sighing, standing with her purse in her hands, eyebrows raised. She looks like a tiny prison matron. I catch my-self thinking of Sister Therese in third grade and the ruler she'd tap against her thigh just to remind you it was there, and I have to bite my cheek to keep from laughing.

No thank you, she says, and it's so clear that I'm stretching her patience beyond all reason—This really isn't that kind of night. We're just going over some stuff so everyone knows what they're looking for when we get library time.

Not that kind of night. It's preposterous how convinced she is of this, and my heart breaks a little for History Research Mark, whom I picture in the back seat of his mother's car, spiffed in hair gel and mouthwash and fancy kicks, hurtling toward disillusion-ment as we speak.

Greta checks the time on her phone and the eyebrows go up even more and I land a kiss on her forehead, careful not to muss her hair.

Go, I say, stepping aside so she can pass, and she's on her way, a smart chick herself but serious, so careful, cautious in a way I learned early not to be. She is afraid of mistakes. She still believes some are insurmountable.

I should be happy about this, because this fear will keep her safer, longer.

Except that it won't and I know it. I know better than anyone how little *safety* means.

◎ ◎ ◎

We had a predicament, Spencer and Libby and I.

We wished for what we dreaded. Privately. In what passed for our prayers, we hurried it. We didn't want the dying to drag on.

We'll kill you ourselves, we'd say, when my brother shook a can of Sprite before opening it to spray us. This was both a joke and not.

But maybe we didn't dread it, exactly. Maybe what we dreaded was the relief we knew we'd feel, the exhalation, the sound and waveless sleep.

What passed for our prayers shouldn't have.

The end of August and it was cool enough some nights to drive the extra fifteen minutes to the firepit in the park, to steeple new twigs in the leftover ash.

Our daytime skin smelled of chlorine and coconut and our nighttime skin smelled of smoke. Our dilated pupils reflected flames and our open mouths found one another's lips and necks and shoulders.

All of us queasy, alcohol and cigarettes or nerves or Cisplatin, the leaves above us rustling clocks, ticking toward crimson.

◎ ◎ ◎

That poor kid, Charlie says through a mouthful of toothpaste. He spits, grins. He didn't look happy when I dropped him off.

History Research Mark? I say, and Charlie looks at me, perplexed.

Never mind, I say. Was she still downstairs when you came up?

He shakes his head and slides into bed next to me. She said she wanted to get to school early tomorrow. Some library thing.

Right, that's the history research part. I lean to kiss him. Of Mark, I mean. I'm going to check on her. One minute.

Charlie reaches for a magazine from the pile on his nightstand. He subscribes to so many he can never read them fast enough, always pulling the oldest issue from the bottom of the stack, climbing his way up through what mattered last week or last month.

She's sleeping already, again. How much time do I spend watching her like this? Enough that I should be able to see every change, miniscule until they're huge; enough that the invisible becomes perceptible; that I will catch her in the act of disappearing.

It will never be enough. Right now her legs are longer than they were yesterday, her face rounder than it will be tomorrow. Her breath is the only constant.

The truth is I want to climb into her body and take it out for a spin myself, dress it in something just dangerous enough and spritz it with vetiver, walk it through beastless woods to a firepit by a ball field, bleachers and picnic tables and a closed concession stand just visible beyond the flames.

I would bring it home safe, hardly touched, none the worse for wear.

I made that body, it's my right.

◎ ◎ ◎

His tongue sharpened as his body swelled and withered. He called our mother stupid and our father useless and they ignored this because the fact of his voice mattered more to them than the words.

He could have said anything, as long as he said something.

He called me a slut and a fool and I ignored this because I believed, in my bed in the dark alone, that he was not wrong.

In my bed in the dark alone I waited for him to crawl in beside me, to wrap his arms around my waist in the same way I'd wrapped mine around his when I was six and he was eight and we'd shared a tiger floaty in the shallow end of the pool. In my bed in the dark I waited for him to cry. He cried until he dry-heaved. He tried to puke the death up.

In the water my feet had paddled, touching nothing: the shallow end may as well have bottomed dark miles below me. But my brother could swim and I clung to him.

In my bed he pinched me, he left pansy-colored bruises on the backs of my legs, the fleshy tops of my arms, and I didn't make a sound.

He whispered how fat Libby was, and ugly; how he'd never have been with a girl so disgusting if he hadn't been sick, and I didn't disagree or argue.

This is just one of the regrets that I am lucky enough to have. There are others, a wealth of them, ordinary and beautiful as blades of grass.

◎ ◎ ◎

I never asked Libby what she did or didn't do for him, with him. When she asked me one Sunday morning that October after she'd been with him the night before—Do I look different?—I said no, and changed the subject turned the channel left the room.

This is another.

◎ ◎ ◎

There are days when I miss my campfire hair and marshmallow heart, my sunburnt cheeks and bony knees—my every breathing minute under every roof before this one.

This roof, these walls. Greta sorts the recycling and Charlie cleans the gutters; Charlie power-washes the deck and Greta packs her sweaters in vacuum bags.

There are days when I choke on everything my brother would have hated, and hated missing.

I want to say to him *power washers and vacuum bags. You didn't miss anything.*

And then I look at my husband and daughter and am ashamed.

The retired stuffed animals on a high shelf in her bedroom and the neat line of her shoes, toes an inch away from the back wall of the closet; the chair by our dresser on which we toss our clothes at the end of the day. The vermeil box with her baby teeth; the wedding china we've never used. The photos in the upstairs hallway: Faro and Lagos, St. Thomas, the sky the same violent cobalt in every shot, so much deeper than the lazy blue of my brother's last summer.

Another truth: he wasn't kind. Even before he got sick, he wasn't kind because he didn't have to be, because the girls who wanted him didn't care, because what they wanted from him wasn't kindness. They were stupid children like the rest of us. He wasn't kind and he wasn't patient and he wasn't gentle. He barely had a chance to be anything at all.

Libby's ex-husband never won a Grammy or played a sold-out stadium. What he wound up doing is playing midsize clubs, which are usually packed with middle-aged women like us. We know this because sometimes, a few drinks in, Libby and I queue up the YouTube videos and watch. There he is on a stool with an acoustic guitar, passing a tambourine out into the crowd. You can see the women trying to be cool about it, restrained and a little ironic, even as they reach far enough for the tambourine that their shirts ride up and expose soft flesh, even as they gasp and squeal like the dauntless girls they used to be. And he is charming; he winks and banters and shakes his head, laughing at the ridiculousness of his own forty-something self in skinny jeans and a shirt with the sleeves cut off.

You two should get back together, I say on this night, meaning to tease, to joke, and am surprised when Libby sighs instead of laughing.

He wasn't a mistake, she says, but sometimes I think if we'd both gotten all that shit over and done with other people first. If we'd only met ten years later. Or now. And I'm not drunk and maudlin, if that's what you're thinking, she adds.

I wasn't, I say, and rest my head on her shoulder, and we watch a kind and gracious man who's a stranger to both of us now and a roomful of women we've never met but know, but know. We watch them, every one filled with the joy and abandon of people who have been on this planet long enough to appreciate absurdity and revel in it anyway.

⊚ ⊚ ⊚

I turn off the TV and close the laptop and ease the sliding glass door open, slip out onto the deck. My skin marbles up; it's chilly and damp, and there's a gray float of mist above the grass. I'm surrounded by sleep—Libby on the couch in the living room behind me, Charlie and Greta upstairs.

How time works: against you, against everyone. Every photograph is proof. The grass is wet, my fingers cold, my face.

Inside I tuck the blanket around Libby's shoulders and climb the stairs, sail straight past Portugal and the blinding Caribbean.

There are days when I worry what my husband and daughter see when they look at me and there are days when I don't fucking care.

Greta is sprawled and motionless, earbuds still in. I listen but can't hear whose voice is in her sleeping ears.

My brother and I had Walkmen, stiff metal headpieces and spongy earphones that disintegrated in bits, spring-loaded doors that broke and trapped cassettes. We turned the volume up, filled ourselves with roar and distortion. Seismic things happen in lyrics. In life, we go about our days.

Like we did. There are days I wish he were here only so I could sweep my hands wide and say to him *What are you missing, really?* and there are days I want to keep from disappearing.

Charlie is sleeping with his glasses on and a magazine open across his chest. I ease both from him and lay them on the dresser and kill the light. When I slide into bed he sighs and turns into me without waking.

These walls, our lives. We breathe against them, into them. We go about our days.

The Anniversary Trip

The three of them are sitting in a café on the Boulevard Saint-Germain, not far from the Odeon metro stop, the wife with her husband, the husband with his mother, not inside the café but at one of the tables on the sidewalk where the prices are exorbitant but the view of the passing crowd is almost enough to counter this. It is November and Paris should be cold, damp, the sky a low gray sheet, but instead it has been sunny and too warm for the cashmere and corduroy they packed. Their collapsible umbrellas have been useless. The wife—Monica—is damp with an unpleasant sweat most of the time, wet skin cooling at the small of her back and between her breasts every time she stops moving.

It is close to four in the afternoon and they are drinking: red wine (*vin rouge*, Monica thinks, corrects herself) for Carolyn, the mother; *un espress* for her son Martin. She herself is sipping an Evian though what she really wants is a bourbon and soda, Jack Daniel's, please, but she is in no way brave enough to order such a thing, such a crass American drink, at one of these cafés, in the presence of her husband's mother, of Carolyn.

The older woman finishes her wine and lights a cigarette, gestures to the waiter. *"Encore,"* she says, smiling, lifting her empty glass for him. He takes it and rushes off.

Carolyn is angular, her cheekbones jutting, her mouth wide, lips glossy red and thin. She wears her silver hair in a neat bob, pulls it up and off her face—her cheekbones—with enameled combs. She is more beautiful now, in her sixties, than her son's wife has ever been, or will be. Monica recognizes this and accepts it. Her husband Martin does not notice or, noticing, does not comment. Or at least has not commented, not in the five years they've been married or the five of on-again, off-again dating before that.

Monica has never quite been able to think of Carolyn as a mother-in-law, as someone for whom birthday greeting cards are designed with stamped gilded roses and unctuous sentiments in pastel script.

"I should've ordered a half-carafe instead," Carolyn says as the waiter returns with another small glass and a new ticket he slides under her ashtray. "You would've had a glass, Martin?"

He shrugs, eyes his wife's bottle of Evian. "Are you sure you don't want anything else?" he says, and she shakes her head. "Maybe I'll stop on the way back to the hotel for some wine to keep in the room," he says to his mother.

"Darling," she says, "do whatever you like. If you'd rather drink in the room than go down to the lounge that's perfectly fine with me." She pulls at the cigarette—*how is her skin still so lovely?* Monica wonders—and tilts her head back to exhale against the awning above them. "You can drink from those awful bathroom glasses and Monica and I will go down for aperitifs and pâté." She reaches for her daughter-in-law's hand and squeezes, her grip firm and cool. "Don't you think, my dear?"

They are on this trip to celebrate an anniversary of sorts: it has been just over a year since Martin's father died of pancreatic cancer, sixth months from diagnosis to death. The perfect length of time, Carolyn pointed out at the reception after the funeral, long enough for the two of them to say their goodbyes but short enough that there was no protracted decline, no months or even years of false hopes and setbacks, no extended physical humiliation or dementia. He was an efficient man and he had been efficient in his dying. A professor of acoustics, retired but for the occasional dissertation advice for a particularly promising doctoral student. His son Martin has a beautiful singing voice, an ease and grace with stringed instruments. Monica herself is tone-deaf, as unmusical as it is possible to be. When she confessed this at one of her first dinners with Martin's family his mother had laughed in delight. "Finally, someone like me," she said, and raised her glass to Monica. "My dear, you have no idea how happy I am to hear that." Even now it is hard for Monica to imagine how two women could be less similar than she and Carolyn.

So they are in Paris for two weeks on a trip that Carolyn planned and booked and paid for, a trip that Martin and Monica would not quite have been able to afford on their own. Their hotel is small but elegant, close to the Seine and Musée d'Orsay. On their own they might have afforded five nights there, seven if they ate from markets. To manage two weeks they would have had to stay in one of the outer arrondissements, by the *peripherique*, in a hotel with toilets in the rooms and communal showers down the halls. Their budget is not unforgiving, but it does not have room for extended or luxurious travel.

"I don't want an argument about this," Carolyn said after a dinner of salad and grilled shrimp one hot night in August, when she handed them their tickets and itineraries. "This is something I promised your father I would do," she told Martin, her voice free of unsteadiness or sentiment. "We'd planned to go to Paris for our fortieth anniversary," she explained to Monica, "which was obviously impossible under the circumstances. So I told him I would go anyway, but I don't relish the idea of traveling alone at this point."

"I don't know what to say," Monica said, and looked at Martin, whose face was impassive, his eyes focused out beyond the hedges in his mother's backyard.

"I think I'll be having aperitifs with you," she says to Carolyn now. They have all finished their drinks and Carolyn tucks bills under the ashtray, stows her cigarettes in her bag, and arranges her shawl over her shoulders. It is a lovely piece of fabric, purple and brown paisley shot through with gold, rich and exotic. No one guesses she is American until she speaks, and even then her imperfect French charms waiters and taxi drivers. "Dinner is at nine tonight," she says. "I have a few shops I want to browse in the meantime but you two go along. Take some time alone." She smiles at her son, a smile Monica recognizes, distant, chill. "Find something spectacular for your wife, Martin." She slips through the narrow space between tables, the fabric of her slim black trousers whispering. "*À bientôt*," she calls to the waiter, who salutes as he rushes past. *À bientôt*. Monica will remember this.

"I wouldn't mind just heading back to the hotel for a nap," Martin says, watching his mother as she crosses the street. "You don't have to come with me," he says. "You can do whatever."

Monica waits for him to finish his sentence—*whatever you want, whatever you feel like*—but he does not. To find the right words would fatigue him, as many such efforts have since his father died, since long before that. As many efforts always have. They both stand and sidle along the neat narrow row of chairs, each one turned to face the street. She looks for their waiter but cannot find him; she imagines him pouring wine and uncapping bottles of Stella Artois somewhere in the dark interior of the café. Martin kisses her cheek and moves off in the direction of their hotel, his head down. She stands on the corner, out of the way of the waves of people moving past, and tries to decide what to do. The sun is dipping behind rooftops and she finds herself in sudden shadow, though the light ahead of her is still gold and long. She will walk to the river, stroll back to their hotel along the quay. She wants to be sure, these two weeks, of seeing the Seine at every time of day, in every available light. She'd known before she came that Paris was beautiful but she had not been prepared for how unforgiving that beauty was, how overwhelming. She had been struck by the lack of what she understood as *charm*: it was not a charming city because it did not need to be.

She chooses a street she has not walked before and starts toward the river and falls into a peaceful near absence of thought, a calm she associates with childhood. She does not know when, exactly, she became unable to love her husband. She knows only that she woke one night and looked at him, at his face, lovely as his mother's but grave even in sleep and thought *I am finished. I am empty. I have nothing left for you.*

She reaches the quay and draws her coat more tightly around her. At this time of day she cannot tell which looks deeper, the Seine or the sky.

Monica's own mother is not beautiful. The most Monica can say honestly about her, looking through old photo albums and clumsily framed snapshots, is that at one time she was pretty enough. She lives alone in a ranch house with a finished basement that she paid for outright with her settlement from the divorce. Monica sees her once a year, or once every other. She has been in Carolyn's presence only a handful of times, and each time Monica is tense, alert, watching for the signs that her mother has had one beer too many: the incessant brushing of imaginary crumbs from her lap, the damp-sounding exhale of breath, somewhere between a sob and a sigh. On these occasions Carolyn has smiled and sipped at her wine and smoked many more cigarettes than is usual while Monica's mother eats peanuts from a glazed ceramic bowl, a wedding gift from one of Carolyn's friends. "These are really good peanuts," Monica's mother might say, or "Aren't peanuts just so good with a nice cold beer?"

She pauses at the window of a narrow shop along the quay. Crowded in the doorway are spinning wire racks of postcards and flimsy chiffon scarves, magnets on easels and tote bags stamped on their sides with disproportionately squat images of the Eiffel Tower. All of these items are helpfully priced in both euros and dollars. She can hear nothing but American-accented English coming from the shop and is moving away from the door, embarrassed, when she sees that some of the magnets are in the shape of pretty little baguettes, webbed *saucisson* and surprisingly realistic cheeses, and she smiles in spite of herself. She loves her mother and her mother would love one of these magnets, probably more than she would love to actually be here, eating food that Monica is certain she will never have the opportunity to eat. She waits until the group of Americans has left before slipping inside the shop. She will be sure to say *à bientôt* when she leaves.

◉ ◉ ◉

Martin dresses for dinner in neat gray trousers and a jewel-blue shirt. "You look very handsome," Monica says. It has become easier to compliment him with every day that passes, with every day closer to her leaving. "I bought a few little souvenirs for my mother today," she says. She sees that he did buy wine; there are four bottles lined up neatly on the desk she has been using as a vanity. Her leaving: to where? She has not allowed herself to think of this yet.

"Have you bought anything for yourself? You should pick something out—you know better what you like than I do."

She has not. But she has, wrapped in fragile tissue and tied with black silk cord, a package tucked into the corner of her suitcase, a pair of jade and sterling cufflinks she bought for him the day they arrived. They struck her as exactly the sort of gift Carolyn would have bought for her own husband, striking in their anachronism. What Monica's mother would call *a conversation piece*. The elderly man whose shop it was complimented Monica on her taste as he wrapped them, his English as archaic as his merchandise, and for a moment she was proud of herself: of finding the shop, going in alone, of counting out euros. She has no idea when she will give them to Martin, and only after she had got them back to the hotel and hidden them away did she become convinced that he would be disgusted with her, that he would think she meant them as some sort of awful consolation prize.

"Are you coming down for drinks with us?" she says. She has dressed carefully, in a simple black dress and red shoes, the shoes bought as a surprise by Carolyn earlier in the week. "No woman should have to go through life without a spectacular pair of red shoes," she said, handing the bag across the table where they'd met for lunch. "If they don't fit we can exchange them," she said, but when Monica tried them on in the hotel later the fit was perfect.

"In a bit. I might have a glass here first," Martin says, and gestures toward a pile of academic journals on the nightstand. "There's an article I've been wanting to finish."

Monica nods and takes up her satin purse. "Then we'll just be down in the lounge. We should get our cab by around a quarter till." She knows better than to try to coax him out. She knows enough to leave him to whatever abstract imperative he has decided upon.

In the hallway by the elevator is a narrow mirror. Monica stands in front of it and waits. She is thirty-four years old; since high school she has always looked her age, or older. Her mother is fifty-two. When Monica was in her twenties they were often mistaken for sisters. Her mother was delighted by this; after her divorce she went out every Friday night and every Friday night she asked Monica to join her. "Why don't you put your party clothes on?" she liked to say. "Let's have a girls' night out on the town."

The elevator arrives and she tucks herself into the tiny space. Her mother was divorced at forty—"Free as a bird," she liked to say. Monica imagines she herself will be able to say the same by thirty-five.

◎ ◎ ◎

"My son won't be gracing us with his presence?" Carolyn says. A cigarette is burning in the crystal ashtray and she lifts it to her lips, inhales once and stubs it out.

"He wanted to get some reading done." Monica settles on the sofa—*chaise longue?*—next to her and crosses her legs so that one pretty shoe is visible. Carolyn lays a warm hand on the ankle.

"Lovely," she says. "Really. They suit you—you shouldn't be shy about wearing beautiful things, my dear," she says. She fishes in her purse and draws out a tiny vial of perfume, presses it into Monica's hand. "And this I think will suit you as well—a sample from a little *parfumerie* I found today. If you like it we'll go back and buy some tomorrow." She finishes the drink in front of her and the waiter appears immediately. "I think we're ready for that champagne now," she says, and the waiter bows, collects her glass and ashtray and turns on his heel. "Reading," she says, and shakes her head. Her hair is loose tonight, spun silver. Amethyst drops sparkle at her neck. "Why would a man want to read when he could be sipping champagne with his wife?"

"I'm leaving him," Monica says, and once she speaks she is amazed, ashamed by how delicious the words taste to her, exotic and heady like the truffle shavings on her galette at dinner last night. "I'm leaving him. As soon as I can—he doesn't know yet," she says. She is racing to get the words out before Martin appears; she feels as though she is running for a train she cannot afford to miss.

The waiter returns and sets the champagne flutes down with a flourish and Carolyn says "*Merci bien, Monsieur,*" picks up the glasses, and hands one to Monica. She does not speak, not yet. Her face is still, open and waiting. Monica takes the glass.

"I need you to help me," she says to her husband's mother, though she has no idea what kind of help there could possibly be.

◎ ◎ ◎

Monica was twenty-five when she met Martin.

A serious student, a quiet man, educated, intelligent, everything about him exotic to her, seductive. So dedicated, not yet thirty and a doctoral student in the philosophy department where she worked as a receptionist. He smiled infrequently and she thought him intense, reflective; she had been smiled at all her life by friendly neighbors in the small town where she'd grown up, by schoolteachers and shopkeepers, by her reckless father and barely grown mother, she had had her fill of smiles.

She was the one to initiate. She was the one to stay at her desk until his Thursday seminar broke at five-fifteen, to pretend to sort through phone messages and interdepartmental mail until he zipped his coat and shouldered his bag and nodded at her on his way past the desk.

"Martin," she said, and he turned, surprised.

So then: drinks late that Friday afternoon, informal, noncommittal. He was reticent, he talked comfortably about only his research. But he reciprocated the invitation and she was surprised: a foreign-film matinee the following Sunday, then drinks again, then lunch, weeks of quiet meetings—dates? she was never quite sure—for an hour or three and then then *then*, finally, a Friday night that bled into Saturday morning and Saturday afternoon, his apartment dark, shades drawn throughout; his bedroom small and kempt and severe, his body also small and kempt and severe. His mouth unyielding, his skin so too, somehow. He was nothing like the boys and men she'd known growing up, affable in their baseball caps and worn jeans, their coolers of beer and soda on the porch or in the truck bed, ready for anyone who might happen along. They were expansive, they were as undemanding as a soft May sky.

When Martin kissed her she felt a weight of gravity she had not felt before. When he touched her she felt, somehow, solemnified.

The question she finally asked herself was not *Do you love him?* but *Can you love him? Will you love him?*

Yes. I will be able to do that.

So then.

◉ ◉ ◉

"There are some promises," Carolyn says, still holding her glass aloft, "that will ruin you. If you keep them past the point of—" she stops, searching, and Monica can see the echo of her son in the upward glance of an eye, the slight tension of the jaw as she thinks, "I don't know," she finally says, laughing. "If you keep them past their own point, I suppose. Past their point of usefulness."

"I tried," Monica says, desperate, close to tears, "I can't even tell you how long—" but Carolyn shakes her head, silver hair and amethyst earrings swinging, and holds up a hand to stop her.

"A toast," she says, "to my son, who was your husband for longer than I expected him to be." She touches her glass to Monica's and sips, sets the glass down and leans forward to rest her hands on Monica's knees. "I know Martin," she says, "and I believe you did the best you could. Drink, my dear," and Monica does. The lounge is filling, couples dressed for an evening out and a few single men in narrow dark suits, but Martin is not among them, not yet.

"It's difficult to imagine now," Carolyn says, "but this is not a tragedy. Not for you, certainly, but not for Martin either." She smiles. "And I think you know this, don't you?"

Monica nods. She is still watching the staircase for Martin, for the lovely peacock-blue of his shirt. She will give the cufflinks to Carolyn to give to him as her own gift—they are beautiful enough that Martin will not doubt his mother chose them, and she allows herself another moment of pride in this.

"Then I want to ask you something," Carolyn says. "A favor," and although Monica cannot imagine what she could possibly do for a woman like Carolyn she does not hesitate before saying, "Of course I will."

"I want you to wait, if you can," Carolyn says. She touches Monica's cheek with a soft fragrant hand and Monica imagines for one moment that the two of them are in this city alone; that they found each other independently of Martin, of anyone; that there is all the time in the world for Carolyn to teach her how to be someone completely different from who she is. "Wait until we get home to tell him—think of the rest of this week as a gift to me. Can you do that, my dear?" and Monica nods, lays her hand over Carolyn's and closes her eyes and thinks *I would wait as long as you asked me to so please ask for longer* and when she opens her eyes she sees Martin on the staircase, she sees her husband, his face pale and solemn above that lovely shirt as he walks toward them.

He never pretended to be anything he wasn't. I did. I am guilty of that.

Carolyn stands to greet her son and Monica does as well. He kisses both of them on the cheek and accepts a glass of champagne from the waiter before they all sit again and touch glasses—"To happiness," Carolyn says—and they drink and Carolyn speaks easily, casually, of an exhibit she is interested in seeing. The room is warm and candlelit and filled with the bright ring of crystal on glass and the low rush of laughter and Monica sips her champagne and though it is not something she has been in the habit of doing recently it seems right to take her husband's hand, slip her fingers through his. He neither resists nor responds. She remembers that first night with him, how cool the tips of his fingers were against her collarbone, how light their touch, as though he was somehow surprised to have found her there, naked and breathing in front of him.

◎ ◎ ◎

The last man Monica dated before Martin was an old acquaintance, someone she'd known vaguely in high school and met again much later, after graduating from the small college she'd driven ninety minutes each way to attend but before taking the job at Martin's university. She was working in a stationery store when he came in to buy a birthday card for his current girlfriend.

"I remember you," he said as she took his money. "Weren't you a few years behind me in school?" He did not have to specify which school. There was one high school in that town and no university.

His name was James—"But call me Jimmy," he'd said—and in addition to the girlfriend he had a three-year-old daughter by a woman he no longer dated but whom he still counted as a friend. The daughter's name was Polly, and that day he bought her a tiny stuffed rabbit, pink and yellow. This was James: a man who remembered birthdays and marked them with cards, a man who bought his daughter gifts for no reason, who found excuses—wrapping paper, masking tape, felt-tip pens—to come to the store during Monica's shifts. A man who made sure to tell her, one day a few weeks after that first meeting, that he'd stopped seeing his girlfriend, that he wanted to ask her out properly. She said yes. And at the end of that first date, after a steak dinner and a stop for ice cream, when he asked her out again before he'd even got her back to the house she still shared with her mother, that was also James: a man who understood exactly what was possible for him and was happy with that, a man who had no need of exceeding his reach. Monica was within his reach. And later that year when she told him she'd found another job and would be moving, he was genuinely puzzled: "But why would you leave? You *belong* here," he said, gesturing as if to take in the entirety of that town where he lived, where everyone he knew lived, smiling, happy, and Monica could not disagree. *That is the reason why, exactly.*

◎ ◎ ◎

When, eventually, Monica talks to her mother about Paris she will not even realize how completely it has slipped away from her, has become again what it was before she saw it herself, the images hazy and lucid all at once in the way of any vivid dream. She will sit in her mother's kitchen drinking coffee and describing the soft facades of buildings, white and gray and taupe, the faded red awnings of cafés, the boulevards and gardens and cathedrals, everything warm and inviting and unreal. She will mention Martin only offhandedly and Carolyn not at all and when her mother finally tires of feigning interest she will be secretly glad, relieved that time is passing, that Paris is again becoming nothing more than a word she might see on the cover of a glossy magazine or hear on a cable travel channel, certainly not a place where she once spent a few breaths of her life, and she will hardly remember the way the Seine sliced the city in half, a radiant curving knife, merciless and perfect.

As Though I Have a Right To

boys

We loved those unpretty boys, bony chests mushroom-white, Bic-barrel and burnt-wire tattoos crawling across pocked and blistered shoulders and backs. We loved their cheeks, scabbed or scarred, and their teeth, crooked and silver-filled but never capped or crowned. They wore jeans from the JCPenney and bandannas from the army surplus, T-shirts with the sleeves torn off and flannel shirts over them ten months out of twelve. Soft pack cigarettes in one back pocket and a Velcroed nylon wallet in the other.

They wore Wranglers and smoked Winstons: everything about them was one-off. Their skin was bad and their teeth were bad and if they managed to avoid being expelled before graduation it was not for lack of trying; if they found and kept a job that paid more than minimum wage they did so in spite of themselves.

They ate white bread, slippery and gritty with margarine and cinnamon sugar; frosted cornflakes and frosted wheat shreds; flimsy paper boxes of doughnuts from the grocery store, three for a dollar on a table by the checkout, the plastic window on the lid glazed and sticky. Those boys had a sweet tooth like you can't imagine and still they had to hook their belts to the last, still their backs were knobbed down their ribbed white undershirts.

But we wanted them for our own, their malty lips and chapped grabby hands and small small promises, and so we smacked cardboard tubes of cookie dough on our mothers' counters and sliced them onto metal trays, peeled the circles of dough half-scorched half-raw onto racks. We wrapped them in paper towels tied with whatever lengths of ribbon we found in kitchen drawers, took the bundles to homeroom or the weedy basketball court on the corner where no one played or Friday night parties where we shoved handles of Jack Daniel's and empty plastic cups aside to make room for them on kitchen counters. We mixed Jack and Cokes and lit cigarettes and leaned against those counters in twos and threes, in our discount designer jeans and bouclé sweaters, in our ankle boots and Jontue. We tipped our chins to the ceiling to exhale and from under our blue-mascaraed lashes we watched the boys tilt in, laughing, stumbling, reaching for everything at once: beers from the cooler on the floor and cigarettes from our open packs, the cookies broken and misshapen on paper plates.

They smoked our cigarettes and ate our food and reached for everything but us and we told ourselves we did not mind.

We did not expect much—torn sheets of loose-leaf taped to our lockers with instructions on where we would meet, a soda at the movies, a ride home from a party across town. We gave them our history notes and bought them slushies and peanut butter crackers at the 7-Eleven, wore their down jackets and rawhide bracelets, followed them into borrowed bedrooms and locked the doors ourselves. We had their babies because they wanted us to.

Our mothers hauled up from basements the strollers they were smart enough to keep, and we passed them among ourselves until the seats were torn and the wheels rusted, the plastic cracked and warped. We shared our tiny clothes until the fabric began to disintegrate, until the flannel shredded pink and yellow and we could not wash them anymore.

We propped the babies against kitchen cabinets and let them chew on the dolls that were not our favorites while we graphed $y = /x + 2/$, while we conjugated verbs in Spanish and tried to get our minds around the difference between *saber* and *conocer*: to know, to know.

We taped songs off the radio and painted our nails, curled each other's hair and left the babies with our mothers in the overly warm front rooms of our houses. We left them dozing on afghan-covered sofas and pulled the doors shut behind us, every block the same, one long sloping roof over eight square brick porches and eight sets of brick steps down to eight card-sized lawns, December grass chewed and brittle. We took those steps two at a time, bright parkas flying open behind us. We took those steps like they'd burn right through to skin if we touched them for too long.

mothers

They complimented our pretty hair and shiny lips, our belts and bracelets and polished nails, the way we set a table. They taught us to cook the bacon first so we could fry eggs in the grease, to iron cuffs and collars last, to get the dinner rolls from the day-old shelf at the market: if you rubbed them with margarine and wrapped them in foil and put them in a medium oven for fifteen minutes no one knew the difference. They bought us deodorant and training bras before we thought to ask, sandal-toe pantyhose and hairspray.

They taught us to layer rice and canned chicken and bright squeaky slices of cheese in casseroles; they bought us French manicure sets and Midol. They wore too much makeup or none at all. Their laughter was quick and rough and not always kind and their faces were lined or swollen, creased and brown or puffy, as though they carried every slight and disappointment in the skin itself. They kept their yearbook portraits on the wall with ours.

They were neither jealous nor demanding. They did not ask to see our corrected homework or graded tests; they looked at our report cards just long enough to sign them. They complimented us on the poster boards we markered and ribboned, pinned with magazine clippings and ticket stubs and mounted on our bedroom walls. They complimented us on our boys.

And those Friday nights when we called back over our shoulders that we would not be too late we didn't wait to hear the response, which they may not have been bothered to give in any case: what did it matter if we came home late or drunk, clothes stained or torn or crooked, gasping with laughter or tears, hungry, spent, sick; if we came home soaking from the fog that floated up from the river below the expressway after midnight or squinting against a cold yellow sun in the hard glare of a Saturday morning; if we came home used and wet and aching, wrung?

Our mothers didn't care as long as we came home, and as long as when we came home we didn't carry back into their houses with us some joy or fear or wonder that they had never seen or heard, some new want clinging radioactive to our flushed cold skin, filling the house with longing until there was no room for the old familiar air, until there was nothing else to breathe. They didn't care as long as we came back to them unchanged, their own, still dumb.

As long as we had tasted nothing new.

When we came home they locked the doors behind us, fluffed pillows and smoothed sheets and dabbed away our smeary eyeliner with the same damp wipes they kept to clean the babies we found so easy to forget. They brought the babies to us if we asked, but we rarely asked.

fathers

Our fathers kept their distance. They wore reinforced boots and reflective vests to work, carried clipboards and flashlights, insulated thermoses and extra gloves. They washed their big hands with Ivory soap, lathered the backs of their necks over the kitchen sink and dried off with torn lengths of paper towel. They drank soda by the liter and ate sleeves of saltines with mustard and salami. When they offered a cracker to us we choked it down and smiled though we preferred our saltines with peanut butter and apple.

On black winter mornings they sat across from our bowls of cereal with their peppers and eggs and bacon, their Ovaltine. They drank their coffee standing at the sink and kissed the tops of our heads as we slurped at our milky dripping spoons. They left in the gray freeze of night before it turned and came home in the gray freeze of the collapsing day, kissed the tops of our heads as we sat with our math workbooks and vocabulary lists. They drank Sunny Delight from the jug and cracked the kitchen windows when they lit their cigarettes, exhaled into the rattle and whine of traffic on the overpass, the red echo of sirens, and we shivered: so much cold from such a small gap.

They were not sure how to love us and so we did our best to make it easy: we climbed in footed pajamas onto their denim laps and nudged them awake with picture books, we modeled the uneven pigtails we'd scraped our hair back into and wrapped in mismatched ribbon, we twirled in our confirmation dresses and then our prom dresses, our pantyhose and heels.

We practiced for the boys on them. We folded their laundry although we could not be bothered to fold our own; we emptied their ashtrays and served their dinners first, jumped up for salt or ketchup. We folded the afghans up over them when they fell asleep in a living-room chair. We woke them with kisses on their rough and shadowed cheeks, we set their breakfast places with placemats and folded napkins.

When they touched our mothers we looked away until we began to watch, from tented blankets on the floor and half-closed doors, from outside the bathroom and down the bedroom hall. Our houses were so small. We watched until they saw us, until they swore and slammed doors and caught us by our skinny wrists to haul us to our rooms.

In our rooms we brushed our hair and glossed our lips and rubbed our wrists with new perfume. We opened our windows to light the cigarettes we'd taken from them, one at a time from crumpled packs left by the toaster, and exhaled into our own piece of sky. We watched for them in the narrow strips of grass behind the kitchens, lifting knotted trash bags into the garbage cans lined up by the alley, standing too still for too long in the dark starry cold, in the halo buzz of highway billboards.

When we looked at them we did not see their thinning hair and blurred tattoos, their hitched and limping gait. We did not see how they bent to drop their clothes where they stood by the bed at night, how they fell heavy into it and exhaled the day, its dull dragging minutes. We had no idea how sweet their sleep was, licorice-dark and thick enough to suck away everything they'd made themselves forget to want.

We could not begin to imagine what they wanted, or that they wanted. They *had*: jobs they'd held for twenty years, that they could perform with one eye closed and leave behind each night; brick houses in a block-long row of them filled with soft shag carpeting and recliners, full refrigerators, coolers and plastic chairs with waterproof cushions in the backyard. Wives who did the shopping the dishes the laundry; who made sure there was always a fresh unopened pack of cigarettes hidden away until they needed it. Us.

They had us, thin and quick and willing. If they drank through a Saturday afternoon or until a Sunday night was pretty we stayed close and quiet on the carpeted floor, folding construction paper into creased and flightless birds and ready to listen to any stretch or bend of truth they needed to tell, to believe.

They had been wronged. They had been overlooked and mistreated, snubbed and humiliated, by their employers, their government, their wives. Taken advantage of, used, cast aside. By cruel fate and bad luck. By their own trusting natures, their self-sabotaging kindness, their lack of killer instincts. And we listened, rapt, with ears too new to recognize the hollow ring of mawkishness, enraged at how the world had used them.

We seethed on their behalf. We wrapped our arms around their thick guts and pressed our faces to their gray and faded cheeks until we were no longer so thin or young, so credulous; until we began to tire of their blurred and slurry misery.

Their nose for injustice extended to us: when they thought they saw the shadow of betrayal in our eyes they began to twist their faces away from ours and push us from their laps. They let the coffee we brought them go cold and the beer go warm, they ignored the trays arranged with sandwiches and pretzel sticks, the ballpoint hearts on torn-off note paper tucked beneath the plates. They were the first to see right through our breathing skin to our cheap and fickle hearts, and they were the first to scorn what they saw there.

We fucked the boys to punish them. We made them disappear.

absolution

Our babies: gasping hot tears and red waving fists, ears like beans and thimble feet, mouths always open and wanting. We balanced them on our laps until our mothers, impatient, lifted them away from us and tucked them in the crooks of their sure arms. We did not protest or argue. We were clumsy with them, slow and awkward, no good at swabbing crusted black umbilical stumps or snipping toenails we could hardly see, no good at breathing calm against their mottled skin.

Our mothers freed them from our shaking grips, handled them as though they were at once miraculous and unremarkable; as though their very ordinariness was a wonder.

We handled them as though they had not nearly finished ruining us.

We sucked our deflated bellies in until we could get our jeans zipped up and over them; we wrapped our burning tits flat until they were dry and ours again. We stepped out of our sour wrinkled clothes and stared naked into mirrors until we convinced ourselves that what we saw was no different than it had ever been, no more spent or used. We tried to forgive our babies but it was so much easier to forgive their fathers. Our world was as wide as their smiles.

We forgave the gum in our hair; the snapped rubber bands in class and the snapped bra straps at parties. We forgave the scrawls on bathroom walls; the twist burns on the kickball diamond at recess and the cigarette burns on pull-out sofas in borrowed apartments. We forgave the stretch marks and stitches, the half-crushed boxes of chocolates from the express checkout in the drugstore and the scratchy rayon scarves from the two-for-five-dollar display, and when we brought their babies home and waited for them to collect us and bring us to the life they had no intention of building, we forgave that too.

◎ ◎ ◎

I say *we* as though I have a right to.

As though I don't still look for her everywhere, that baby I was too careful for.

As though I did not chew my own heart out to wake beneath a new sky.

joy

What bodies they had, stringy and loose and indolent, free of apology or guile. They slipped electric through our empty hours. What they wanted they got, without wheedling or compromise.

They did not need to bargain or beg: we made it easy. What they wanted we gave.

Quarters for air hockey at Eddie's Pizza and two-for-one pitchers on a Wednesday night, kung fu movies from the video store, clumsy joints that popped with sticks and seeds. The babies to carry like trophies into homeroom and hold for five minutes before handing them back to us and slipping down the hall and out the gym doors to the parking lot beyond. Us on our knees in someone's back hallway on a Friday night, hair damp and jaws aching, pants stained with spilled beer and mildew.

We didn't understand how much so little could cost.

If we had we wouldn't have cared: they belonged to the world in a way that we did not and we were happy to ease their already effortless way in it, to catch, if we could, the velvet smoky wake we could almost see behind them. We switched cigarettes to the brand they smoked. We waited for them in their mothers' kitchens, arranging slippery ribbons of pasta in casserole dishes and tearing lettuce into bowls; after dinner we jumped up when their mothers did to clear the table and spoon instant coffee into cups. We followed them out to underfurnished apartments with scavenged hubcaps piled in the living rooms and stolen electronics in the bedrooms and choked down the shots they poured for us, swayed against their skinny flannel heat. Sometimes we got drunk enough to believe that we were somewhere extraordinary, to forget how easily they tired of a room, a record, a game of cards, to protest when they jerked us up to leave and hardly feel it when they caught us backhand on the mouth, knuckles scraped and scabbed over, our own names inked across their fingers.

We loved the taste of their taut flesh, blood and nicotine and the powdery vanilla of our perfume. We loved the sound of their begging voices, thick with shame every time and every time vowing, swearing, on their mother's life on their grandmother's grave that it would never happen again. We loved that we were the only ones to make them sound that way. We loved it enough to believe them.

And when our ankles turned beneath us they carried us from the apartments and down greasy metal stairs, across volcanic parking lots. They folded us into the cars they'd borrowed for the night, cracked leather seats and taped windows, broken wipers and broken taillights and just enough gas to make it home. We let them slide their chapped hands into our corduroy laps and work the glinting zippers down, we let them lick the bruises they never meant to leave, we let them pry us wide and open as our pink and beating hearts. And when they were finished and asked us if we wanted more, we refused to understand the question. God yes, we said, and they lifted us back on their damp skinny hips. We closed what we could—our mouths, our eyes—and let them boil through the rest of us.

They broke us like kindling, like matchsticks for the bridges they wished they could burn.

Undertow

He is still my husband. What is left of him.

His body is a map of what has been lost.

The first things were sneaking, invisible—stamina, energy. It took him ten minutes to get out of bed, to the bathroom. He had to lean on the vanity to catch his breath, to rest on the lip of the tub after a shower. The distance from the driveway to the front door became interminable.

Next, peripheral vision. Balance. Little falls, the tip of a shoe caught on a curb, a treacherous doorway, a chair that tilted, spilled. His sides were blue with bruises. Smell, and with it taste—roasted quail, risotto, chilled Orvieto on the back porch in June—cardboard, cotton, water.

How could we have been so foolish, then, to complain? June was flawless, an idyll.

Next: fine motor coordination. Keys, pens, forks—fumbled, dropped. The remote control, his socks. My hand. My breasts.

For our honeymoon we rented a cheap apartment at a fading resort. The boardwalk was bleached and splintery, lined with penny arcades and taffy stands and ear-piercing pagodas. We dressed for dinner in cutoffs and clean T-shirts, we ate out of oil-spattered paper bags: waffle fries and funnel cakes and mint-chocolate fudge. We smelled of patchouli and sunscreen and by dusk our skin blistered, or flaked white, a harmless insult.

Mornings we woke to the smells of bacon and clean laundry coming from the apartments on either side of ours. We stretched and wrapped arms and legs, tangled, eyes still closed and sticky with dreams. The walls were thin but we were not quiet. His fingers, after they'd been inside me, tasted dark and salty-sweet.

What else? Haunted houses, miniature golf and bumper cars. Briny steamed clams, and sliced tomatoes, and beer. Soft-shell crabs and daiquiris at ten a.m. and anklets strung with bells. His body, still new to me, his hands greedy and generous, fast strong legs, sunburned shoulders. The sofa cushions were damp and sandy and I wore a necklace of pink shells and a pink skirt, gauzy, insubstantial. We fucked there, on the sofa, my skirt pushed up and my underwear aside, like that.

And? His voice.

◎ ◎ ◎

My parents live in a gated community—Gracious Living for Active Seniors, the sign says, by the mechanized gates, by the keypad, the electric eye that reads the sticker on their car window. The houses are new and hideous, carpeted and skylighted and landscaped, all single story, all wired to a central station staffed with private security and medical personnel.

They swim in too-blue water, they golf on too-green grass. They work a community garden with other community members, they harvest beets and parsnips and salsify and prepare them for elaborate potluck dinners, roasted and herbed and dressed with fine aged vinegar. Their eyes are bright; their skin is burnished wood, glowing. They wear linen drawstring pants and silk button-front shirts, hand-tooled leather sandals, cashmere sweaters in the evening chill; they drink martinis and Manhattans on their stamped-concrete patios. They do not talk about politics or religion or any subject that might provoke discord or require nuanced thought—this is their reward, now, for having made it intact to this flat sunny place.

These are my parents and their shining friends. They are pleased with where they have landed. They are wrapped in safety upon safety.

What right have they, at eighty, to such a life?

They go cruising on luxury ships that are overdecorated and overstaffed. They spend days shopping for coral jewelry and black pearls in the Bahamas, the Virgin Islands. They go on safari and write checks to the World Wildlife Fund and hang calendars with glossy photos of oryx and cheetahs on their kitchen walls.

They are well insured, with access to peerless health care— what some of my mother's friends call *Western medicine*. My father's internist is on speed dial, as is his cardiologist. My parents take medication for blood pressure and osteoporosis—*We are lucky, they say, We are blessed*—such minor ailments. They take multivitamins and various herbal supplements. They meditate, they receive acupuncture, they practice yoga. Even so, there is time for more indulgent pursuits.

My mother calls me every Friday and talks a wall, a tidal wave; she tells me about her cooking class and movie club and reading group and when she has exhausted her trove of stories from her week of cultural and aesthetic improvements she asks how I—how *we*—are. And I tell her.

You should really consider yoga, she says, when I have finished. She is so gentle, so concerned. She is filled with such serenity. She has no idea.

I would sooner saw off my feet than leave him for one unnecessary hour.

Perhaps you should speak to a priest, she says—or some other spiritual advisor.

What right has she to her sun salutations and warrior poses, her centering breaths, her tinctures and aromatherapeutic wraps? What right to coffee and croissants by the pool, to card games after lunch and tennis, to manicures and the new *gelateria* next to the nail salon? What right to private screenings of foreign films, to discussion prompts and journaling assignments?

I cannot help it: I wait for the day when what lives in my house comes to stay in hers. I wait for the day when she sees my father try to stand and fail, when his hip refuses to flex, his knee to bend. Or the day like any other when he wakes in a panic, his bedroom a place he does not know, his wife a woman he does not recognize. I wait for the day when she cannot deny what I already know.

◎ ◎ ◎

My own body is a fine machine, every part a model of competence, of efficiency. His body is erasing itself. His legs are white and wasted; his lovely arms curl inward, empty parentheses.

Even so, I am the one who is insignificant, who is useless.

He taught in jackets he'd owned for twenty years. His paperbacks were sun faded, bloated from damp, underlined and dog-eared. He corrected essays at the kitchen table with the radio blaring, he slashed red through usage and punctuation errors.

You'd think by the time they got to college they'd know this shit, he said, shaking his head.

Girls called, freshmen, their voices high and breathy and anxious, to ask for extra help, and he referred them to the writing center, and they protested: couldn't they just meet for coffee and talk about the paper then, instead of going to the writing center? Couldn't they just talk to him?

He was young enough, handsome enough, and they called and called.

We sat on our front porch barefoot and ate oranges and nuts. We drank wine from squat heavy glasses and tore stale bread into pieces for the cardinals.

I don't change the bedclothes nearly as often as I should. A compromise: I change the pillowcase daily. I change it before the saliva and sweat and watered-down juice can dry and stiffen. His head in my hand is fragile as a wasp's nest. He twists to look up and over at me and his neck is skin and sinew.

When we met I was with someone else, and one month later, I wasn't. It was the easiest thing I ever did, leaving, and the cruelest.

You'll live to regret this, my mother said when I called to tell her. That man is the best thing that's ever happened to you, she said, and she was right: he was a kind man, hardworking and conscientious, and wanted only to take care of me and the family we would have, the family I did not want with him.

Throwing all that away, she said, and for what? For some teacher without a pot to piss in.

His hair and nails have gone brittle and grayish, his lips have cracked and faded. But his eyes are still his eyes, sometimes.

◎ ◎ ◎

My mother calls to tell me they are going to the beach, she and my father, my sister and her husband and their baby. My father has rented a condominium, four bedrooms, three baths, a wraparound balcony five floors above the Atlantic sand. It will be the baby's first time seeing the ocean, my brother-in-law's first real vacation in years. He works in the financial industry; he sits behind a lovely lacquered desk and conjures money out of the air while my sister walks their teething daughter over the shining marble floors of their house. Her husband smokes Kools and eats a meatball-and-cheese sandwich for lunch every day and brings gourmet jelly beans to the office staff. His employees adore him. He is generous with their bonuses and vacation time. He takes pills for high blood pressure and cholesterol, his skin is soft and pink, and money cannot keep away from him.

My sister sets the baby in a carrier on the kitchen table while she prepares dinner, complicated vegetarian dishes that involve rare spices and obscure cooking vessels. When the food is simmering she takes the baby into the master bedroom and they nap, the baby wrapped in flannel and my sister in a velour throw, side by side on the king-size bed until her husband comes home.

I imagine the one I left in a life like that, now, whole and sound and healthy. I imagine him lifting his wife to kiss her, the wife he deserves, the wife who is not me.

He's better off without you, my mother said, and she was right.

You'll wish you never left, she said, and she was wrong.

Our bed is where my husband lives now. Occasionally, an outing: the chair by the window.

So they go to the beach, the four of them and the baby, and every day in my inbox I find pictures attached to my mother's brief notes—the baby in a terry-cloth hat and plastic sunglasses, my brother-in-law with a cigar on the balcony, my sister squinting at a magazine.

Everything is wonderful, writes my mother, *the accommodations, the weather, the food.*

Delete, delete, delete.

I puree carrots, I drizzle fruity green olive oil over them and tell myself it matters. I hoist his shoulders with one arm and stack pillows against the headboard with the other. When he is upright enough I spoon orange mush into his mouth.

He can still swallow, though I think he would rather not.

What he can't finish I store in the refrigerator, or scrape down the drain, or hurl against the kitchen wall, against the spot where the glossy animals would hang.

Save the Wildlife. Donate Now.

What my mother does not write: *Wish you were here.* Or *We miss you.* Or *Sweet Jesus how can you bear it?*

Every day he grows more still. As if practicing, or rehearsing. He has always been a perfectionist.

◎ ◎ ◎

He loved candy. Peanut butter cups, Snickers, handfuls of M&Ms—cheap sweet chocolate, childhood. Foil-wrapped Kisses rattled loose in his desk drawers. At the ends of semesters he worked through the night. He drank coffee with milk and three sugars and used a green marker to grade final papers and ate bags of miniatures—Milky Way? Almond Joy?

I am already forgetting him.

I warm chocolate in the sun and touch my finger to the melting surface, let him work the gloss of it from my finger. This takes time. His lips are slack, his tongue slow—not sluggish. Slug-*like*. There is a difference; one he would appreciate.

My hands become sticky, my fingers as clumsy as his lips.

Except, not really; not nearly.

The messages, the photos, keep on.

Dinnertime! my mother writes, and attached is a picture of my niece, grinning through a smear of soup.

I look at this picture and imagine sending one of my own, imagine forcing his flapping matchstick arms through pajama sleeves and propping him upright, head lolling on the stalk of his neck and eyes darting, the left one faster than the right, the right one drooping, closing.

Allthetime!

I used to be kind, but there is no room for kindness here.

◎ ◎ ◎

I used to be many things, before him—before *this*—but it is an effort to remember what.

Kind—yes, that. What else? Patient, until there was no time for that.

I sleep on a cot at the foot of what used to be our bed. I can reach him from here, arm stretched, fingers extended, and sometimes, waking, I do. And sometimes, waking, I find myself on the bed next to him, curled against his bones, the mattress a floating white raft around us.

How did I get here? I whisper, but he does not move and it does not matter. The floor pitches and rolls beneath us.

I used to dress in the morning, twist my hair in a lacquered clip and spray perfume on my throat and wrists. I left lipstick marks on my coffee cup. Five mornings a week, I went out into a world that I can't remember; I came home to one that no longer exists.

What was I? I whisper. Neither of us knows. I can see my cot in the dark; it is farther away than when I left it. There must be an undertow.

I used to line my eyes with kohl and stack bracelets up my arms. I used to make preserves of lime and orange. I used to be afraid of deep water.

At dawn the beach was empty and we walked along the surf line as though we could never use up the day, as though we had years of mornings.

As though grief were not lapping at our feet.

He is disappearing. He is taking me with him.

◎ ◎ ◎

My mother calls when the trip is over. They are home, she says, they are tanned and rested and renewed.

This is the word she uses: *renewed*.

She tells me that my father, my sister and her husband have decided to make the trip to see me. She has agreed to watch the baby.

I told them you would be fine, she says, and her voice is dry and light as a leaf, and from our bedroom I can hear his breaths, the marble-rattle, and the silences between, too long.

When I told her we'd got married she said it wouldn't last a year.

His breath, like tearing paper. We have had five.

I have to go, I tell her. I can hear him dying.

◎ ◎ ◎

In our kitchen is a bottle of wine, a bowl of pomegranates. On his desk a stack of notebooks, a chocolate bar, a pen gone dry.

I brush his hair, touch balm to his lips with my finger. I smooth the sheet across his shoulders. I sit in the chair by the bed where I used to read to him. I don't, anymore; he is too busy leaving me to listen.

I slip my hand under the sheet, under the thin cotton of his pajama bottoms, and when I close my hand around him he jumps, chokes a sound out from somewhere I have never been. He lurches in the bed, twists to face me, and his eyes are silver pebbles, his eyes are full of hate like I have never seen.

Like this he is only mine: no other woman has seen those eyes. I lean to kiss him and he tastes like a panicked animal, bitter and delicious.

Better

My father-in-law is drunk. This is something only my husband and I know: the old man does not stagger or flail, he is not vacant; neither too friendly nor hostile to the woman who shows us to a table and sets down three bundles of silverware wrapped in paper napkins before disappearing behind a counter.

We know he's drunk because he always is, in that low-grade way of the long-term alcoholic. Low-grade, like a fever—on a day like today he is just feverish enough. He prefers rye—an odd, old-fashioned preference—but drinks vodka on the days we take him out. This is some combination of cunning and vestigial thoughtfulness: the smell of vodka disappears into the drugstore aftershave he pats on in his bathroom at home, hands trembling.

The woman who seated us returns with three oversize plastic cups of water bunched against her apron and I see that she is not a woman at all, she is maybe eighteen, or twenty, almost pretty and young enough that for a moment her worn face takes me by surprise until I remember where I am—this is a neighborhood I used to know well, the streets and houses and the girls in them, girls who are flawless at twelve, bruised at fifteen and ruined at

94

thirty. I smile at her and she smiles back, spreads three laminated menus on the table and touches my shoulder. "You let me know when you're ready to order."

The menus are sticky, cloudy in spots and smeared. "Raymond," I say, "can you read the menu or do you need one of us to help you out?"

"Dad?" Michael leans across the table and grasps his father's narrow wrist. "Do you know what you want to eat?"

"Chicken," the old man says. "And a beer. Some bread." He shakes Michael's hand free and feels across the table, knocking into one of the glasses. Water splashes, an ice chip skitters to the floor. "Where's the peanuts?" he says.

"How about a sandwich?" I say. "Chicken parmigiana? I don't know if they have peanuts." We're careful where we take him; the list of what's risky is long—steps and stemmed glasses; candlelight; carpets and upholstery and linens; daily specials that might run out; a back door, a liquor license—and so we end up in places like this one, with plastic cutlery and paper napkins, a stack of Xeroxed to-go menus and a Styrofoam cup with Tips markered on it next to the cash register. It's safe—safer—this way.

"Sandwich?" Raymond says. There is a slight but visible tremor in his neck and he steadies himself, focuses on me with an effort before turning to his son. "She must be extraordinary in the bedroom," he says, his enunciation careful, precise, "otherwise, you'll have to explain the appeal. The appeal," he says, "escapes me at this moment in time."

"Jesus, Dad," Michael says. He scrapes his chair backward, rubs a hand over his face. He is a patient man, usually, forbearing and stoic, but he hates these storefront eateries with their uneven floors and sticky tables and exhausted staff, hates every minute that he is obligated to spend in them, hates that they are what his father is left with even if the old man is beyond caring, or noticing. "Can we get through one goddamned lunch without this? Can we try, for once—"

"Michael," I say to him—our waitress is coming back, pen in hand—"It's okay," I say, my voice low, and turn my attention back to her, to this girl who will pocket the pile of bills and coins we leave her gratefully, whose beauty was ground out of her before it could open and bloom.

"I think we need a few more minutes," I say to her, "but maybe a soda for my father-in-law and when we're ready I'll just come up to the counter with the order?"

She nods. "Absolutely," she says, "you take all the time you need," and there again is her hand on my shoulder, easy, familiar; she touches me as though she knows me. "I'll be right back with a soda for you," she says to Raymond, who does not acknowledge her presence at all.

"Thanks," Michael says to her. I reach for one of his hands but he shifts away from me. He would never admit it, but still: in places like this he hates me as well.

"Dad," he says, "They've got subs and sandwiches. There's egg plates—" he glances at a menu, "tuna salad, chicken salad—the usual. What do you want?"

"God rest your mother's soul," he says. "God rest her beautiful soul, and Deirdre's." He jerks his chair in staccato scrapes so that he can look at me without moving his neck at all. "Those two are in the great embrace of light and everlasting—" he hesitates, his eyes glassy-bright, "everlasting grace." The waitress returns with his drink, a paper-tipped straw bobbing at the top. She places it an inch from his splayed fingers. "Right there, on the left, sir," she says, as though it is the most natural thing for her to direct a customer's attention to something right in front of him, and my heart cracks. This girl has not yet given up on grace.

"Thank you," Michael says, his face stiff—he hates, too, her kindness—and she waves him off, the universal gesture: *of course, my pleasure, no problem.*

"The problem, as I see it," his father says, "is one of decorum. Of decency, which I recall from some days and years ago. That young lady," he says, gesturing vaguely toward the counter, where our waitress has gone to begin preparing our trays, "who is properly neither young nor a lady, and who would be more appropriately employed in the privacy of a gentleman's quarters, is at present a walking affront to the memories of those who have gone, more modestly, before her."

We have only been sitting here for five minutes. Less. My father-in-law's hands shake, his throat pulses. His thirst must be enormous. "Do you think my son is aware of the magnitude of his compromise?" he says to me, this man whose floors I have mopped, whose linens I have washed. "Do you think he understands the enormity of his loss?" I don't speak, and in the silence that follows I smooth the napkin in my lap and wait for Michael to say whatever it is a husband should, in such a circumstance. I could wait for this until the walls crumble around us.

◎ ◎ ◎

Michael's first wife died on a bathroom floor. She died in cotton underpants and an old oxford shirt, the underwear hers and the shirt his, paint-spattered, blood-soaked, the paint dry and the blood not, legs and arms bare, splayed on a mint-green rug on a white tile floor, twenty-three years old. A beauty, a painter, her parents' only child, with long pale hair and a scar by her lip from a bicycle accident when she was a little girl, with a silver band on her finger and a cellophane-wrapped lemon candy in the shirt's breast pocket.

She died with the water running in the sink, with her head tilted back over a folded towel on the lip of the tub, with a mostly full can of root beer on the vanity, with a pile of Michael's laundry in the corner by her foot. Her foot was bare, her feet and legs tanned, like the rest of her. This was August, a Monday morning in August ten years ago, this was in their first and only house together, a duplex on a wide sunny street with cracking sidewalks and smallish trees.

She took tranquilizers, just enough to calm herself, not enough to vomit back up. She cut on the vertical, deep gashes in each narrow wrist, three inches long, parallel and evenly spaced. She meant it.

What kind of man tells his second wife such details?

My husband, who was still her husband when he kissed her goodbye and left for work that lazy August morning, decided to come home for lunch, and this was when he found her, not in the tiny spare room she used as a studio but in the bathroom, on the floor like that, not quite dead yet, not quite, not yet, and because she was still alive he believed that what he did—the call to 911, the towels pressed to her cooling arms, the mouth-to-mouth—might make a difference. Might save or keep her. He did not consider the possibility that someone unhappy enough to do such a thing might not want to be saved, or kept.

What he did—the call, the towels, the breathing—was not even close to making a difference, though what he did was right. The doctors told him this last, thinking it might bring him comfort. I cannot imagine anyone who would take comfort in that, in knowing that the right thing was useless.

So that afternoon he left the hospital with his dead wife's, his first wife's, clothes in a sealed plastic bag inside a larger paper one, with her wedding ring perched on the tip of his smallest finger, with the phone number of a support group on a card in his pocket. He did not go back to work—he would never, in fact, go back to that particular job—and he did not go back to their house, his house, that duplex, the front door of which he had left not only unlocked but open. He sat on a wooden bench some few yards away from the emergency-room doors and waited in the melting August light for his father to arrive, and when the older man pulled up in his dark-blue sedan he got into the car wordlessly. They drove in silence back to the apartment where his father—a drunk even then, a widower himself—lived alone. The elevator often stalled between floors, so they walked the five flights up, stopping on the landings so his father could rest. Once inside, Michael—I suppose at that point he was no longer, really, her husband—sat at the small kitchen table and placed the bag of clothes in front of him. His father filled two tumblers with rye and set them on the table, lowered himself into a chair by his son.

"Listen to me carefully," he said. "You will come to understand why it was better for this to happen now—better now than later. Before there was an opportunity for a profound variety of attachment."

The old man, even then.

For the next few weeks he slept on his father's sofa. He slept from dusk until midmorning, when bright daylight burned its way through the thin woven curtains, and in the early afternoon, when the sun had passed, he slept again. During his waking hours he listened to—or did not listen to—his father's unending recitation of his mother's virtues. She had died of a stroke, after thirty years of marriage—enough time for countless virtues to be made apparent. During his waking hours he considered his own dead wife, and he became furious with her, not for the commission of the act itself so much as the timing of it: they had been married barely a year, and because of this he would have a paucity of stories to tell about her virtues, about her. During his waking hours he felt himself rotting from the inside.

At some point, during this time, he became the man I would marry.

What kind of woman marries such a man?

◎ ◎ ◎

"I wouldn't even bother with that," Michael says. I'm wrapping what's left of his father's lunch, which is most of it.

"What are you talking about?" I say. "This is a lot of food. It's enough for dinner, at least." I glance up toward the hall to the restrooms, where Raymond has gone to drink from the flask he carries when he's forced to leave his apartment. "He's so thin, Michael. I think since we saw him last—"

"Jesus, Sue, I know," Michael says. "I know he's thin, I know he doesn't eat, I know. You can't force him."

"I'm not forcing him, I'm just making sure he has something if he wants it." A Styrofoam carton of potato salad, one of green beans, a turkey sub with a few bites gone. I wrap the sub in foil and pack everything into a white paper bag. "If he gets hungry, he'll have it."

"Has it not occurred to you yet that he doesn't want it?" Michael says—what he means is *he doesn't want it from you*—and gets up to collect his father from the restroom. We've played this scene before: at some point during lunch Raymond excuses himself to the restroom and doesn't come back, won't come back until Michael goes to get him. *One of these days I'm just going to leave him there*, Michael sometimes says, and I let him think I believe he means it.

The two of them come out of the restroom and I stand, collect Raymond's soda and the bag with his food. Michael has a hand under his father's elbow, a rudder, and the old man moves forward steadily, spine straight and chin out. A stranger would imagine him to be nothing more than frail.

I'm thinking this, relieved that we've got through as well as we have, when they pass the counter where our waitress is sorting silverware and Raymond reaches into a pocket for a handful of change and tosses it in her direction. The smile on her face freezes as coins skitter and bounce across the counter, to the floor at her feet, and she looks up, confused. "To keep you in the manner to which you are accustomed," Raymond says, melting into laughter, and Michael tightens his grip, moves them forward faster. "Meet us at the car, Susan," he says, but I hesitate—she is looking at me, our waitress, the corners of her mouth trembling, and all at once I see that I was wrong: there is nothing left in her to save. Here is her life, in its entirety, and we are no more nor less of an insult than anyone else.

"Susan, come *on*," Michael says, and I push through the door ahead of them.

⊚ ⊚ ⊚

He slept on his father's sofa and listened to the old man's stories and drank the old man's rye and his grief shrank and hardened, became a throbbing clot. It burned to the touch and so he stopped touching it. It refused to heal and so he stopped nursing it. It took root, a live thing, an infection, *his*.

He left his father's apartment for one of his own and slept in a bed but did not always wake in it, waking instead sometimes standing in the bathroom, the clean empty bathroom, gasping, choking on what he was sure was his dead wife's blood. He worked for a custom cabinet maker and sometimes coughed out his own blood, the sawdust and particulate matter in the shop abrading his sinuses, his throat. His palms calloused, his hair grayed along the nape and behind his ears, his shoulders broadened, his waist thickened. His wife remained twenty-three and blonde and tanned, remained perfect, remained dead. His heart, traitorous, continued to beat. Time continued to pass, months of it, years, and he began to feel a strange ache that he eventually came to understand was loneliness.

It was at this point that I met him and began to love him. His ruins. I was ready to save him. I was not ready to see that he didn't want saving. And so when he showed me his heart, the hollow yaw of it, I refused to see. Blind, I began digging at a stranger's grave.

⊚ ⊚ ⊚

We load the old man into the back of the car for the drive to his apartment. I open the rear door so he can drop backward onto the seat and Michael helps him lift and bend and swivel his legs into the footwell, then pulls the seat belt to and secures it. Even with both of us it takes some minutes—Raymond is slight, but leaden. Michael pulls out of the parking place and into traffic and already his father is slumped, eyes closed, mouth open, anchored by the seat belt. His breath rattles gently, and by the high thin sound I can tell his teeth have come loose, have opened up a thin whistling space between plate and wet pink gums.

"Do you want me to wake him?" I say. Michael looks straight ahead, his hands light on the wheel.

"For God's sake, why?" he says. "So he can shower you with a little more love? You in the mood for that, Susan? Because I'm not. I'm about finished for the day, I think." He glances at the rearview. Raymond's head lolls, bounces. The seat belt has caught his shirt, bunched the collar up toward an ear. His undershirt is grayed. Before he was a drunk he was a professor of history. *Which area*, I'd asked Michael once, years ago when I still asked questions, and he'd looked at me with pity: as though the answer mattered.

"I don't want him to choke," I say, and Michael laughs, mirthless. "When he chokes it won't be in the back of our car," he says. He taps the brakes, flashes his lights at the car in front of us. "I hate this road," he says. "Goddamn."

It's a city street, two-way, one lane of metered parking and one of traffic in each direction, lights at every block, sidewalks, bus stop benches, the concrete stained and cracking, the wood warped and peeling. Raymond's breath catches in his throat and he starts; his teeth click back into place.

History: he was a professor and a husband, then a professor and a widower, then a widower and a drunk.

"I should have taken the highway," Michael says.

"Faster this way," I tell him.

"He's in no hurry."

Intersections, crosswalks, this neighborhood is still full of pedestrians, old women wheeling canvas grocery totes, younger ones in housecoats and cardigans, men with newspapers rolled and clamped under frayed jacket sleeves. Teenagers, girls in too-small shirts and boys in too-large pants, smoking, shouting, in and out of the storefronts, the Baskin-Robbins and Epstein's Drug, the Park Avenue HiFi Palace, napkins and flyers and promotional circulars spinning, shredding at their feet. I know this place. I know it the way only someone who's tried to forget can know a place.

"How is he with his meds?" I ask Michael.

"What?"

"Does he have enough?" Heart disease—dilated cardiomyopathy. This will kill him well before the cirrhosis does.

"Shit," Michael says. He rubs a hand over his face, eyes the rearview again—he's hoping to look and see that somehow, there is nothing in the back seat but sweet empty space; I know him the way I know these streets. Raymond's slipped lower under the shoulder harness and there's a bubble of saliva on his lips, quivering. "I have no idea," Michael says. "He was supposed to get a refill last week, I think—can you—"

"I'll check when we get him home." It is my job, keeping track of the prescriptions, and has been for some time now. The diuretics, the beta-blockers, the multivitamins. The blood pressure monitor, the laundry and groceries, fragrance-free detergent and high-fiber cereals, salt-free seasonings, antibacterial wipes and disinfectant sprays: the procurement and maintenance of these things, too, my job. Medication, nutrition, hygiene; clean folded towels, cases of Pedialyte and Ensure, cellophaned three-packs of Ivory soap. No mouthwash, no cough syrup, no acetaminophen.

We stop for a red light and there's a rustle from the back seat, Raymond pulling himself straighter. "I see you've decided on the scenic route," he says. His eyes are bleary, his skin papery, dull.

"Did they deliver your refill, Dad?" Michael speaks to the rearview mirror. I keep my eye on the traffic light, counting seconds.

"When I was a young man a friend and I would come, on occasion, to this area," Raymond says, "for what we liked to call excursions." The windows are closed and his breath fills the car, denture adhesive, weak mint. The light changes; bent men in threadbare pants climb back onto the sidewalks. My own father died before I could speak. "We would come with pockets full of cash and clean handkerchiefs," he says, turning his head from side to side as Michael eases the car forward.

"Your pills, Dad," he says again, his voice louder, tensing, "the refill—"

"Sectral," I say. "I think that's the one." Three more blocks, then the turn, the crosstown acceleration.

"We would come for a dose of what we liked to call fuckery," Raymond says, "from the kind of girls I'm sure you have not encountered, Michael, but whom your wife could perhaps explain to you, seeing as how she is familiar with our immediate environs."

"Don't," I say, low enough that Raymond won't hear, but it's unnecessary: Michael does not respond, just drives, chasing yellow lights until the traffic thins and he can swing the car onto the smooth new blacktop, the bypass. My father is dead and my mother is tight in a senior housing complex she can just barely afford.

I see her twice a year, on her birthday and the day after Christmas, when she sets aside the presents I bring and works crossword puzzles while I sit in the armchair I remember from our front room when I was a little girl. When it is time for bingo, or *Wheel of Fortune* in the sunroom, she marks her place in the crossword book with her pen and stands, accepts my kiss on her cheek. She is finished with family, what's left of it.

Bright green exit signs blur by. This car can move.

"While you get him settled I'll check the medicine cabinet," I say to Michael, who drives, drives, and I am almost ready to press the radio on when I hear a choke and gurgle from the back seat and there is Raymond, eyes closed and mouth open, a thin brown bile pooling behind his teeth, under his tongue and finally spilling over his chin and I lurch over the seat back with the clutch of napkins I've been holding all along. He hiccups and more comes and when the napkins are sopped I use the front of his shirt.

"Jesus," Michael says, "*Dad*—"

"Just drive," I tell him, "he's fine, just go," I say, and it is true: this, right now, is what has come to pass for fine. I drop the napkins to the floor and press his shirt to his chin, to his slack lips, whispering the usual nonsense: *it's all right, it's okay, we'll be home soon, soon, soon.* He jerks his head away from my hands, from me, draws back so that his eyes can focus and his gaze is clear as the vodka in his flask. "What you do," he says, "means nothing. You know that, don't you?"

Michael exits the bypass—*cities, hearts*—and I brace myself against the back of my seat.

"Of course I know," I say to Raymond. He allows himself a smile and lets his head fall back.

"Michael," he says, "tell your wife she can sit back down. Tell your wife I am quite through with her services. Such as they are." He looks at me and all he sees is who I am not.

◎ ◎ ◎

I am not a second wife anyone would imagine. There is nothing of the prize in me—I am not some golden thing, newly forged, barely breathing. When I met my husband I was already thirty years old, worn smooth in some places, rough in others. I was kind.

Thirty—seven years luckier, then, than she had been. Deirdre.

The yellow hair, the green rug, the white shirt and white tile, and the blood an exclamation over all of it—he told me this at a patio bar, fizzy drinks on the table and a basket of popcorn, in the soft sweet dusk of early summer. He presented all this to me, a gift I didn't want wrapped in twilight and tonic, muscle and skin. We were barely more than strangers.

When he finished the story, he drained his glass and reached for my hand. I had to fight not to pull it away. At the table next to us three boys in baseball caps high-fived one another, clinked their beer bottles together and chanted something unintelligible.

"I don't ever want you to think I wasn't honest with you," he said, and I nodded, dizzy, struck dumb. "It's important that I tell you everything," he said, and I nodded, a puppet, an idiot girl I had never been. Everything—I didn't know his mother's name, or his father's birthday; I didn't know his face in sleep. All that was nothing.

He squeezed my hand, leaned over and said "And I don't want you to think I kept anything from you, because I didn't. I won't. I can't be with you if you don't know."

I finished my drink and he stood, lifted me by the hand to lead me between the tables and the boys in baseball caps kept on, drinking and laughing in the fading pink light, oblivious to death slipping by them.

◎ ◎ ◎

Raymond's apartment is dark, too warm; it smells of living things. The walls are thin, the paint scuffed and stained and cracking. The windows vibrate with music coming from the neighbor's stereo. The couch is the same one Michael slept on, some dozen years ago.

We put Raymond there, on the couch, and stand for a moment, breathing.

"I don't think we should just leave," I say. Yeast, I'm breathing; mildew. Bath towels are piled on the kitchen table. How long since I've been in this place? Two weeks? Not quite?

"I am fully cognizant of your words," Raymond says. I look down: everything about him is skewed, sideways, one shoulder high and cramped-looking. His eyes flutter open. "You are not the first woman to express *thought* in this place."

"Leave her alone, Dad," Michael says. "For Christ's sake." He makes a move toward the kitchen area—tiled floor, shrunken appliances lined against the wall—and stops. He has no idea what there is to be done.

"Here," I say. I hand over the bag of leftovers. "Why don't you see if anything in the fridge needs throwing out? And whatever he needs—if you make a list—I can get to the store tomorrow." On the couch Raymond tugs at a pants pocket, curses. The flask is caught on a seam. "Bring him some ginger ale, if there's any, or some juice," I say to Michael. "You do the kitchen and I'll take care of the bathroom, all right?" He does not respond, only shakes his head. The counter is covered with dishes, plastic cups and take-out bags. "The ginger ale," I say again, softly, and he looks at me as though he has never seen me before.

The bedroom is spotless, the bed covered in a white chenille spread, pillow shams fluffed, needlepoint bolster centered in front of them. A flimsy dresser with a crocheted runner over the scarred top, an armoire, a straight-backed chair. This room has not changed since the first time I saw it. It is the bedroom of a husband, a sober man; one who is grieving or ready to grieve. It is the room of a man I do not know. The only sign of Raymond is the carpet, plush and deep green but worn in a narrow path from the doorway to the bathroom: cigarette burns, torn and matted pile, stains.

The bathroom is where I find what I expect. It's a small room, a rectangle with a toilet and bathtub, a built-in vanity along the short side and plastic shelves screwed into the plaster next to an oversize mirror. The floor is slick; there are stacks of magazines and old academic journals piled along the side of the tub, bloated and warped, some sopping, some only damp and curled along the edges. Condensation runs down the sides of the toilet tank, disinfectant fumes burn my sinuses. I flip a switch and the fan sputters into life. The vanity is covered: sodden napkins, and plastic cups, used razor cartridges, the blades thick with rust. On a shelf by the mirror is a row of women's perfumes, the bottles old-fashioned, glass heavy and faceted and golden, capped with stoppers meant to look like birds and ribbons, a thick layer of dust on their shoulders. Black plastic combs, three for ninety-nine cents, eye drops, ear drops, Poli-Dent. Gauze pads, Ben-Gay. No orange plastic pill bottles, no prescription inserts or pharmacy envelopes. I kneel to look under the sink when he appears in the doorway.

"Can I be of some assistance?" he says. He is wavering, just balanced, gripping onto the door frame. It is filthy, the paint along the jamb a greasy brown.

"Raymond, your medication," I say. "Your pills, from the doctor, from the pharmacy—where are they?"

"Perhaps you can be of some assistance to me, then, seeing as to how your husband has recused himself from the situation at hand."

"What are you talking about?" I say.

"Right there, where you are, is a good place to look. Your husband. My son. It seems he has decided his presence might be better appreciated elsewhere."

"Did he go to the grocery store, Raymond?"

"Under there," he says, gesturing at the door beneath the sink. He lowers himself onto the lip of the bathtub, braces his feet against a pile of magazines, and he's close enough that I can see how bloodless his lips are, how opaque his eyes. "I keep all my medication under there." I pull at the vanity door and it swings wide, loose on its hinges. The cabinet is filled, bottles of bourbon and Scotch, none full, crowded all the way to the rear wall, tilted under the pipes, wedged into a pile of towels, and in a corner the pills, a jumble of bottles and wadded pharmaceutical inserts. Months' worth, every bottle labeled and sealed and full to the top.

"Raymond," I say, "I don't understand—haven't you—"

"You do understand," he says. "You are in possession of more insight than my son." He reaches toward me and in the instant it takes me to know what he wants I understand what he means.

"You'll die," I say, and he smiles, his hand still extended. It is mottled and gray and gaunt, as though the skin itself were exhausted.

"Susan," he says. It is the first time he's ever called me by name. "Please, dear girl." I pick a bottle at random from the hoard and hand it over to him. He unscrews the cap and drinks and hands the bottle back to me to hold. "Your life with him will eventually come to seem impossible," he says. "In the meantime—until such time as we both know will transpire—I am going to dispose of these pills at their regularly scheduled intervals. You will not tell him this." He extends his hand again and when I offer the bottle he curls his hand over mine, hard-knotted and cold. "He will love you as much as he can and it will not be enough. Nonetheless." He eases the bottle from my grasp and sets it on the floor, takes my hand again. "I don't know if you deserve better than him. I suspect you don't. But then again, I have encountered very few in this life who deserve better than—" he pauses, searching. "Better than. Just that."

When he begins to shudder I move next to him, guide him so his shoulder is against the wall, brace my arms on either side of him. He shakes; his breath smells sweet, too sweet, turned fruit. It is the only sound in the apartment, this rattle and rasp. I hold him while his heart goes about the business of using itself up, not nearly fast enough. When he quiets I help him lift the bottle to his lips, and when he is finished I drink from it myself. There are no ghosts here. I hold him and we wait for his son to come back to us.

A Little Mercy

What will you want to remember?

The way they look at you: the boys like prisoners and the men like thieves.

The feel of your skin, tight, taut, radiating heat and shining after the sand and salt water and too-hot shower, the coconut lotion. How brown your stomach is, how flat; how red across your shoulders, the bridge of your nose, the sting of it. Your hair sopping the back of your shirt and the rubber smack of two-dollar flip-flops against your calloused heels, your cutoffs. Your sixteen-year-old ass and the cherry-red sun dropping into the bay and the smell of low tide.

The comfort of all this, the insufficiency.

The splintered boardwalk and the drunks beneath it, the barkers, too loud, with their parachute pants and Parliaments, their water rifles and clammy plush alligators, understuffed and so much lighter than they should be, than you want them to be. The goldfish in their rows of bowls, dazed and still or circling, panicked.

The mosquito bite you scratched bloody, the scab on your arm, your paua-shell bracelet, your best friend Heather grabbing your hand to pull you after her, up the metal ramp to the last car on the Matterhorn. The sandy bar across your laps, the suck of damp vinyl on the backs of your legs. How you loved that last car: when it went backward there was nothing between you and the air and the lights and the strobing beat from the speakers, all of it rushing ahead and ahead and ahead.

◉ ◉ ◉

I spent my twentieth birthday in a bar, goat-thin and half naked in a sky-colored satin dress, stained along the hem and wrinkled, blue as a dream. Three dollars at the Goodwill. A man with coyote teeth bought me lemon drops, sugar-rimmed and stinging. He kept buying and I kept drinking and I led him through the churn of bodies on the dance floor to the back stairwell door, to the high buzz of dim wattage above them and metal steps below.

I spent my thirtieth in the top-floor suite of a hotel in Paris where a lifetime before German soldiers had played skat, eaten bread and chocolate and traded women like matches across the card tables in the smoke and quake of the occupation. I wore gray lace stockings and satin shoes, plucked cashews from a porcelain bowl and licked first-class salt from cabin-cracked lips. I'd eaten Valium for dinner on the plane. The man who'd paid for everything I touched watched me pour Chateau Mouton Rothschild into a tumbler I'd carried from the bathroom vanity, watched me drain the glass and pour another, eight hundred dollars gone in the time it took to slip the scarf from my neck. I toed my shoes off and raised my perfect legs for him to peel the stockings down.

And the birthdays in between, New York and Toronto and Nassau, dainty spoons for caviar, cocaine; orchestra seats and penthouse suites and roped-off blackjack tables where wide men in tuxedoes stood tree-still, staring at nothing, seeing everything. Black chips, black tie, black eyes, but not often enough to matter, or beg to be tied to the mast.

◎ ◎ ◎

Heather's mother was like no one's I had ever seen: I could not understand how such a narrow strip of land could contain her. Her hair was long and dark and permed into springy curls and her earrings, a cascade of white shells, flashed from the thick of it. She wore white tank tops, spaghetti-strapped and edged in lace across her freckled brown chest, a rose-gold cuff on one arm and a chain bracelet on the other, two tigereyes set in silver, one at her wrist and one on her finger, linked and glinting on her narrow hand.

When I had dinner at Heather's I loved to watch her mother moving in the kitchen, that hair pulled back in a leather barrette, no apron, a cigarette burning in the ashtray on the counter, a pretty ring of flowers on the filter. She drank white wine while she cooked and hummed along to the radio and moved her hips as she stirred, swayed when she leaned to adjust the flame beneath a saucepan. I watched and wondered what had kept her from the highway anyone could see.

Come on come on everyone, we've got something new tonight, she'd call, carrying paella or jambalaya or cioppino to the table in a deep stoneware bowl with a loaf of bread split horizontally and smeared with soft margarine and minced garlic from a tiny jar, gleaming from the broiler; a salad of iceberg lettuce and quartered tomatoes and green pimiento-stuffed olives and three kinds of dressing on the table, the bottles cold from the refrigerator door.

Heather and I sank damp from showers into chairs around the cluttered table, feet bare and eyelids glittery.

Looks like someone got into your makeup, Heather's father said. A couple of someones. He sat for dinner in a baseball cap and flannel shirt undone to the third button and when he reached for the bread the shirt fell away from his chest and the thin twist of beaded leather around his neck swung forward before coming back to rest.

When he caught me looking he winked, unembarrassed; unselfconscious in the way of a man who was used to being admired. He worked days at the marina and weekend nights at a bayside bar, he smelled of patchouli and clove and he looked at his wife the way the boys on the boards looked at me.

Sweet Becky, he said to me, squinting over his can of beer, when did you get so dangerous? and Heather rolled her eyes and kicked at my sunburned shin with her sandy foot. Dad. Ew.

Leave them be, Joey, her mother said, brushing her hand across his shoulder before she sat. If you behave yourself I'll let you take me over to the east side and buy me a drink with an umbrella in it.

Wednesday's ladies' night, Heather said. Free drinks till ten— that's a deal, Dad.

And you know that how? her mother said, her eyebrow a perfect raised arc.

Oh my God they advertise on channel sixteen all the time—tell her, Becks!

They did advertise on channel sixteen but we would have known that anyway, lingering as we did by the bleached wooden patio overhanging a pizza-and-stromboli takeout Tenth Street and watching women stagger out in rope-heeled wedges to light cigarettes, sweat drying on their necks and shoulders, lamb-eyes bleary. The men who followed them had their pick.

Educational programming, Heather's father said, leaning across the table and burying his hand in his wife's dark hair, lifting it from her neck, and I brought a napkin to my burning face, ashamed of what I wanted.

Okay, we're outta here, Heather said, pulling me up after her and into the kitchen to dig through the freezer bin for the crushed box of Popsicles.

Not too late tonight, okay? her mother said. We're going to your grandmother's tomorrow.

Have fun, her father said, but not too much. And Becky, you be gentle with those poor boys. Have a little mercy.

We slapped the screen door open and slipped out, lemon ice pops dripping. Three short blocks toward Ocean Highway past the rows of trailers, all of them set at angles to the sidewalk, their walkways edged with pansies. The bayside was quieter than the beach and people kept their front door jalousies cranked open: through the frosted glass we could hear laugh tracks and newscasters, card games, babies crying, the pop and hiss of opening cans.

We tossed our sticks and wrappers in the trash can at the edge of the highway and I smacked the metal dome on the damp wooden light pole, waited for the light to change.

If they go to the east side they'll come home shit-faced, Heather said. Streetlights and traffic lights swept north, a blinking chain that stretched to Delaware, where we'd gone more than once, to shop tax-free. She worked a lip gloss from the pocket of her jeans, unscrewed the top and rolled a slick of cinnamon over her lips, held it out for me. And if they come home shit-faced we can probably head back out after they pass out. Probably. She leaned out over the bus lane and fanned her hair up from her neck, as pretty then as she would ever be, her shoulder blades like wings.

The light changed and we crossed six lanes at a run, tumbled onto the splintered boards, into the neon and sugary grease, the thumping bass and spinning rides and crash of waves beyond. We twined our fingers together so we wouldn't fly apart.

Mercy for whom? Sunburned fathers in plaid Bermudas who pretended not to see us when they bent to scoop their screaming children up; middle-school boys in seething packs who tripped and pushed one another into our path, terrified, elated? Or the ones in between, feathery-lashed and barely whiskered, teeth white and fingers quick, foolish and hungry and reckless as we were?

They were already more dangerous than I would ever be.

◎ ◎ ◎

Those birthdays: by the thirty-fifth the slide had started, merrily relentless; the march and tick of indifference even though my hair was still shiny my legs still long my mouth still warm and wet.

I knew it, I could see it in what was missing and in what was there instead—a room in the airport hotel for the left-bank suite, a forty-dollar bottle of brandy for the wine.

There was the visible, and the rest: the blood-leather gloves with holes worried through the lining, the resoled boots and the scarf just beginning to fray.

I told myself the brandy tasted like apples, I slipped plastic bottles of milky lotion from the bathroom into my purse. I'd wrapped that scarf tight around my throat in Venice in a blue November and tighter still in the back seat of a taxi idling at four a.m. in Knightsbridge. How many seasons before? The fabric was musky-sweet; rose and oud, skin, years.

Happy birthday to me. The fifth-floor room, two double beds, built-in console desk and television in the armoire; a man with scarred cheeks in expensive shoes and monogrammed cuffs and on the bed by the window a shirtless boy not quite young enough to be my son, long hair twisted over one skinny shoulder.

I'd opened the curtains first thing to watch the lights pulsing on the runway below. My bag was suede, oversize and filled with everything I could hardly bear.

We'd shoved the phone and lamp to the side. The desk was covered, trays of wilting sushi and pink ginger petals, a jar of candied walnuts and a cake topped with crushed rosettes, the bottle. The man poured glasses for me and the boy. The other guests had left.

My associate, he said, or maybe just my nephew. He grinned, he leaned and tugged at a lock of the boy's hair. Which is it? he asked, but the boy only watched the muted TV, one hand curled light around the remote. His pretty lips were slack and I wondered what they could do.

Myrrh, bergamot. An apothecary in Venice; then bitter thimbles of espresso, *amari* burning flowers down my throat in the morning damp. Everywhere a *chiccetteria*, a church; the pews filled with tiny stooped women and the bars filled with their sons and husbands and the alleys between them stone-slick and cold. Smoke was all around, cigarettes or incense or the sizzling fat of spitted meat.

The boy on the bed stretched and sat up, dilated pupils and rabbity hands. The room was overwarm but I drank that brandy down. Even then, already, I knew better than to expect the maître d'hôtel to present me with hot scones and clotted cream, a newspaper cone of chestnuts, a quiver of beating hearts.

There is something to be said for clean-enough sheets and a wallet full of twenties; for knowing the trajectory of your economic and aesthetic worth. And the boy was so sleepy.

His mama is a dear friend of mine, the man said to me, and I promised her I'd take good care of him—she's away for the next three to five. He chuckled. But I've been thinking he's a little old to need taking care of. The way she had in mind at least.

What do you think? he asked me, running a hand over my dying hip. You think he needs taking care of?

First things first, I said, and cocked that hip right into the spread of his fingers, their bite.

Something to be said for meeting expectations, or exceeding them.

◎ ◎ ◎

Twenty years old in candy-red stilettos and someone else's dress, in a room full of beautiful strangers, in the beginning of everything, and those lemon drops went down like sunshine.

The blood sang fearless in my veins and when the man who was buying the drinks leaned down to shout his name in my ear I nodded as though I heard or cared, as though a name could make a difference. I led him through the smoky crush, through a graffitied door to the stairwell and my shoes clanged, echoed. I hooked my peppermint heels onto a metal step and vined my arms around him and his hands whispered over me in the hum and thump of music behind the wall, in the green exit glow.

I hiked my lying satin dress up and the tips of his fingers were dandelions.

I didn't care what he thought of me and I didn't care what might or might not happen in an hour or a day. I was afraid of nothing, I was still too clean for that. I didn't care what fucking a stranger in a stairwell made me. I was too busy making myself.

◎ ◎ ◎

What else? Newports stolen from Heather's father and No-Doz crushed and snorted in her bathroom after dinner, patchouli oil in a brown glass vial, shell-pink soap in a dish on the vanity and Zest on the shower shelf. I loved the smell of her bathroom, that Zest, balsam shampoo and the bay, always the bay, the jalousie window cranked open and the water slapping at the wooden pier beyond. We hooked each other's necklaces, squinting through watery eyes.

Caramel corn and funnel cakes and Heather's special floats: vanilla soft-serve in a cup doused in the root-beer schnapps she carried in her salt-stained denim bag. The curve and knob of her shoulder bumping mine, her strapless sundress, yellow with blue daisies, and the flannel shirt she wore over it, the fray of the collar.

The boy who worked Skee-Ball on Tuesday nights, his winking earring and the scar below one gold-flecked eye. We gave him sips of schnapps and he let us play for free, and when his shift was over he followed us out onto the boards and we followed him to where his friend was waiting, a sunburned boy in painter's pants slouched across the bench by the Tilt-a-Whirl. Scar was Heather's and Sunburn was mine and we trailed in pairs down the boards to the pier, sharing cigarettes. The boys pitched the butts out into the water and settled back against the rough wooden rails, V'ed their legs and drew us between them, against their chests and hard stomachs and zippers. They opened their mouths against ours, tongues flicking, impatient on our lips. They pressed their hands on our backsides and we let them, they pulled our own hands to their zippers and we let them. We let them and let them until they were almost weeping, until Heather pulled back from hers and reached to pluck at my arm—We gotta go, Beck, or my parents'll *shit*.

Which never happened: we were quiet enough sneaking back in that they could pretend not to hear us even if they did.

My own parents were gray and slowing, refugees from narrow houses on city blocks gone cracked and buckling, from low ceilings and small windows, from corner lots scraped vacant. They slept long and deeply. They woke to surf and seagulls they never quite came to believe.

The front door left unlocked and the stove light on, Heather's mother's empty wineglass in the sink, her father's library book open on the coffee table, two-page diagrams of suspension-bridge design.

Heather's bedroom, the floor strewn with piles of clothes that we added to, hanging on each other for balance while we tugged shorts and shirts off and dropped them where we stood, where we swayed. Her white rattan bed, rumpled. We collapsed into it. Her sleeping breath, a pause and rasp. She slept on her stomach, arms flung wide, unmoving, deep and as far from me as she ever was. I had a hard time sleeping even then and watched shadows on the ceiling, watched the ghost boys sigh above us with their snaky tongues and hooded eyes, their sweet dirty promises. I drifted off and woke. Before dawn I slid from Heather's side and felt my way along the short hall to the bathroom, the shag damp under my bare feet, the wall cool and rough along my fingertips, half-asleep but not dreaming the sigh and squeak of sheets and springs in the master bedroom.

I saw Heather's mother on her father's lap, hair spread across her back, legs wrapped, feet locked, rocking, and her husband's face over her shoulder. His eyes were open, and his mouth, his hands on his wife's hips, the sheets pooled white around them. I did not move. Her breath caught in what sounded like laughter and he smiled, sweet and slow. He murmured in her ear but he was watching me. I did not move. He wrapped his arms around her back, under her hair, his lips moving against her shoulder but his eyes on me, my face, my brand-new heart.

He closed his eyes, still smiling, still seeing me, I knew. I would have stayed until the ocean came rushing and roared me away.

◎ ◎ ◎

When they disappeared I didn't miss them. I didn't miss their bespoke suits, their manicured nails or capped teeth. I didn't miss their voracity.

I didn't miss their generosity, the sky-blue ribboned jewelry boxes dropped carelessly onto armrests, the lobes of foie gras tossed on the empty bottom shelf of my refrigerator, the town cars and drivers that idled at the curb for me, the maid service that scrubbed my clean sink while I stood by, cringing.

I didn't miss the lectures in first-class airport lounges, the too-patient instructions of how I could avoid sinking into ruin along with the rest of the fools who trusted the government, the treasury, the media. I nodded, I watched the departures board, the list of destinations that cycled from potential to imminent to impossible as the minutes ticked past.

The rocks glasses in those lounges were heavy and cold and too big for me to wrap my fingers around. In the restrooms I ran warm water over my hands and slathered moisturizer over the damp, dabbed balm on my lips and under my eyes and perfume at the nape of my neck. I swallowed half tablets of Valium, I twisted before the full-length mirrors to be sure seams were smooth and hems were straight. In my carry-on I kept a roll of bills tucked into the toe of a shoe.

They loved that I never checked baggage, that I could sail through concourses on four-inch heels, that I took the time to learn at least a few phrases in any language I did not know. They loved my sense of the understated, the appropriate.

When they disappeared I did not miss their hands on my elbow, just firm enough that I would not misunderstand, lifting me up from orchestra seats from luxury boxes from limousines and into penthouses, into hotel suites, into dust.

I did not miss their monstrous certainty that nothing and no one was worth what they were worth. I did not miss the green leaf of their aftershave, or the charnel-house stench beneath it.

Even so. When they disappeared I did too.

◎ ◎ ◎

Rain, pocked gray water and cold sand, wind enough to shake the pier apart. The wearying summer stumbled and we pulled damp sweatshirts from the back corners of our dressers, waited for Heather's mother to warm milk in a saucepan and shave chocolate into it.

Where are my socks? Heather crowed, stomping through the trailer, and her father looked up from his tackle box, open on the kitchen table. Good lord, flower, it's not that cold, he said, and Heather flung open the hall closet doors, muttering.

Oh you know what they're all in a huff about, her mother said, while her father made a show of checking his watch and I curled myself into a corner of the sofa.

As a matter of fact I do, he said, winking at his wife, I think they've got about fifteen days and fourteen hours until homeroom. That sound about right? and Heather's mother laughed. That sound.

He had never mentioned that night, never acknowledged having seen me watching no matter how hard I wished, no matter how I lingered at the kitchen counter shucking corn while he sorted his spinnerbait at the table and the bay pulled the sinking sun into it.

I could not look at him without seeing, without wanting, and he knew. I ached and he knew, I could not breathe and he knew.

◎ ◎ ◎

Of course there will be a last one, and he will destroy you, or not. He will give you a necklace to wear over the place you used to keep your heart or he will fashion one of his own two hands. Either way the sky outside the windows where you are will be high and bright at midnight, pricked with stars that are not yours. Either way the ground below will be treacherous as quicksand.

The last one will be no different from the rest, but you'll know he's the last before he even touches you, before he tosses his wallet and keycard onto the bedside table, before he loosens his tie and pours the wine and forces you to the plush plush carpet in front of the floor-to-ceiling windows and the riot of lights beyond them. You'll know by the way he looks at you: like the ghost of someone he has already forgotten.

Outside those windows will be Tokyo or Toronto or Barcelona but where you are will be on your best behavior, on your guard, on your knees: where you have been since you came to understand the concept of an exchange rate. Since you decided on a fair one. Be honest, there in that sumptuous room, in your floating hair and dissolving skin, in the cold burn of irrelevance.

Be honest, under that borrowed sky, under sheets as heavy and smooth as cream, under everything that is not yours.

Be ready to be over.

Au revoir, arrivederci, auf Wiedersehen. So many endings at the beginning of the alphabet.

◎ ◎ ◎

I see Heather's father at two o'clock on a Wednesday afternoon in Dmitri's Tap & Package, the last stop on my rounds after the VA, the supermarket, the pharmacy, the last stop before I deliver the carload to whomever the eldercare agency has assigned me for the month. Dmitri's is one long room with stools and high-backed booths, dusty windows and cracked vinyl and curling linoleum. Some days there is a plastic-wrapped tray of moussaka behind the bar, or Crock-Pot of potato soup.

The bartender's name is Patrick. He spends the quiet of the afternoons in a square of sun by the register, sweater buttoned to the throat, the morning paper open to the crossword and a cup of tea at his elbow. When Patrick looks up he smiles, eases himself from the stool to pour me a seven and seven and collect my lotto tickets and cigarettes. These will go into the back seat of the agency car, along with the groceries and stapled prescription bags and case of vanilla Ensure. This month, it is the Sperrys who are waiting.

Heather's father is sitting at the edge of the bar, almost directly below the television he'd have to crane his neck to watch. Pale jeans and a darker denim shirt, a plaid wool jacket, hair pulled back into a tufted curling ponytail, graying but thick enough. Sturdy moccasins, rubber-soled, new-looking; an empty shot and full pint in front of him. His face is blurred and rough, just out of focus but still his.

"Here y'are, sweetheart," Patrick says, setting my drink on a napkin in front of me. "How are Mr. and Mrs. Sperry?"

"Keeping on," I tell him. "Their son is coming next week so I might get a few days off." Heather's father lifts the pint glass and his sleeve pulls back to reveal a wrist as fine and graceful as any boy's.

The last I heard from her was my sophomore year of college, a water-stained envelope tucked into my mailbox in the student union, lines scrawled in soft pencil on a page torn from a spiral notebook and signed *Mrs. Hemmert*, a Polaroid of Heather and a boy with his arm in a cast in front of a narrow brick duplex, postmarked Youngstown, Ohio.

Guess who's an old married lady! I folded the paper in half and again around the photo, around the Hemmerts of Youngstown. I slid them back into the envelope, the envelope between the onionskin pages of my Norton anthology and the anthology into my backpack, and at the end of the semester when I crated my books for exchanging at the campus bookstore I didn't think to shake the pages out or remember why I might want to.

Heather's father drains his glass. I pick up my own and move down the bar and lay my hand on his sleeve like the kind of whore I wasn't. He looks up, and time slides beneath us, a tide rushing out.

◎ ◎ ◎

I will not remember how we agreed to be strangers that day, or who moved first, or how we knew which places were too damaged to touch.

I was lucky when I was younger, he says to me, I was—it's important, anyway. To know what you have.

I was never lucky, I say, and smile, so he knows I am asking for nothing. But I was dedicated. I was conscientious. I was good enough until I wasn't.

I don't believe that, he says, and I say You don't have to. That's the thing.

This is as close to the waiting graves as we are willing to go; we are not ready to dig and sift that soil. We know what we would find there.

The skin of his chest is puckered, paler than it used to be, leathery and worn; his hands and knuckles scarred: fishhooks, gutting knives, fire. My front door is locked and every window closed; my bedroom is a music box, an abattoir. His stomach is soft but his legs are tense, still muscled.

I will not remember how we agreed to pretend that all we knew was in that room, that the world went black beyond it.

I lower myself onto him and he pulls back to look at what's left of the girl he remembers, or doesn't, or won't allow himself to see, and I don't know which I am to him, but I have been invisible for such a long time that it doesn't matter.

⊚ ⊚ ⊚

The Louvre, the Prado, the Uffizi; blood oranges and figs sticky and sweet as lies; kidskin and cashmere and water I will never see again. I am years from everything but him. He smells of salt, of the hot wind that blew east over the bay and burned through me, of before. He sleeps like Heather did, arms thrown above his tilted head, palms up and empty and smooth as driftwood. Heather's hands were full of stars; I could feel their bright sweet prick when she twined her fingers in mine and pulled me across the sand.

His sleeping breath is ragged, frayed as the cuffs of his shirt. If I lifted it from the floor and went through its pockets I would find nothing worth taking, no broken shells or arcade tokens, no freshly turned earth or feathered lures or hooks sharp enough to pierce.

Outside the afternoon bleeds away, the sky cotton-white, cold and heavy with water. In Venice the lagoon is milky green; the Seine roils gray, and darker. My dresser holds a shoebox filled with cash, bills rolled or stacked and banded. I was good enough.

The Sperrys must still be waiting, anxious in their living room, stubbing their cigarettes into the red aluminum ashtrays they bring home from the flea market by the dozen. Sometimes, when I drop off their groceries and medications, I tip the full ashtrays into the kitchen can filled with empty deli containers of pineapple-chicken salad and boxes of graham crackers. I tie the plastic liner shut, take the bag out the back kitchen door and toss it into the metal can by the alley. I am conscientious still.

In my bed he sighs and twists beneath the clean white sheets, knotted in his futile sleep and far from any rest: there is neither comfort nor distraction here, no limestone bridge or doge's palace, no gondoliers or chandeliers or bitter-almond thighs. There is nothing here but what is left of us.

My lips on his neck are split and dry as moths' wings and when he lifts himself to me his mouth on my throat is a waking ruin. We are beggared vampires, here in this mausoleum with its clock that won't stop, needle-hands circling while our skin peels away in carnival ribbons and our barbed-wire fingers draw blood.

◎ ◎ ◎

What did you wish wouldn't end, those nights, your face tucked against Heather's warm neck, the two of you draped across the sandy boardwalk railing like some perfect vine, twin-blooming and only a little poisonous?

The burn of caffeine in your nostrils, patchouli oil in the crook of your elbows and the hollow of your throat, the hanging shard of moon. The crash of surf, the switchgrass and petrels, the pink dawn that lifted itself from the edge of the Atlantic and spread up and across the breathing sky.

The press of new skin, tobacco lips, denim worn snow-pale and soft, Old Spice and Irish Spring. The spit and sizzle of tongue and hands on your blistered skin, the vanilla melt of sticky lips and fingertips past midnight.

The pines across the bay that caught the night in their feathery branches and held it. The foam white against black sea, black sky. Delaware, and the rest of everywhere, waiting.

Other People's Children

Paul does not love me, and when he touches me I can feel all the lies he can't be bothered to tell. He is fifteen years older than I am and wealthy, for now. He lives alone in this town I've never left, where he moved his family when his family was whole. It is not, anymore. His son is in a locked hospital and his wife is in Boulder with a river guide and six Basenjis. The guide is not much older than the son; he is strong, broad-shouldered and smiling. He ties bandannas over his tangled hair and shepherds breast-cancer survivors and middle managers down rivers not nearly as dangerous as they would like to believe, as they will tell their friends. Paul knows this because his wife sends letters, and photos.

The son, Alex, is a junkie. Before this he was a college student and a classical pianist; he made dean's list and volunteered at an after-school program for at-risk children, guiding them through "Chopsticks," through "Heart and Soul." At night he sold his perfect body for plastic bags of poison bliss. He is a dark-eyed beauty, blade-thin with broken hands, sedated in a locked white room.

He owed money he did not have. He was thrown down in the alley behind his favorite vegetarian restaurant, his smooth cheek crushed in oily gravel, his arms yanked up and out and his hands bound at the wrists. If he had seen the faces of the men who did all this he would have recognized them. No matter: one sat on his back and the other slid behind the wheel of a metallic blue Nissan. This one steered, rolled forward and back, careful and slow, and the son's fingers were not so much broken as crushed, pulverized, skin split and bones powdered, and in the restaurant behind them pretty servers carried mâche salad and parsnip-potato soup to undergraduates.

When Paul called his wife to tell her she was serene. She would channel healing energy to his chakras, she said; she would meditate under the new moon. She had faith that he would emerge transformed from this obstacle in his karmic journey.

She writes Paul letters on handmade paper, pale green, fibrous and thick. The envelopes smell vegetal.

I know this because Paul tells me, late evenings like this one in my too-warm house, drinking bourbon from the good bottle he keeps here. His white shirt is damp at the collar, the monogrammed cuffs.

He'll need to be on a strict macrobiotic diet, his wife said from Boulder, and I think he'll need chelation—but this is a blessing for him. You can't see it now but you will, she said. Her voice was sweet as bells and certain, buoyant with confidence. It was the voice of someone Paul had never met and would never want to know.

He pours another drink. "They didn't even know he plays piano," he says, his mouth wet and weak. We are in the peaceful clutter of my living room, surrounded by tilting stacks of magazines and DVDs, scraps of paper with phone numbers and recipes written in smeared ink. The kitchen is dark for the night and clean, the calendar and order sheet cross-referenced and balanced, towels folded and apron hung. "Of anything they could've done to him," Paul says, shaking his head in bewildered fury, "why that?" He is waiting for me to acknowledge an injustice I cannot bring myself to grant. If they had known, those men with their benign and ruthless smiles, their insulted dignity, would it have stopped them? Would they have, for instance, wrapped his hands in batting and moleskin before cracking his ribs or puncturing a lung? Broken his knees or ankles, knocked out his teeth instead?

Would you rather that? I think, but instead I say, "What's important now is that he's safe. He's safe and getting better—the doctors said so. You told me. Focus on that."

Paul looks at me with loathing. "You have no idea what this means," he says, and stands, begins rifling through the books and cups on the end table for his keys, "what's been lost."

"You're right," I say. It's true. I have no children, have never felt that panic, the gnaw and chew of it, and there is only so much comfort I can give to him, in his vain and helpless love.

His wife told him that this was his chance for transcendence: Give yourself over to the pain, she says, and it will fill you with the purest light.

He loves a woman who could say such a thing.

◎ ◎ ◎

By six a.m. I'm pulling four dozen cupcakes from the top oven and sliding a sheet cake into the bottom one. The stand mixer is ready for the next order, loaded with a pale soft mound of butter and drifts of sugar, eggs cracked and waiting in a bowl on the prep table. My laptop is safe and clean on the far counter but the open pages of my organizer are coffee-ringed and sticky.

I have appointments with potential clients at nine and ten-thirty, then a wide-open stretch until three. Some are easy—the administrative assistants tasked with organizing the postmerger meeting, with reserving the conference room and stocking the bottles of water, ordering the laminated name tags and trifold packets. I'm the quickest call they'll make: two pans of lemon bars and two of peanut butter squares, childhood on plastic plates. As though this will make the rest of it any less bitter.

There are the easy ones, and then there are the rest, the frantic brides and their anxious mothers, the panicked husbands staring down their calendars, the birthday or anniversary looming, inevitable. When I give my quote the mothers will haggle, will argue and fuss, but the men will pay anything. They pick up the orders themselves, and when they do they throw their credit cards down and sign the receipt without even looking, hold the white boxes away from them on the way out, stiff-armed and irritable. They are afraid of ruining their only chance. They cannot get away fast enough.

The women are another story, from the first phone call on, the engaged girls breathless and scattered, relaying questions from their mothers to me and back again until the mothers finally snatch the phone, exasperated and efficient—this is what they've been waiting for, after all, from first communions or bat mitzvahs or sweet sixteens through homecomings and graduations and every other occasion rendered with disproportionate enthusiasm in the window displays at the mall. This is the curtain all the dress rehearsals have been building to. They sail into my kitchen with their daughters behind them, shellacked and taut and ready to make one right decision after another. The girls themselves are interchangeable, beautiful in a way I can recognize without understanding, with their French-tipped nails and glassy sheets of ironed hair, waxed brows and lined lips and clouds of designer perfume. They are perfect American daughters, energetic, acquiescent; easy to admire and easy to forget. They hug me when they leave.

The drama doesn't start until after they've gone, with rambling voice mails and updated head counts, with second thoughts and third and fourth: *maybe not the carrot-coriander maybe that's too much please call as soon as you get this message* and I do, I call, and when I do I hardly have to speak: they will talk themselves back around to where they began, eventually, if I let them; to the almond-apricot or the key lime chiffon; the bride or her mother in a circling tumble of indecision and uncertainty.

They talk themselves out, exhausted, teary, skittish as horses. The girls are terrified and they are right to be. Like horses they can smell the threat they cannot articulate: that one wrong decision will lead to another and that to a worse one, will set off a landslide of mistakes, unstoppable and crushing.

The timer buzzes and I ease the oven door open. I touch the heel of my hand to the top of the cake, slide it onto the cooling rack and collect a bowl and whisk, the glaze. I brush the first layer on while the cake's still warm, a thin sheen of caramel, sugar coaxed to the bare edge of burnt, and then another layer every fifteen minutes, and a crackling frost deepens, becomes pearl-smooth and perfect.

The mothers don't quite trust me, with my ringless finger and unstretched belly. They look at me too long, too close; they can see the years behind me. If I am not quite old enough to have a grown daughter I am too old to have none at all.

They stiffen when their girls hug me, they haul them out of my kitchen, fingers hooked and suspicious in cashmere sleeves.

The doors click locked when they put the car in gear and twist to back it down my drive—they cannot get their daughters away from me fast enough. When they look at me they see what the girls here used to be, all of us rough and imperfect, our cheeks slick and shiny in the heat, our hair tangled and damp. We lived here before they came, before they parked their Range Rovers in front of the Tyvek-wrapped houses that overlook the highway I have only been so far on. We smelled of sweat and chlorine and bruised strawberries. We were nothing like their daughters, these girls with ironed hair and diamond studs who teeter on stilettos in my kitchen, unlikely as unicorns.

We stretched ourselves across hot grass on melting afternoons, waiting for the spill of dark, for the pool on St. John's Lane to close so we could climb the chain-link fence and drop soft on the sloping grass above the deep end, the lounge chairs and furled umbrellas. We passed flasks of root-beer schnapps and smoked Benson and Hedges Ultra Lights and waited for the boys to come and slip their hands between our bare hot knees, for the sudden punch of joy that was almost too sweet to bear.

Those boys were seal-smooth, at seventeen all sharp teeth and ragged nails and hurry. They whispered exactly what we didn't know we wanted to hear and no more, words slipping from their smoky mouths, slithering along back decks and bleachers, over rec-room sofas and cracked front seats, floating through sticky midnights, tree frogs and crickets, cicadas, before they came to rest, untrue and irresistible, on us.

On our sunburned arms, our pastel halters and peeling shoulders. Our feathery hair, our coconut lips, pink and shimmering. Our concave stomachs and denim skirts, our flowered cotton underwear with its frayed elastic and the glass beads of our bracelets. Our pink-painted nails.

They breathed the words into our mouths, they fed us and we swallowed, gulped. What was true didn't matter; we were too hungry for it to matter.

⊚ ⊚ ⊚

Paul tells me that during morning visits the common area is bright with sun and loud. Donated televisions are balanced on gouged tables in distant corners of the room, chairs filled with other people's children circled around them, around the basketball scores and talk shows, the newscasts and cartoons. Paul surrenders his coffee at the reception desk before he is granted entry—he never remembers to leave it in the car—and pours himself a Styrofoam cup of hot water from the station in the corner, floats a dusty teabag on the top. He stands by the long bulletin board, by the frayed and faded posters of sand dunes and sunrises, of mountain ranges at dawn; by the laminated schedules and their color coded blocks of time—orange for group, gray for meditation, a long rectangle of dark blue from ten p.m. to morning. Every hour of the day is saturated.

While I froth eggs and sugar Paul waits for his son in his coat and his smile, in his desperate good cheer, his obduracy. I calibrate the ovens and Alex emerges from the stairwell, rested, damp and eager. From this distance he is so close to the boy Paul remembers. When they hug he rests his cheek against his son's clean hair, eyes closed. He can feel on his back the pressure of the boy's brick hands, dull and blunt and heavy.

My own hands are hatched and laddered with scars. They were pretty once, and less than useful.

Paul draws back to admire his son. Alex's smile is wide, snow-globe vacant. His breath is sweet and hot, turned fruit; his hands float safe in their hives. The days drift past and he is monitored and counseled, fed and washed and supervised; the hours enfold him, soft as cotton.

My kitchen smells of almonds, white. When my phone rings I let it go to voice mail, pour coffee and work my thumb under the thick peel of a grapefruit.

"I want you to come next time," Paul says on the message he leaves. I can hear traffic in the background; he must be on his way to work. "I think it would do him good and I want him to meet you anyway. I got another letter from his goddamned mother—"

I slide the phone back into my pocket without listening to the rest of the message. He won't expect me to call back—the words themselves, flat and hanging, are enough: *I want*. He is comfortable with wanting and accustomed to getting. When he is away from me he does not cajole or coax and when he is with me he does not profess or promise.

My heart has never known such awful gaping ease.

I put my sunglasses on and wrap myself in a heavy scarf, collect deposit slips and the metal cashbox, a paper-clipped stack of the checks the women scrawl and tear off and slap down on my sugar-gritted counter before rushing their daughters out to their appointments with the florist or the photographer.

When Paul came to pick up the cake he'd ordered for his wife's birthday she was already gone, already waking in the pined dry air of Boulder, in the bed of someone else's healthy son. He stood in my kitchen in his cashmere scarf and polished shoes, his bewilderment and fury, and decided I would do.

⊚ ⊚ ⊚

Paul's house is on the way to the bank. When it was the Jensens' house my mother drove past to have her hair cut; when it was the Humphreys' I drove past to pick up bushels of corn for my father's Labor Day parties.

The Jensens put up the basketball hoop and the Humphreys planted the forsythia, and in between a couple whose name I don't remember hung wind chimes from the eaves and spent the summer on the front porch sprawled across brown wicker chairs, bottles of beer and a portable radio on a table between them where they rested their tanned bare feet. In September they painted the front door indigo and in October they let the fallen leaves spin and flip from their drive to the street and in December they packed a van with sagging cardboard boxes and folded quilts, crude wooden end tables and fringed wall hangings; they backed down the driveway in the first spitting snow and in the dark of the van the tips of their cigarettes flared and dimmed like beating hearts.

What Paul doesn't know could stretch for miles.

He has never brought me to that house, has never held the front door open and waited for me to slip into those winter rooms, cold and waiting. He has never done this and those rooms are still more mine than his.

He does not know, for instance, that the neighborhood boys played basketball in the driveway even though the Jensens' son Stuart could not; that Mrs. Jensen served those boys cherry Kool-Aid and oatmeal cookies while Stuart sat strapped in his metal chair, eyes crossed and drifting, hooting with excitement and delight. His arms slapped the plastic tray like hooked and thrashing fish. He howled with joy and his mother looked straight through him to the boy she had never stopped imagining in his place, who was sloppy and surly and vertical, who tied his own shoelaces and drank milk from the carton and sneaked breathless giggling girls to the finished basement no one used.

He does not know that Kathy Humphreys and I crouched beneath the forsythia while her parents slept, waiting for those boys to coast down the street in cars borrowed from their parents or bought used and rattling, to slow enough for us to run light across the grass and launch ourselves up and through an open door. Inside the car they smelled of Flex shampoo and Zest soap, the least-used letters of the alphabet made common on drugstore shelves. We emptied our pockets of everything we'd brought for them—cinnamon jawbreakers and crooked cigarettes and perfect aching secrets. Closer in they smelled of impatience, of promises. We climbed on their laps and dipped our heads so our hair fell tangled and warm against their stubbled cheeks. That close, they smelled of escape.

He does not know and does not care about the people who moved through that house before him, who slept wrapped warm in secrets and woke terrified or careless, who lied because they could or because they had to, who were strange and beautiful beyond imagining. Who were breakable.

He thinks there is no room for any grief in that house but his own.

Kramer: that was their name, the couple with the wicker and the indigo. Their wind chimes were strung with shells and driftwood and velvet curtains blew through their open windows. Stuart

Jensen lived longer than any doctor expected he would, longer than his mother thought she could bear, and the only thing worse than his death was the wave of relief that came after, tidal and brute. Kathy Humphreys' parents took her baby away before she was even stitched up and when she came home the priest was waiting for her with his keys in one hand and a vial of holy water in the other, a towel for her to sit on spread across the back seat of his car. Mrs. Jensen burned Stuart's clothes before her husband could stop her and Kathy Humphreys bled across three states before sneaking through the back door of a roadside convenience store and I stretched myself wide under the soaking sun, I slept under the only moon I knew.

◎ ◎ ◎

In the evening it's another story. In the evening the air is roiled, sour; the girls stalk through the common room in dirty slippers, trailing ashes and laughter, a mean ripping sound. The boys keep their distance, keep their dead eyes down; they flatten themselves across tables over cards meant to hurry the night along. I wait with Paul for his son in the watery green light of the hallway. Paul paces, in his coat and his dread and his hope, but the night does not hurry, nothing here does.

A metal door clangs open and his son comes shambling, cheeks slack and eyes hooded, smiling around the bent white stick of a lollipop. His hair is overgrown and curling; his bandaged hands hang gray as wasps' nests. Next to me Paul stiffens, a marionette jerked taut. His fingers on my arm squeeze and lift and the heels of my shoes come up off the floor.

"Jeannie," he says, "this is my son. This is Alex."

Alex shakes a twist of greasy hair out of his eyes and works the lollipop to a corner of his mouth. "I knew a girl named Joanie once," he says to me, "and that did not end well. One of many things that didn't." He is wracked and haggard and thrumming with a feral heat: it comes off him in sugary waves.

"How are you?" Paul says. "I talked to Dr. Patel and he said we'll be able to get you out of here and back home soon. And I thought I could call Lerner and talk to him about next semester." The words fly, the fingers on my arm press and dig, and around us the boys slide down the hallway, hands dragging along the walls that the girls press themselves flat against, their smeary eyes hot on Alex, on us.

"Jerome Lerner," Alex says to me. "That would be my advisor, whose advice was sorely lacking. Meanwhile—" he says, and lifts his chin and tongues the stick so I can see the lollipop between his teeth, "—help a guy out?" He waggles the stick and grins and Paul reaches up, snatches the candy from his mouth and tosses it at the metal trash can against the hallway wall where it clangs in the ashtray on top.

"They sugar us up in here," Alex says to me, and I understand that he has no intention of speaking to his father, he has angled himself away enough that Paul is leaning, straining to stay in his son's field of vision. Alex's eyes are red-rimmed, too shiny; his voice goes lilting and musical. "Sugar and caffeine and nicotine, yes. Haydn and crystal and pussy, no."

"I'll have the piano tuned," Paul says, and his fingers knead my arm through the heavy fabric of my coat, hard enough to hurt. He has not looked at me since we've been in here. "I can arrange for the sheet music—"

"None of the good stuff," Alex says to me, and his eyes dart to a knot of girls down the hall in pajama bottoms and stretched-out shirts and too much eyeliner, cheap rings on every finger and cigarettes burning low at scabbing knuckles. They huddle and preen like wet birds, all knotted hair and spotty skin and buzzing nerve. They are nothing like the girls I see and nothing like the ones he fucks but we both know them, Paul's ruined son and I. When we look at them we can see everything they are afraid of never having and everything they wish they were.

"I can get the syllabi from Lerner," Paul says, the words light and useless, so easy for Alex to bat aside, "I could have him come to the house after you—"

"I'm sorry, but I have to ask," Alex says, leaning toward me, "I apologize but I have to know—you're not actually letting him fuck you, are you? You're not letting him anywhere near that gorgeous—" and quicker than I have ever seen him move Paul is between us, his thick heavy hands on me for what will be the last time, shoving me back and away from his son, who is looking at me like a starving dog. My back hits the wall and the girls down the hall shriek and explode in a burst of feathers I can almost see and a giant of a man in bright white scrubs shifts his weight from one massive leg to the other before settling back into his spot by the water cooler: we are no worry to him. He pulls a chocolate bar from his breast pocket and begins to unwrap it, his face serene and shining.

Alex is grinning, almost panting; his skin is glazed and his sweat smells electric, marine. There is no breath or echo of Paul in his face and I wonder what it must be like, to look at your child one day and see in his place a stranger, perfect and whole and unfathomable. "I could make you forget all about him," Alex says, with the limitless confidence of a boy who is still young and foolish enough to think this would be difficult for anyone but him.

◎ ◎ ◎

A partial list of what Paul's wife did not want:

Block parties. Weekend swim meets at the club and potlucks after, citronella torches and burnt hot dogs and foil trays of potato salad. Wednesday bridge, Sunday brunch, Christmas open houses. The fireworks at the park on New Year's Eve and Labor Day.

The wall-to-wall carpeting in the living room; the finished basement and jukebox there; the chest freezer in the garage filled with boxes of stuffed mushrooms and miniquiches, family-size lasagna and chicken pot pie. The parties at which these items were served. The basketball hoop, the forsythia. The brush of high grass and hazy press of sky in summer, the trees that closed around us.

Car pool on alternate weeks, revolving lunchroom duty, attendance at the holiday assembly. Fur-lined driving gloves and eighteen inches of Tahitian pearls. Her son's bright and fevered eye and the weight of her husband's heedless sleep.

The house whose door is no longer indigo whose eaves are free of wind chimes whose rooms are empty of broken children. The line of trees behind it, the shadows we slipped under and into before we had daughters or didn't, before our sons disappeared or didn't, before we understood how much hurt there was in the world that was pressing in around us, humming and insistent.

She exhausted herself, not wanting these things we hardly knew to dream of.

The river guide does not own a piano and his dogs do not bark and the sky in Boulder is a high blue dome and beneath it she has pared herself of years, flayed seasons from her skin. She has let her hair go gray and long. Her son is just now broken but he will fit himself together. She is his mother: she does not doubt what his father despairs of.

◎ ◎ ◎

The weather warms and my appointment book fills with orders for engagement parties and weddings, for bridal showers and bachelorette brunches, inevitable as the thaw and bloom. It is like this every spring, as though the ballast of ceremony is all that keeps the stretching days from floating up and dissolving in the pale sky.

Papaya and mimosa and violet, candied ginger and orange blossom and lavender honey, all familiar as vanilla to these girls, as unremarkable on their tongues. They are serene in first-class lounges and three-star restaurants, conversant in macroeconomics and Aristotelian tautology but in my kitchen they are fretful as horses, as easily spooked; in my kitchen they can think of nothing but the minefield of time to be got through before they see their grooms in their morning jackets or black tie or wrinkled linen and stubble, with their waft of cologne and whiskey, waiting for them at the foot of altars or the banks of streams, under chuppahs or the beaming sun.

I serve crumbly samples on rose-faded china, two forks on a plate: they chew and smile but taste nothing. The girls are terrified and their mothers are vigilant: everywhere they look is the threat of the imperfect, ticking and ready to detonate: a too-warm banquet hall, a wrinkled dress, wilting flowers, rain. They lay the forks down—*it's wonderful*, the girls say, and their mothers nod, *it's fine*—and they swallow what I've made them and it tastes of dust, of dread.

At night the kitchen cools and I lock the doors, climb the stairs and throw my bedroom window wide. In my bed Alex has kicked the sheets into a wrinkled twist; his breath is quick and shallow. He wakes when he hears me. His hair is damp and overgrown and his fingers are crooked on my skin, stiff and bent; they creak and pop when he tries to spread them, to grip. They announce their intentions, they fall on every right place.

He is empty of secrets and unable to lie, this beautiful boy with his tracked arms and perfect manners, his candy lips and ketamine eyes. He has climbed Machu Picchu and swum in the Bosporus, he has trekked the glacier at Denali. He has decided he loves me and though I know better I say nothing. I know how fast a summer burns.

◎ ◎ ◎

He will realize soon enough how much he misses what he had, the summers in Europe and Thanksgivings skiing, the girlfriend with the hybrid car and tiny diamond in her nose, the Negronis and Haydn and handblown Turkish pipe. He will realize all this when he's well, but right now he opens his eyes and pulls me on top of him and he is nothing like those boys I knew, with their stolen cigarettes and borrowed cars, their need. He opens my lips and he tastes of the widest world.

His mother is so pleased he has landed in safe arms, so happy he has found a place to cleanse himself of those hospital days, those dragging rainbowed hours. She thinks of this time as an incubation of sorts, a needed respite, and from it he will emerge resilient, transformed.

I know this because she told me. Her handwriting is looped and swooping, the letters of my name pressed into the soft envelope in ink thick and sticky as pine resin. Her letters are a commotion of exuberant serenity, a spill of confounding joy: It is so peaceful here, she says, on the other side of expectation.

Tell him that, she says. Make him understand how little he needs, she says, and how can I hate a woman who believes such a thing?

The brick-walked campus and polished practice rooms, the girls wrapped in suede with their bindles and vials; Vivaldi and clean needles like water drops, like bells. When Alex realizes that none of this has disappeared he will slip back into it, full of stealthy grace, and his mother and I will wish only to believe he is safe.

The boys I knew were nothing like him: they were shy and rough and kind, they mowed lawns and pumped gas and bagged groceries for the money they spent on records and baseball games, for movie tickets and milkshakes. They were quick to provoke and easy to soothe and their dreams were too small to be dangerous.

They dreamed of girls like me and for that I climbed on their backs, wrapped my nicked and fearless legs around their waists and let them carry me into vacant houses, quick and light as an arrow.

Alex gathers me to him, a sleepy thief: his ruined hands know nothing about me. There is so little to know. He will blink this town away, once he is back out in his bright world.

Outside the waiting streets are warm. I know them like I know the trace of veins on my arms, river-blue and pulsing.

Dinosaurs

It's the end of August, the first night the temperature has dipped below seventy since—when? The Fourth of July? Memorial Day? Wendy can't remember. Since she's had the slatted lounges out on the deck, at least, and Kath and Matthew came back from Paris. Since Matthew died.

This deck where the two women are sitting is not a mile from where they grew up, across the street from each other, Wendy's family in a ranch house and Kath's in a split-level, driveways soft and black and new. Their parents chose the houses from the eight models available to them—the ranches and split-levels, Colonials and Georgians, all white siding and red brick.

When they moved in it was hardly a neighborhood. The streets petered out into dirt and lots were covered in mulch and hay, the woods crept up into backyards. Wendy believes she remembers that first Sunday drive out from their duplex in the city, stretched across the long back seat of her father's Buick with a stuffed gray poodle in her lap, a red vinyl purse hanging from a loop on her wrist. She remembers staring out the window at unfamiliar highway, monotonous and flat; guardrails and dense trees, an exit and then cornfields, pasture, silence; thirty minutes that felt like thirty days to her. Her father turned the car onto an uneven road and they lurched and bounced their way past construction trailers and stilled trucks and half-houses, and just behind all of it that wall of trees, impenetrable, shocking.

By the time she graduated high school the trees were sparse, decorative; behind the rows of houses were rows of newer houses and driveways, newer cars, newer families and children.

Wendy still lives here; Kath lives someplace else.

It's just the two of them tonight. Wendy's husband has taken Kath's son out to a pizza and video-game emporium and the women have been sitting on this deck for the past few hours—long enough to empty one bottle of wine and start another. They are two glasses into it. Kath is smoking, steadily but without savor. She quit five years ago, before Eric was born, and hadn't touched a cigarette until she was on the way to Matthew's funeral. She'd noticed the rectangular bulge in the soft seat pocket of the limo and how could the driver refuse her?

"I wish James would've at least let me give him the fucking roll of quarters," she says. She sips and Wendy sees the slight purse of her lips before she swallows. They're drinking the best wine she has, a twelve-dollar California chardonnay. She bought it because she'd wanted something decent in the house but even with the case discount she'd felt extravagant, foolish. Now she feels foolish for entirely different reasons.

"He loves Eric," Wendy says. "He always says how he wishes he could spend more time with him." This is true, and not. What her husband wishes is more complicated than that.

"First, that's not the point." Kath crushes her cigarette out and Wendy wonders if she recognizes the ashtray, a hot-pink ceramic boomerang they kept on the coffee table in an apartment they'd shared—fifteen years ago, or more? Wendy had kept it in a kitchen cabinet even though no one really smokes anymore. "Second . . . " Kath's voice trails off and Wendy waits. "Shit, I don't know what's second." She drains her glass and shakes her head, pours with a steady hand. "Second, it doesn't matter anyway, you know—extra cheese and Asteroids. Donkey Kong. Does anyone play those anymore? Do they even make them?"

"I have no idea," Wendy says. At the gravesite Matthew's parents stood on either side of Eric, the three of them weeping silently, a fragile swaying monolith. Kath sat alone, her face impassive, half-covered by black sunglasses. They were no affectation; at one o'clock it was ninety-five degrees, cloudless, the sky almost white. Wendy's hand was wet in James's; her arms and chest prickled with burn.

Summer afternoons they'd played in the cool of the darkened den at Kath's house, tossing dice and moving plastic markers over game boards while Kath's mother cried in the master bedroom. They made up new lyrics to cartoon songs and sang and pretended they did not hear the sobs, the whispering, the sound of Kath's mother vomiting into a powder-blue toilet bowl.

"Me neither," Kath says. "Matt didn't like the idea of them. Video games, that kind of thing. We don't have any at home." She lights up, tosses the match at the ashtray and misses. "Jesus, Eric's probably so happy right now he can't even think straight." She plucks the match from the table and drops it in the ashes. "I bought fourteen lip glosses today." She looks at Wendy as though she expects an argument but Wendy is silent. "I was at the drugstore getting Eric's ointment and they had one of those little racks by the register with all the eyeliners and stuff and I saw this gloss that looked pretty and then another one did too, and there were people in line behind me and I couldn't decide so I just got one of each color. Fourteen fucking tubes of lip gloss," she says, and laughs a laugh that Wendy has never heard. "The clerk must've thought I was crazy."

When they got hungry they spread apple jelly on English muffins they hadn't bothered toasting. They drank grape juice, they arranged the play money in a rainbow spray. They were careful never to be too quiet.

"So now I've got a bag of cheap lip gloss in the car," Kath says, jerking her head toward the dark driveway. "You want one? You want all of them?"

In all the years she and Matthew traveled Kath never failed to bring back a gift for Wendy, something small and exquisite, perfume from Milan or lipstick from Paris, a scented candle from an apothecary in Geneva. None are imperishable but all are too precious to use. Wendy keeps them in a drawer in the bedroom, a cache of small failures, of places she has not been. She thinks of the plastic drugstore bag tossed in Kath's car. She would never take something from Kath she could provide for herself.

"Look," she says, and raises her chin toward the road, the headlights moving slow. "They're back." They watch the car until it turns into the side drive and they can no longer see it. Doors open and close and Wendy listens for her husband's voice, tries to imagine what it would be like never to hear it again.

James slides the new kitchen door open and Eric squeezes through as soon as he can fit, runs for his mother. "Hey boys,"

Kath says. She smiles at James and opens her arms and Eric hurls himself onto her lap, presses his face into her shirt. "Was it a screaming success? Did you laser pizzas and eat intergalactic mercenaries?"

"We slew many a dragon," James says. Wendy tries to catch his eye but can't; she tells herself it's too dark, too late, too soon.

"That's what I like to hear," Kath says, bouncing her knees, and Eric giggles, whips his head from side to side. "It was cool!" he says, and tilts his face at James, flirtatious as a kitten.

"It was *totally* cool," James says, and Eric erupts in hiccupy shrieks. Kath lowers her chin to his head, tries to settle him by running a hand down his messy hair. *Thank you,* she mouths to James. She stands, Eric wrapped around her like a monkey. They are sleeping in the spare room downstairs, a room with a sleep sofa and television and desk to which neither Wendy nor James lays claim—the de-militarized zone, James calls it.

"I think it's hammer time," Kath says, hoisting Eric higher. "Say good night," she murmurs to him, "say thank you," but he has shrunken into himself again, his face tight against his mother's shoulder.

"Yell if you need anything," James says. Wendy drains her glass and pours another as Kath slips into the kitchen, carries Eric down the back hallway. She watches her husband watch them.

"Want a glass?" she says, and James shakes his head, lowers himself into Kath's empty chair.

"She's still smoking," he says, and Wendy shrugs.

"What do you want me to do, tell her she can't? Take her cigarettes away?" She stops herself, breathes, asks the question he's been waiting to answer. "How was Eric?"

"I think they should stay," he says. "I think you should talk to her about staying around—he's got, what, at least two weeks till school starts? Why go back?"

Because that's their home, she thinks. "Kath mentioned something about stopping over at Matt's parents' for a few days. So she's not planning on going straight home." She waits for him to acknowledge this but he is silent. "They're his grandparents, James," she says. "They want some time with him."

"I know that," he snaps. "Jesus. How far are they, an hour? They can still see him, he can visit. But wouldn't you rather have them here with us, instead of with strangers?" He looks her in the eye for the first time since coming home, ready to fight, but she will refuse him this. New grief pours over old like lava over hot stone.

They ate ice-cream sandwiches in the lacy shade of a dogwood tree and played at what they would be when they grew up: a sales clerk, a bank teller. *My God,* Wendy thinks, *is that all we wanted? Even then?*

What they wanted, what they got, what they still have. She reaches for James's hands but he pulls away.

"They're not strangers," she says. Inside the house a light comes on, a faucet runs, and it is dark and silent again. "They're family," she says, her voice soft, inexorable. "James."

"I'm going in," he says, finished with her for the day. She watches him. She has done so for ten years, longer; she has seen his shoulders broaden and his legs become more solid, the skin around his eyes crease.

They poured warm water from yellow plastic teacups and played at being married, being wives, mothers. They clucked and scolded at imaginary children, welcomed invisible husbands home from work.

James slides the kitchen door shut behind him, turns off the track lighting and disappears into the darkness. She closes her eyes: *Dear God*, she thinks, *let him grow old. Grant me that.* She has watched him for more than ten years, from the time he was an overgrown boy just out of college, eager, so desperate for Kath to notice him, to *see*; but Kath was oblivious, so desperate then herself for a life far from the one she'd had, for a future of something other than master bedrooms and two-car garages.

How many nights the three of them staggered from bar to bar, drinking, dreaming, until Kath met Matthew and in a matter of weeks was gone, on trains to Philadelphia, New York, Montreal; and Wendy was left with James, chastened, resigned, but ready, finally, for her to love him.

Let him grow old, even if it is not with me.

She has loved him since they met, since he sat down next to her and Kath in a club where his friend tended bar and bought them soft pretzels and black licorice. She was twenty-three years old, too thin; she'd been dancing and was chilled sitting still. The pretzels were warm and salty, the licorice squeaky against her teeth. She saw the way he looked at Kath and didn't care. She was young enough not to care. She remembers thinking *It doesn't matter, I can wait. I will wait.*

◎ ◎ ◎

Eric is asleep, his forehead damp, mouth open. Kath strokes his cheek and he furrows his brow, presses his lips together and swallows. Once he turns on his side he won't move for hours. She settles next to him, her back propped against sofa cushions, the remote on the arm. Their bags are piled in a corner, by the closet; Eric's bright blue duffel and backpack and her small suitcase and satchel. The satchel is beautiful, Italian leather, hand-sewn, deep and soft as chocolate. In it are Matthew's clothes, the shorts and shirts she pulled dirty from the laundry room, a full week's worth.

She clicks through channels, settles on an infomercial for a closet organizer and reaches over to the coffee table for her glass, half filled with the Pastis and water that settles her stomach.

Eric turns onto his side and draws his knees to his chest, his hands up under his chin, and presses his back into her hip. Like a periwinkle, she thinks, curled and clinging. He can still sleep, he has slept every night since Matthew died, a sudden and heavy unconsciousness that seems almost willful. It's as though at a certain point each day he decides he's had enough, enough of this new life with no father, this new mother with no life, and he shuts himself down.

It is an ability she does not have. She has Valium instead.

Eric sighs; his foot twitches and she slides closer to the edge of the mattress, away from him. She reaches to the floor and gropes through her cotton toiletries bag until her fingertips brush the pill bottle. On the screen a woman is running her hand over padded silk hangers. Her nails are long and polished, the color of cherry cough syrup.

Kath mutes the television, swallows the Valium with a sip of her drink and settles back into her pillow to wait. Beside her Eric is still, his breath deep and damp and even. She stares at the screen, at the padded hangers and cedar-lined shelving, the delicious order of it all, and thinks of wrapping her arms around her son's wiry shoulders, his narrow chest; pressing her cheek to the top of his head and drawing the blanket up, up tight over his face that she can hardly bear to look at because it is Matthew's face, the features smaller and the years unwound and smoothed out but Matthew's face all the same. That perfect face: her husband's, her son's. She thinks of erasing it and smiles. The shame is burned out of her.

The shelves are adjustable, and the shoe racks, the lingerie bins. The hangers are wrapped in satin. She drops a hand to Eric's head, lets it rest, but he does not stir. His trust is the size of the universe. She could do anything to him, her son, her beautiful wound, her perfect grief.

◎ ◎ ◎

They called each other on Christmas mornings to catalogue and compare what was tucked into stockings and left under trees, to arrange for their new dolls to meet.

After trick-or-treating they upended their orange vinyl totes onto the kitchen table at Wendy's house into one magnificent pile and began the distribution: dark chocolate and nougats for Kath, fruit chews and marshmallow for Wendy, bubble gum and peanut butter cups apportioned evenly.

Summers they wore matching flip-flops, yellow plastic flowers over the toes and white rubber soles that went gray by July. They painted their toenails with the dregs of Kath's mother's polish, they rubbed lemon into their hair.

They dressed as cowgirls but didn't trick-or-treat. Instead they walked the murmuring streets to the park and waited for boys with cigarettes, boys with bottles of beer, boys with soft lips and sure hands.

They rubbed baby oil into each other's shoulders, untied their bikini tops to lay on their stomachs. In the late afternoon they dabbed Noxzema on their burned skin in the chill of Wendy's bathroom.

They lied for each other, to their teachers and their parents, to the boys they no longer wanted and the ones they still did. They waited up for each other, for the bars to close and the sound of keys outside the door, for the early-morning stories, breathless, abashed, thrilled. They jumped when the phone rang and despaired when it did not. They carried their pillows into each other's bedrooms, they shared packs of cigarettes and bottles of wine, they cried until they could no longer remember what there was to weep for. They kept secrets.

They fell drunk into each other's arms outside the door of the last apartment they shared, laughing, staggering; a sweet cloud of jasmine and smoke, the jingle of dropped keys and coins, purses spilling open, their hair a pretty tangle. They struggled with the knob, the lock. They promised: *You will always have a home with me. You will always be my sister.*

◎ ◎ ◎

James is not awake. Wendy knows this before she even opens her eyes—she can hear the sleep in his slow breath, feel it in the heavy stillness of his body next to hers. She tells herself it is too early to wake him, and on any other morning this would be true.

She slides from under the sheets, slow, quiet; grabs her robe and steps light on the balls of her feet to the hallway, pulls the door just closed behind her. The house itself seems to breathe differently with strangers in it.

But that is absurd; there is no one less of a stranger to her than Kath.

When she passes the door to the spare room she hears movement, murmurs. She pauses, touches her fingertips to the knob and brings her face close to the frame.

"Kath?"

"Yeah," Kath says. "It's okay, come in."

The sleep sofa is closed and cushioned, the coffee table pulled back in front of it and the bedding folded and stacked against the wall. The television is on, the volume close to mute, and Eric sits on the floor just in front of it, flipping between two cartoons.

"Remember how they said if we sat that close we'd ruin our eyes?" Kath says. She's on her knees, stuffing clothes in Eric's duffel.

"What're you doing?" Wendy says. The room is warm and bright with sun.

Kath zips the duffel and tosses it into the corner with the rest of their bags. "Yeah." She nods toward Eric, who is transfixed by the screen, and to Wendy she mouths the word *Dover*—where Matthew's parents live. "Eric, you want to hang out here while Aunt Wendy and I have coffee?"

"Okay," he says. He does not turn. Kath stands and brushes at her knees, squeezes past Wendy. "I'll get the rest of this later," she says. Her handbag is open on the coffee table, a makeup case and hairbrush on the arm of the sofa, a few magazines on the floor. She pulls the door closed behind them. "Is James still asleep?" she whispers, and Wendy nods.

They sit with their coffee at the kitchen table, the sliding glass door cracked open so Kath can blow her smoke out onto the deck.

"I can't not go," she says. "They know we're here. And I can't even begin to express to you the drama that would ensue if I didn't take him." She shrugs. "They haven't seen him since the funeral."

"Why so hush-hush?" Wendy says. "Doesn't he want to go?"

"It's not that, exactly—it's more . . . they look at him and they cry. And of course I understand that and I would never fault them for it but he's better, you know, he's getting better, and he doesn't need that. I mean, Jesus, maybe I'm a terrible person but when they start that I just want to say to them look, I manage to stay in control every minute of every day he's awake, so the least you can do is keep it together for a few fucking hours." She shakes her head. "He sleeps through the night now. And he needs that, you know? He needs the normal stuff again—his friends, and school, and . . . anyway."

The summer they were thirteen Kath's mother went to the hospital, and so Kath spent weekends at Wendy's house. On Friday evenings her father walked across the street with her, waited on the porch with a hand on her shoulder. Wendy's father let them in, her mother insisted on pouring glasses of iced tea before Kath's father left. The drive to the motel near the hospital grounds was over an hour. The four of them sat around the kitchen table and talked about the sweetness of the corn at the stand behind the firehouse, the new construction at the end of Hearthstone Drive, the misman-agement of the restaurant where they sometimes ordered pizza and fried shrimp and pit beef sandwiches to go. Wendy could hear them from her bedroom, where she waited for Kath. She knew better than to join them, she knew Kath did not want her to. She heard the scrape of chairs, the clap of a hand on a shoulder. She heard her mother tell Kath's father to drive safe, to *give Louise our best.*

Louise. Kath's mother, whom they did not talk about over their iced tea, who was sedated in a bed with metal sides, a feeding tube up her nose, her eyelids bruised and her hands wrapped in gauze, mouth working, soundless, dry.

"Thank you," Kath says. "You and James both, I mean it. I needed this, you know?" She runs a hand through her hair. Her wedding band, a circle of perfect diamonds, sparks daggers in the sun. Her hair is still long and gold and lovely but her fingers look stiff, the skin rough and red. "I should probably collect Eric and get going."

Her mother's hands were wrapped because after she bit off her nails she chewed at the fingers until they bled. Kath had seen the bright red blooms on the gauze the one time her father took her. She told Wendy this one Friday after her father had left, the two of them sitting cross-legged on Wendy's bed. *She was eating herself,* Kath said. And then: *She didn't recognize me anyway.* Wendy did not know which was worse. Her own mother insisted they all have dinner together on these weekends, the four of them passing platters of chicken cutlets and bowls of salad while Kath's father ate takeout from Styrofoam containers next to his wife, who jerked and hummed in her cage of a bed.

"James wants you to stay," Wendy says, Wendy hears herself saying. "You and Eric, as long as you want—he was saying last night, after you went to bed—" She sees that Kath is watching her, all her early-morning vagueness gone, and though she is close to choking on the words she keeps on. She would do anything for him. "—he was saying how good it would be, all of us here, for a while."

He cannot let a day pass without asking her—in the kitchen before work, in the car on their way to dinner, in their bed, in her,

Will you, When will you, and she feels nothing but his want, his desperate want. *Someday,* she says, *Soon,* she says, and what she means is *Not soon, not ever. I do not want a child.*

So no: not *anything,* not really.

"You know, it's a funny thing," Kath says, still watching her, smiling, "in Paris, our last night, we'd made reservations at a new place, a restaurant we'd never been to, and we weren't sure where it was exactly but we knew it was pretty far, and we decided we'd take a taxi." Even now Wendy cannot stand the taste of licorice, though James eats it by the handful. "So we had a few drinks and walked down to the taxi stand—Matt liked walking," she says. "Just about anywhere, and usually I did too. But I had these new snakeskin shoes on and my feet were miserable so we got the cab. And this restaurant is apparently down a side street, and it's narrow, so the driver decides to just let us off at the close corner but it's a pretty busy boulevard—by the Luxembourg Gardens," she says, and pauses, to give Wendy a chance to nod in recognition, *Of course, the Gardens,* but Wendy does not move. Parisian boulevards and snakeskin shoes have no place in this house, this life. She does not know much but she knows that.

"Rue Vaugirard," Kath says. "I was a little drunk and not paying attention and when I got out of the cab I was almost hit by a car. I mean, it was seriously close—inches. Matt was beside himself but I tried to make a joke out of it—you know, what a way to end a vacation, at least I would've died happy, that kind of shit." James keeps bags of licorice in a kitchen drawer, ropes and twists, shiny black and sticky. Wendy hates the smell of it on his breath. Kath spreads her hands, an innocent magician. "That's the story. We had dinner and got a cab back and packed and left the next day. No drama. He was dead a week later." She collects her cigarettes and lighter. "You can thank James for the offer. But I think Eric and I are going to pass. Because the thing is, Wendy, all of us are not here."

◎ ◎ ◎

"Where are they?" James says. His face is slack with sleep but his eyes are wide, avid.

"They're gone. They left," Wendy says. She is still sitting at the kitchen table, her feet propped on the chair where Kath was. The room smells, just barely, of smoke. "I told you last night—"

"You told me—what—how could you let her leave?"

"I didn't *let* her do anything, James. I can't keep her here. I don't want—"

"No," James says. "You don't *want* much of anything, do you?"

Under the smoke is a breath of verbena, of Kath—her skin, her hair. She used to sleep with it in a braid. She used to sleep on her side, one arm thrown over her head. She used to tap on Wendy's door when the sleep wouldn't come, whispering *Hey can I come in, hey can I come in there with you*, and the two of them would stretch across the pillows and dream awake of what the world might bring them. There were no ghosts, not then, not yet.

"I want to be enough for you," Wendy says. James says nothing, he does nothing. He is the whole of her grammar and she is an ellipsis.

"Was I ever?" she says. She waits, and his silence fills the world she knows. There are so many places she has not been.

◎ ◎ ◎

"I like Uncle James," Eric says. He is belted into the seat behind Kath, plastic action figures spread around him, their arms and legs in the air, battle-weary.

"Yeah? He likes you too. So does Aunt Wendy. Did you have a good time with them?" In the rearview mirror she can see the top of his head, the crooked part and cowlicks. Half of his reason for being is gone.

"Uh-huh."

"Good," Kath says. It's still early enough on a Sunday for the highway to be mostly empty. The median is wide, the grass there long and feathery, but the shoulders are well trimmed, lush green dipping shallow into a bright bed of calendula and coneflower before rising up again. She glances in the rear view, catches a glimpse of his brow, damp and knotted. "So listen, I need you to do something for me, okay? When we get to Gramma's? I need you to be really nice to them, because they're sad."

"Because of Daddy." It is not a question.

"Because of Daddy," she says. She can hear the cheerful click of plastic, of tiny knights and dinosaurs and astronauts fighting to the death in her son's lap. "Look how pretty," she says, and he raises his head from his toys just long enough for her to notice.

"Do we have to stay long?" he says.

"No, baby." He is everything that she loves, that she grieves. He speaks and his voice cuts; he sighs and his breath burns. "Are you about ready to get back home?"

"I guess," he says. "Uncle James said we can go to their house whenever we want." She glances behind her and sees that he has pulled the center armrest down to arrange his dinosaurs on it but they won't stand, won't stay; they wobble and tilt and topple with the motion of the car. The knights and astronauts are forgotten.

They are the only ones on the road; she could ease the car into the breakdown lane, let it roll until the wheels touched the earthy shoulder.

"He did, huh?" She'd put the car in park and the dinosaurs would settle. And then out of her seat to stretch, to open the rear door and unfasten Eric's belt for him.

"Uh-huh. He said not to tell Aunt Wendy, though."

She remembers Wendy on mornings like this one, sitting at a wooden picnic table and weaving God's-eyes with vivid yarn, arms and hands brown, her fingers quick and sure; or in the damp grass by the Oakmede pool, stringing beads and bells onto skeins of leather for anklets—identical sets, two of everything. And she remembers Matthew, the morning after their last night in Paris, the window open but the pillows warm, their arms and legs in an exhausted tangle, his heart beating against her, through her. *Don't ever scare me like that again*, he said.

I won't. She hadn't—it had been impossible.

"I think Aunt Wendy's sad too, baby." She'd lift him from the back seat—*Want to play with your toys in the grass?*—and take his hand, help him out of the car and lead him around to the grassy slope, a perfect place for dinosaurs. "We used to say we'd go everywhere, your Aunt Wendy and I," she tells him, but he doesn't answer. His focus is unwavering. Wendy's skin at the end of summer was soft and coconut-sweet; it shone with possibilities. Her own was a paler gold but just as ready, more. *Everywhere, till we run out of places to go.*

Eric repositions the bright plastic reptiles when they fall, setting them upright over and over again. He arranges them in complex patterns, lips moving silently. "You okay back there?" she says. He does not answer, does not stop. He would not stop, she thinks, would not give up pressing their hard feet into the crumbling earth by the side of the road, would not notice that she had slipped away until he saw the car moving away from him, smelled the exhaust and heard the tires grabbing asphalt. She imagines what he would look like, growing smaller and smaller in the car mirrors, his face shining white by the road, a relic, a ghost. *My son.* The air rushing past is warm and gold and heedless. She imagines what he will look like in five years, in twenty. She imagines what it will be like to see him for the last time. There are so many ways to disappear.

Crestview Way, October 1985

It's Saturday night almost Sunday morning when Jimmy and Abby do it. They're at Ryan from AP European History's house, the front door open and the back patio slicked with spilled beer, an October wind spinning up woodsmoke and brittle leaves. The party's roar has settled into a tranquil boozy purr. The kitchen is fluorescent and empty, the couch in the living room anchored by couples panting at either end, the staircase littered with plastic cups and discarded sweaters and moccasins with the heels crushed down.

Jimmy and Abby have been on the sofa in the den drinking Pabst Blue Ribbon and slugs of root-beer schnapps for hours. They're drunk but not drunk enough to quit looking: Jimmy for KeriAnn with the braid and Abby for Sam who just moved from Chicago. They look furtively, through lidded eyes and over shoulders as they lean together, foreheads almost touching, sharing the bottle of schnapps as they pantomime a serious conversation, laughing too readily and brushing damp hair away from each other's flushed brows to telegraph to anyone passing by how interesting each finds the other.

They know, they do, that KeriAnn and Sam are not looking for them, and maybe they even know that KeriAnn and Sam would go the long way through the dining room for a beer to avoid talking to them, or having to think of a reason not to talk to them.

It's not that KeriAnn and Sam are unkind, or cruel; it's just that they're used to being forgiven their mostly insignificant slights and inattentions, if these are even noticed beyond the pretty hair and awesome accent and the effortless ease with which these two navigate the treacherous currents of eleventh grade.

Neither is it that Jimmy and Abby are stupid. They're just tired of being a little lonely a lot of the time, and pretending they're not, or pretending it doesn't bother them. They're tired of the constant dull ache of the bother they won't admit to, this boy and girl who are smart enough to suspect that this loneliness won't last and young enough to hurt anyway, anyway.

So here they are, these two and a few dozen more, not the football players and cheerleaders who are at a nastier party in a fancier house where already three boys are bleeding and two girls are weeping and a dining-room chair has been put through a window screen; not the crowd with green hair and black nail polish and studded boots and belts who are gathered at the playground throwing the I Ching and smoking clove cigarettes under the bright moon.

No: in this warm and bright and only slightly trashed house are the well-liked and well-groomed, the promising and polite, the goofy and awkward and decent, the ones who might stand in front of their mirrors at night and wish to be special but not odd, unique but not different; the ones who believe this is somehow possible and for whom anything more would be too much, too soon.

They are not long past crying for their mothers if they wake from nightmares—if they were birds they would still be damp. The boys blush, remembering how when they slow danced in middle school they rested their hands on the girls' hips and the girls leaned in just enough for the boys to feel through shirts and sweaters what they dreamed of touching. The girls blush remembering how much they wanted to be touched.

So they pretend not to remember what may as well have happened yesterday, these conscientious girls and responsible boys, curved and muscled but awkward still, hearts stuttering and shy. They try on bravura anyway, shimmying into it together, safety in numbers. When they slow dance now the boys pull the girls hip to hip and the girls wrap their hands around the boys' necks and their sweaters float up just enough: sliver of belly, gut-flutter, butterfly fingertips.

Saturday night balanced on Sunday morning and Jimmy and Abby are teetering between drunk and hungover, their eyes burning with exhaustion but still bright. They're tired and ready to abandon the illusion that if they just wait long enough, smile hard enough, laugh loud enough, KeriAnn and Sam will materialize before them, backlit and gauzy and moving toward them in paradoxically eager slow motion, the euphoric end of a movie they've seen before and can't decide if they like or not—if they *believe* or not. They can't decide if they're hungry or nauseated but they know they're ready to stop pretending to be fascinated by each other in the unlikely hope that this feigned interest will generate around them a radiant orb of irresistibility.

So they sigh and draw back from each other. Abby kicks her shoes to the rug and curls her socked feet beneath her on the couch but not before Jimmy grabs at a toe—her socks are purple; Space Invaders march around her ankles in thready green rows—and laughs.

What's funny? Abby says, annoyed.

Nothing, Jimmy says, too tired to tease, I like them, and Abby smiles, says So do I, too tired to be angry, and once they stop pretending they start meaning it. (Meaning what? They never meant to find themselves doing what they could not have imagined doing three hours ago, not with each other at least, not in this lifetime, and yet here they are, and they are doing it with a heat and urgency they've never felt, shoes off shirts off pants undone, gasping, close to laughing though there's nothing funny about how much each of them wants this person they're suddenly not at all sure they've ever seen before.)

They pull the afghan from the foot of the sofa over them—there are other people in the house, after all—and beneath it they shove at the clothing they haven't got off yet and now they're laughing for real.

What's funny? Abby says again, not annoyed anymore, she's so not annoyed she can barely get the words out,

Nothing, Jimmy says again, and it's true, nothing has ever been less funny, nothing has ever felt scarier or better, nothing has ever sounded like her breath on his throat or felt like her hair on his face or tasted like the soft quiver of her belly.

I think—he says,

I know—she says,

They are in such a chaos of bliss, of relief and disbelief, that they can hardly see, so they squeeze their eyes shut because what good are they now that they have hands and tongues, now that their skin is on fire, now that the dry leaves are blowing cold outside, blowing *before* away.

They will forget closing their eyes before they can regret it.

These things matter: Jimmy and Abby both hate gym class. They're smarter than they let on. They shared a crushed Snickers once in the back of study hall. They've never flown on an airplane. Jimmy works the front desk at the emergency vet on Monday and Thursday nights, and when someone is crying too hard to fill out the paperwork he does it for them. Abby fills take-out orders at the Old Line Cafeteria on weekends, and if a ticket has a senior citizen discount code she adds extra slices of chocolate cream pie in the bags, extra pints of vegetable soup, extra crackers. They've never danced together and they never will.

These do not: the music that's playing in Ryan from AP European History's den—Jimmy and Abby aren't listening to it. They aren't listening to the furniture warehouse commercial on the television in the next room or the choking laughter of the couple from drama club in the yard or the blue sizzle of stars above them, so pretty in their dying. The trig test on Monday doesn't matter and neither does the fight they'll have in the hallway after, Jimmy trying to take Abby's hand and Abby yanking it away hissing *not here* and Jimmy trying to shake the hurt off as he walks past KeriAnn without seeing her and Abby blinks back tears she does not understand.

The blood-pound in Jimmy's ears is oceanic; the hot rush in Abby's veins deafening, and when they finally do what they never expected to be doing the world contracts around them; a hole burned through film, edges black and curling, dust motes dancing in a ring of hot white light.

It doesn't matter that Abby has done it before and Jimmy hasn't, or that neither knows this about the other. Abby decided long before that the two times with the breakfast waiter from the hotel on vacation in August didn't count: the first because she still isn't sure it actually happened and the second because all she wanted was to get it over with.

That's not what she wants now. What Abby wants this third charmed time is *more*, even if she's not sure how to ask, or what that means. What Jimmy wants is to do it right and for her to like it, even if all he can think of now is how he doesn't want to die before he finishes.

What they both want is to know *Have you always been this person have you always been right here?*

What they both want is to know *Will I always be the person you're making me?*

These sweet foolish children in the universe of their bodies, their blood ready to burn through the roof of the sky, their words blown to ash and useless. They still believe it's possible, probable, definite that they'll be happy. They have no idea yet what small things they'll learn to tell themselves happy is made of.

What they want is the next time before this time even ends.

Right now, though, their hearts hammer and pulse with astonishment.

It doesn't matter that there won't be a next time, not yet. By the time they realize this they will have misremembered everything about this night and morning except the saltwater taste of each other's skin. By the time they realize this Jimmy's mother will have passed out in a tub of cooling water with an empty bottle of pills on the rim and a cigarette burning its way to her scraped and twisted fingers and Abby's brother will have sprawled bleeding in a frat house basement while the other pledges close in to spit and kick, screaming *Faggot faggot faggot.*

Right now, though, their fingertips spark and sing: they don't believe yet that everything ends, or that they will greet some of those endings with a relief so vast and blinding it will seem more like death than deliverance.

A car horn honks and the couple from drama club shout, crash and stagger through the fallen leaves to the driveway, to the waiting day that Jimmy and Abby want no part of. No matter: Saturday night has tumbled into Sunday morning. The clocks insist.

They will not remember separating, tugging at their clothes under the afghan, shy again and nervous, wet throats cooling. They will not remember the drive home, Jimmy driving his mother's car alone and Abby squeezed in a back seat between the girls she came with, the radio murmuring over their exhausted quiet. They will sleep without dreaming and wake in their own beds, in their new skins. They will open their eyes and the furniture and walls they've been looking at for years will be funhouse-strange, their own faces in the mirror two mysteries, and they will be elated by this, and terrified.

They will forget, sooner than is imaginable, that for a few October hours the world was perfect, and they were perfect in it. The clocks will not remind them. In one month Jimmy will wait by his mother's naked body for the ambulance to come and in two Abby will sit in a plastic chair bolted to the police station floor while her parents wait for her brother to give his statement. The mirrors will not remind them. In three months Ryan from AP European History will throw a Christmas party and the football players will show up, staggering, high-fiving, shouldering through the door in twos to move furniture from the living room out onto the front lawn. Jimmy and Abby will hear about this on the Monday before winter break, Jimmy in homeroom and Abby in the cafeteria, and they will receive this information with the perplexed frustration of people who cannot understand the language they hear; who are unable to parse the customs they see. When they pass each other in the halls they will suddenly find reasons to rummage through backpacks and purses, heads down, hearts galloping. They will not remember the weightless bodies those hearts lived in.

They will not remember the cold from the open patio door, the crocheted afghan, cigarette smoke and root-beer schnapps, the silvered world stretched wide, branch and star and frost.

Jimmy will learn to clean his mother's feeding tube and Abby will learn to be silent when her brother refuses to press charges and February will erase itself. They will learn to find the derivative of f at the point $x = a$ and they will learn how easy it is to forget what is impossible to have. The snow will melt and freeze again and Jimmy will think *Once she can feed herself—*

and Abby will think *Once he transfers—*

and the last freeze will sink into warm soil and Jimmy and Abby will think

Once the insurance pays

Once we can get away for a weekend get a little time to breathe

Once the home health aide comes full time

Once we find new doctors new lawyers new friends

Once I stop caring I get out I forget

Once he leaves

Once she dies

and they will not remember the fizz and skip of breath and pulse and wanting. Abby's brother will be found with his skull cracked open in the back lot of a package store by campus and Jimmy's mother will drown silently in her own pulmonary fluid and they will accept this as the best ending they could hope for.

And if they accept it, what tired god would intervene?

What Surrounded

I dreamed I couldn't remember my baby's name and when I woke I wept with relief—not that I knew its name, but that I had no baby.

Sometimes, in the dream, the baby was lost, or injured, or I had hidden it away and forgotten where. Worse was when it was none of these, when it was just the happy baby, fat and smiling at my feet and waiting too patiently to be fed while I stared at it, my hands full of nothing but bluebirds.

I reached for the ceramic cup on the nightstand where last night's wine had become this morning's, careful not to wake Peter next to me or draw the attention of any babies that might've found their way into the house while we slept. The house was a mile up a barely paved road so I hadn't been locking the door. It felt safe. *I* felt safe, but all the same. Anything could happen. Anything can always happen.

What most people call *bluebirds* are in fact indigo buntings. The house was my father's, or had been, until it became, per the terms of his will and the laws of the state, legally mine. Things happen—transubstantiation, shape-shifting, metamorphosis—whether anyone notices or not. I had fallen asleep on the floor sorting my father's clothes and drinking the wine and woken in the bed. The sky outside was pinking at the ridgeline. The window was mine but not the cold air that whispered through it. The scraping branch was mine but not the leaf-brown rattle. I half expected a sheriff to show up at the front door bearing papers that outlined the necessity of my vacating the premises immediately. Peter, still next to me, sighed in his sleep and turned to me, reaching. I drew myself away. He is not dear to me. He is nothing to me, he is no one. I am even now my father's daughter.

◎ ◎ ◎

It got easier, closer to the end. Morphine snaked merrily into the blued crook of my father's arm. He never hit me, though he'd wanted to. We all want things we can't have.

It got easier, the less of him remained—*the end* is just a pretty way of saying this. I sat in an upholstered chair by his bed and listened to the absurd machines, their hum and whoosh, their lullaby sigh.

I didn't mind the hospital at all—the microclimate of the glass vestibule at the entrance, the slight astringency of the pumped air on his floor, the floor itself that seemed impossible to slip on. The chair in his room was deep and sturdy and wide enough to wedge pillows against the wooden armrests. His nurses brought those pillows, shoes squeaking, forearms strong as ships. Paula and Marilyn and JoAnne belonged to my father although he didn't know it. They touched him more than I ever had, or wanted to, and every day I brought doughnuts and muffins to leave at the nurses' station.

It got easier with every blue dawn. Time moved through me, a warm and buoyant wind, and I floated on the enormity of it and marveled at the view, his limbs shrunken and wilted, his chest and cheeks caving, every bit of him curling inward as though he could make himself invisible, as though he could hide from what was coming for him.

◎ ◎ ◎

Peter, in the doorway, is nearly vibrating with worry for my state of mind, coffee cup in a two-handed death grip and shoulders shrugged to his ears. Jesus Christ *exhale*, I would like to say, but look at his furrowed brow! So I say nothing. I can be kind, no matter what my father believed.

"Can I help you with that?" he says, and his forehead contorts into a degree of concern previously unreached.

"Oh. No, I don't think so. I'm just—it's fine. Really." I'm on the floor, drifts of clothes everywhere, suits and sweaters and shirts. Truly beautiful shirts, in fact, custom tailored, poplin and herringbone and pinpoint. "But I feel a little like Daisy Buchanan." And his face collapses, this decent man who will not allow himself to be amused or distracted by what he imagines is my desperate attempt to stave off grief with humor; this man who is considerate and generous and utterly unaware that every day he's spent with me is a wasted one. These shirts will end up in a bright yellow bin at the back edge of a drugstore parking lot and this bothers me not at all.

"I can't imagine all this on a rack at Goodwill but I don't—"

He puts the coffee cup on my father's mahogany dresser—*my* dresser—and milky concern sloshes over the side *be fucking careful that dresser is literally irreplaceable* as this man, whose ex-wife has nothing but kind things to say about him, drops to his knees *what the fuck is the matter with you* and wraps his arms around me as though I'm porcelain *don't touch me don't touch don't* but I'm not I'm lava.

◎ ◎ ◎

Paula's son was in prison and her daughter-in-law and grandson lived in her half-finished basement. Marilyn's husband was a public defender who was studying for his divinity degree in the spare time he didn't have. JoAnne and her girlfriend were planning to get married as soon as the girlfriend finished her associate's degree in dental hygiene. Paula and Marilyn and JoAnne said hello to my father's jaundiced body when they came into his room and asked me if I needed anything before they left. I told them no, every time, the pillows were enough, I was fine, I was good, really, and they were too professional or too busy to argue. I wonder now what happened on the shifts when I wasn't there—maybe they moved around his gowned bones in silence, preoccupied with the son or the husband or the girlfriend. Maybe they stood at the window just long enough to catch their breath, the city flung below them, sparkling or fogged; soot-stained brick and on-ramps, Formstone and trundling busses and the exuberant splash of graffiti on underpass walls. I wonder now what they thought on days they walked into that room and saw my chair empty, if they were relieved to have one fewer person to comfort that day, or if they understood they didn't need to comfort me at all.

◎ ◎ ◎

By noon we are at an impasse: Peter does not want to leave me and I don't want him to stay. I have important things to do, such as sitting in this silent room and pretending to clean out my father's desk, or lacing my boots and wrapping my scarf and crabbing my way sideways down the hill to settle on the flat rock that overlooks a hard-frozen gully that will be a stream by April.

"Why don't you take Amanda to lunch?" I say. Amanda is his grown daughter and Peter is *retired* in the sense that he has a staff of people who do the work for him that he used to do himself.

"She's got some chaperone thing at the boys' school today," he says. Of course—the boys. The grandsons. I've seen their picture, six and eight years old in private-school ties and khakis, Amanda and her husband Max in shades of coordinating blue behind them, Amanda's mother Louise draped across the front of the photo, pinkish sundress on green grass, brown legs stretched to the side and brown arm bent fetchingly at the elbow. She's the kind of blonde who looks like she belongs on a yacht. They've been divorced for long enough that they can talk with the ease of affable neighbors.

"Okay," I say, and consider how to get him out and gone in as kind a manner as possible. Ragg wool socks, fleece-lined boots, flannel shirt and a sweater and still I'm not close to warm—the chill comes up through the foundation, through the wet February smell of cold dirt and leaf. It's in my hair, damp and matted. "I have a shopping list. In the kitchen—it's—*wait*," I say, because he's turning around already, as though the slip of paper will spontaneously combust if he doesn't get to it fast enough, "it's just a few things. If you could go into town, take your time, pick some stuff up for me—for us." I correct myself. *Us*: who would I be if that word had ever come more easily to me?

"Of course," Peter says, and his face melts with the relief of having a concrete task that, when accomplished, will demonstrably and qualitatively improve the current situation. He's not a push-over, not a simp or a sucker, a cuckold or a chump; he's a nominally retired and considerably successful investment consultant who can identify and dissect and correct whatever complication is hampering optimal performance and maximized returns. He's considerate and conscientious and I cannot find a way to want anything from him. "Thanks," I say. "You can make dinner tonight. I'll be your sous. You can bark orders at me and I'll yell *oui chef!*"

"An offer no man could refuse." He kisses me, leaves me surrounded by open drawers and mildewed file folders.

Oui chef.

This is my talent: this performative flirtation, this telegraphed coquettishness. I wrap it around my needlessness until it holds its own obscene shape. Until it conjures something out of my nothingness.

◎ ◎ ◎

Pallor, algor, rigor, livor—pretty words all in a row, smooth as tumbled shells and too delicate to carry the dense black weight of *mortis.* Trochaic, archaic.

Paula and Marilyn and JoAnne told me what would happen to my father's body—this seemed only appropriate, given the amount of time he'd spent telling me what should happen to mine.

So much prettier than color, temperature, rigidity, or gravity's last irrefusable request. The flesh seizes before softening. Blood finds its place eventually.

There were dozens of lessons and there was only one: a daughter's body cannot be trusted. It is unmanageable, prone to secrecy and deceit and the most useless pleasure.

Keep your legs together. No man wants the town pump.

I pictured a wooden barrel and metal cylinder, blue-painted handle and spout. The itsy bitsy spider. Sweet clear water, not spit-warm and rubbery-tasting like what dribbled from the green hose when I looped it over its curved and rusted holder. I was eight, I was ten, I was fourteen. My mother had always been dead. It was my job to shut off the sprinkler every night in summer and I dripped starbursts from the hose across the driveway. I pictured my mother in pedal pushers and a blouse tied at the waist, I pictured my mother with dirty bare feet. The sky was pink then blue then endless. Black is the absence of all color and white is the entirety of the spectrum—or is it the opposite? It was a boy who explained the difference to me, somewhere between the black driveway and the high white moon. I don't remember his name; I only remember his fingers under my cutoffs and hooked into the elastic of my underwear, tugging them aside, then the sweet shock of his licked thumb-tip on me, the house's cooling brick against my back and the sound of my father's evening news from the console television in the den, my eyes closed and sparking colors I had no names for.

◎ ◎ ◎

But the corpus before me: twig legs, clavicle narrow as a log fallen across a river. I could have spread my arms for balance and tiptoed across that jutting bone. The bed was not wide but in it he was a marionette. Paula's hands, when she snapped the latex gloves off, were fleshy and pale as ground veal.

"Okay, I'm seeing a little more breathing difficulty today." She squeezed my shoulder. "I can send the doc in if you want to talk to him but honestly, sweetheart, I wouldn't bother. This is just what happens." She glanced at the clock without trying to hide it—it was visiting day at her son's facility. I knew because she didn't try to hide that either.

"Of course," I said. "I mean of course no, I don't need to talk to the doctor. Are you almost done?"

"Almost." She adjusted the oxygen flowmeter and lifted his head to shift the pillow. "But you stay as long as you want," she winked at me, settled his skull back down like an egg in a nest. "Visiting hours don't mean so much around here, you know what I'm saying?"

Yes. Once the care plan had taken a turn for the palliative, all policy bets were off, it seemed. No matter what time of day or night I came, I saw visitors in the hallways and lounges, slipping in and out of doors with damp wads of tissues and blotched swollen faces, silent and foundling-thin. No vampire would have spared them a second glance. Only occasionally did one of them look at me long enough to notice: my pink cheeks, the eyeliner and mascara I put on to sit with him, precise and unsmudged and perfect.

◎ ◎ ◎

A daughter's body—if she is the right kind of daughter—will never be only hers. It will be passed from parent to husband to children, like a precious thing if she is lucky and like necessary filth if she is not. Or do I have that backwards?

In the pictures on Peter's phone Amanda looks sturdy, unflappably cheerful, at home in her skin. Across from me at my father's dining-room table, she looks older than I know she is. Her boys have left their mark. Peter carves the roast into perfect slices; they curve and fall, one onto the next, an open rosy book. Max pours wine. This dinner is happening because the only way I could get Peter to stop suggesting it was to agree to it. It's happening in this house because how else would the right kind of daughter ever sit at my father's table?

The heartfelt murmured condolences, thank God, are over, and there's nothing for me to do but nod and smile and make sure the wine bottle is in easy reach. *Get another one on deck, Peter, time waits for no one!* I put my fork down and lean back in my chair, let my eyes soften. You don't have to touch the walls to know how cold they are but the fire glows behind me. I let my eyes close, for just a second too long, but no one remarks. The bereaved are given such latitude! Their inattention is indulged, their distraction and withdrawal delicately ignored—we could play a parlor game after dinner: *Rude, Bored, or Grieving?*

Next to me Peter reaches for my hand and Amanda clocks this, saws at the tender meat that doesn't need sawing and launches into a new story about the boys, an aggressively complicated anecdote that puts their precocity front and center—there is carpool confusion, a lost cell phone, rehearsal for a talent show at the grade school. Her forehead is knotted, shiny with the effort of turning the familiar annoyances of a day into cinematic slapstick. Peter and Max chuckle and nod, their encouraging smiles supportive as pool noodles, and even through the haze of wine and indifference I understand that their attention means nothing to her, that her labored attempt at whimsy is meant for no one but me.

The right kind of daughter would care, but I am not that. I stretch my arm and nudge the empty wine bottle toward Peter with the tip of a finger and am struck again by the new luxury of not caring where my phone is; not dreading its ring. No one tells you that, and you, in turn, tell no one, and so the delicious secret of postmortem relief is perpetuated. Peter excuses himself to get more wine and I realize that Amanda has stopped talking, is sitting with her lips pressed and hands folded, her own glass nearly untouched. Max leans to wrap an arm around her. "You warm enough, babe?" he asks, and in that moment I long for Marilyn, her box braids and scrubs the color of this wine, her sure hands tucking a blanket over me, waking me when I hadn't known I was sleeping.

◎ ◎ ◎

The Ativan, sublingual. JoAnne had a tattoo of a kitten with wings on the inside of her left wrist. She slipped the pills under my father's tongue, deft as a priestess.

It is not exactly true that every day he became less present, but rather that the nature of his presence refined itself: his outline became sharper, his edges more vivid even as he wasted, as though his body were declaring its separation from what surrounded it.

Sublingual: under the tongue, beyond speech. He knew even before I did that I was the wrong kind of girl, before I understood which parts of me mattered—the brain doesn't, the mouth only sometimes. The hands matter depending on the work they're doing, and the work matters in direct proportion to its beneficiary— ideally a husband, a child. And if no husband or child is available then any acquaintance or stranger in need will do.

This was just another lesson for me to learn. He never hit me, not because he didn't want to but because what good would it have done?

What will not do: work on behalf of the daughter herself.

The markers tied to the dry-erase board were color coded according to shift. JoAnne's was blue. She squeaked her blue notes across the board and capped the marker, let it fall. It dangled by a knotted string from the frame, across the room from the pinging monitors, the obsolescing body. She put her hands on her hips and swiveled her head until her neck cracked.

"Sorry," she said. "Sounds nasty but it feels so good." She peered at the IV, moved in to adjust the flow, then didn't. "It's fine," she said. "I mean all of this—" she gestured at nothing, at everything—"we're doing the minimum required according to his AD. It doesn't change anything, it just drags it out some." She shrugged. "Wouldn't be my choice, but . . . " Another head tilt, this time lateral. "Has anyone from social services called you?"

"No," I said. His right hand, yellowed palm up, fingers curling incrementally more each day like cooking shrimp. "Is that protocol? I mean if it's not required I don't want to waste anyone's time."

"No," JoAnne said, "I know you don't. We all do." She sighed, glanced out the window. "Gonna rain, unless it snows, am I right? Okay, let me see what I can do about social. It's just more paper that no one bothers to read before they file it."

His hand: first a shallow boat, then a bowl, then a cup. The fingertips almost grazed the palm.

"I brought muffins," I said. "Blueberry and carrot and a few lemon poppy seed—did you get one?"

JoAnne laughed. "Do I look like I've passed on any muffins in my life?"

But of course what else have I done but laid waste, to every hour of every day; to the pebbly minutes of mountainous years; to my hollow body. My father saw the wrong in me before I did. And the truth is that he never hit me because he could barely bring himself to touch me, with my greedy flesh and indifferent heart, with my imperviousness to regret or shame.

What's wrong with you, he used to say to me, genuinely bewildered, genuinely wanting to understand as though by understanding he could fix me, *don't you want a husband? Don't you want children? If your mother could see you. Thank God she can't. What do you think you're here for?*

I can no more easily answer that now than I could then.

⊚ ⊚ ⊚

The dark earth has sucked the day into it, but even so I can see where the owl has been by what he's left behind: rabbit scraps and bits of fur, disarticulated legs.

It is difficult, in this place, to hear death coming. It resists announcing itself. It slips its whisper among the groan and creak of branches and bending limbs, the snapping rain. It buries itself in the drifting snow. You have to look to find the damage. You have to want to find it, to dig and scrape at the loose soil and rotting branches until the rock below draws blood, slippery on your paws, on the basalt shear below.

On your fingers, is what I meant. The Ativan has my feral cat's tongue, the bottle having somehow found its way into my bag, after. Along with his rosary, his glasses, his wallet and comb.

Ativan, talisman, atavist. My mouth is full of stones but I am safe in this dead man's house, in this weightless body that has never fed anyone. The feathered sky is locked out, and the trees' chewed roots, and the quaking infant. The nameless baby. I breathe it back into whatever black place it came from.

Penitent is a noun and an adjective.

Slit is a noun and a verb.

My knees are unbruised but my hands are blundering cold, swollen with disuse. Next to me Peter sighs in his blameless sleep and I turn to him, belly-up like an animal ready to be opened, neck to snatch. We are at odds, Peter and I: he wants to nurse me and I want him to reach down my hot red throat and turn me outside in.

◎ ◎ ◎

By the end I could close my eyes and still his body floated, sticklike and insistent, behind the lids. Easier just to keep them open.

What surrounded it: very little. The metal rails and plastic boards of the bed, the wheeled trays and baskets, wall mounts and brackets for wires and cords and monitors. White composite walls and drop ceilings, all of it growing blurrier with the slowing shudder of the chest, as though he were dragging the world with him.

Leave it, I thought. *You can't take it.*

I can, and I can leave you with the nothing you've always had, the palsied hands said, the bluing feet and the sawdust lips.

Not nothing.

I have a ragged heart and a pilgrim's shell. I have knees and ankles that ache and creak but work, but carry me over rock and dirt and entrails steaming in the dark morning.

I have a smile that no one has seen and teeth enough blood enough rage enough. And I have your fury, its savage kick and flail, its undepleted venom. I will never give it up.

You are nothing, the skinned eyelids said, and the yellowed orbs beneath them.

I am made of you. There is no part of me that isn't yours.

What good is a daughter who refuses to use the only part of her that matters?

I kept my eyes open, I sank to the floor next to his bed, one hand around his wrist and the other his ankle, my useless palms burning. I held on until I was sure.

◎ ◎ ◎

There is always the moment when, looking, you see what you did not expect—the black bear in the drive, the hawk in the window, the man dying, the man dead—and you tell yourself you will never forget it, and of course the forgetting begins before the telling ends.

The night is cold and perfect as eternity, the bed filled with everything we don't know.

Peter, next to me, tethered tight to this breathing world. I want to pry his jaws open and howl down the cave of his mouth *What are any of us here for?*

The right kind of girl would know. Would be born knowing. Would have been a daughter a father wanted. Who would I be if I had been that girl? Not his. And I am nothing if not his.

The soaking clouds press down and the fox bellies into its den—bloody snout, musk and funk and muddy tail. It dreams of fat sheep like Peter dreams of prizes less vicious than me.

Accident, Design

In the house that is barely a house Roy kisses June's skin, the smooth dips and raised puckerings, the lilac scars and the furred petals. He kisses all of it. Outside the ground is wet and the sky is lead and inside he runs his hands over ruins and fortune.

The house stands on blocks that are sinking. Its windows are insulated with heavy plastic and the roof with tarpaper. The rooms, front and kitchen and bed, smell of oil soap, apples, and tea. June does not wear perfume. She wears long skirts, wool socks and heavy boots, sweaters whose sleeves reach to her fingertips, wound scarves. She wears a different face every day. Roy loves all of them.

She is both lucky, and its opposite: she has been opened up and rearranged, fixed as far as fixing goes, closed up with pricking stitches. On the way home from a party she'd unlatched her seat belt to reach for a fallen glove and when the car flipped that was enough for her to sail through the exploded window, to land on iced and broken ground while in what was left of the back seat, clothing fused to bubbling skin. She is new but not improved and what does this matter anyway, what difference to Roy, she is exactly as she has been since she knocked on his door and asked if he could call a cab to take her back to town.

Town is far but home was farther.

I'm sorry to bother you, she said that night, but sometimes I get confused. Do you have a phone?

I don't think it was my fault, she said the morning after that night—the crash, I mean—but sometimes I'm not sure.

Roy has been patient, he is patient. It is his nature. He does not know hers, yet.

⊚ ⊚ ⊚

Roy's mother pulls her hair up into a high ponytail, tight enough to smooth her forehead, lift her brows. Eyeliner and mascara but no lipstick, perfume sprayed on her throat, wrists, inside the waistband of her jeans. Hoop earrings, the gold flaking off at the closures. More eyeliner, more mascara.

Lipstick smears off anyway: onto cigarettes, glasses, skin.

The trick is knowing which tricks to know.

She packs her purse with a makeup bag, lighter and cigarettes, sunglasses even though it's November and dark already by five o'clock, a tin of Vaseline, peppermint candy.

Eight ball, nine ball, one-pocket. She'll have a cigarette and then leave for the bus stop to catch the number three and be in the smoky warmth of the Last Resort by seven-thirty, *Wheel of Fortune* muted on the TV above the bar, Boston or Foghat on the jukebox, a spiced rum and Sprite with lime in front of her. The last time she saw her son was when she'd slipped onto a stool beside a wide back in a coat she didn't know. She'd swiveled and laid a hand on that blind and promising expanse of wool, then frozen when he turned to face her. The coat, the beard, the cap pulled low—a mistake anyone could make. She tried to speak and he recoiled as though she were licking flames.

◎ ◎ ◎

Town is six blocks of dollar stores and convenience marts, buffets and drive-thrus, then miles of narrow roads that snake out toward ravines and woods, toward flat-roofed houses set low on shallow lots, a rocky creek behind them and the steep reach of hills behind that, trees bare and damp.

To find Roy's mother on a Friday: go to the Last Resort on the corner of East and Valley, to the short bar next to the pool table.

On a Wednesday: go to the VFW hall, to the card room in the back.

On a Thursday: go to the truck stop at exit 26.

◎ ◎ ◎

Roy dropped out of school at fourteen and no one noticed. He baled hay and handled stock, assembled media consoles on one factory floor, tanned leather on another. He opened an account at a bank across town, kept his deposit slips in an envelope in a box of laundry detergent on his closet shelf. He learned to drive and learned to sew and learned to become invisible in the house he shared with his mother and the men who came and stayed a night or a week or a year, the men who looked at him with contempt if he was lucky and loathing if he was not. He learned to fight back.

He reads the newspaper, he reads the farm report, he reads the turned-out leaves in the saucer of his teacup. He knows that he cannot entirely rely on the information he derives from any of these sources and he knows he has no choice.

He knows the first chapters of *Treasure Island* and *The Old Man and the Sea* by heart, and all of "The Rime of the Ancient Mariner." He knows when to cover the garden rows with soft pine in winter and how to sedate the blind dog to pull a broken tooth. He knows every road that spokes from town: the crumbling asphalt that climbs almost to the ridgeline, the highway to the interstate and the two-lane's graceful swerve into towns that may or may not be like this one, filled with girls that may or not be like her. Except: he doesn't know any girls like her, he doesn't know her. Her skin tastes of smoke and berries, ash and blood.

He doesn't know if her name is really June. When he asked her that first night she hesitated in telling him, just long enough.

◎ ◎ ◎

His mother zips her jacket against the wind at the bus stop and Roy spreads June open in the wide bed while the town breathes under shadows and sky, between mud and mountains. In the spring the sun finds ways in through its long setting, between new green leaves, between carports and fences. In November it fades falling before dinners have been set out. The trees are naked and shaking, too weak to hold it up.

Roy's mother waits in the streetlight's sodium glow, eating peanut butter cheese crackers from crinkling plastic. Her fingers are bright orange and salty. The bus schedules vary by neighborhood: extended nighttime routes by the college to the north, every fifteen minutes starting at four a.m. in a nine-mile radius of the milk-processing plant, a constant eastern curve around the paint factory and the hang of thick pink smoke above it.

She is thirty-eight years old and the wrong kind of thin. Her cheeks and hands are chapped rough and the skin on her forearms and chest is the mottled blue of a waiting bruise. Even so she can remember what it was like to look in a mirror and see nothing that needed fixing, or hiding.

Before her son, for example. She was perfect: fourteen years old, a long dark braid and brown shoulders, sundress straps twisted into uneven bows. The boys in homeroom liked to tug that braid and so did Uncle Al, who was not her uncle but her mother's boyfriend, who had a car that filled their driveway with hot metal, who let her sit in the driver's seat and rest her hands on the leather-wrapped wheel that was bigger than the pizzas he bought for the three of them to eat on Saturday nights. Her mother insisted they eat the pizzas with knives and forks, because Uncle Al was from the city—he had city manners and city money and he left behind a pile of it after bending her over her twin bed with the daisy sheets and the ruffled pillowcases, after doing what all the boys in homeroom must've wanted to do, after easing that bright blinding car out of their driveway and steering it back to the city before her mother even woke.

She hears the bus before she sees it, an oily wheeze; crumples the crackers' plastic wrapper and drops it back into her purse.

Those pillowcases with their pink-and-yellow flowers, Uncle Al's rough cheek against her back, the cedar and musk of his aftershave, his mint-hot breath.

His mother climbs into the blue warmth of the bus and Roy presses his face into the crook of June's elbows, the soft crease of her hips. Her skin feels aqueous against his lips. He has never seen an ocean but her eyes are very blue. Sometimes they lose focus and sometimes they burn straight through him.

◎ ◎ ◎

June: a pile of bloody rags by the skid and muddy rut but breathing, ambulance lights cherry swirls in the smoke, in the gasoline sky, in the melting glass. When they peeled her from the punched earth, quartz winked hot from her flesh.

Paramedics, nurses, surgeons, king's horses and men; articulate fingers, too many to count, all of them gloved and slick with blood but dexterous, precise. Accident, then design.

I used to be pretty, she said to Roy the second night, by way of an explanation he hadn't asked for, her voice empty of regret or grief. I have pictures if you want to see them.

He didn't. What do I need pictures for when you're right here? he said, and she coiled herself around him, her hair matted and dull in the lamplight, honeysuckle arms ragged and veined. She didn't ask to stay and he didn't say to leave and the second night multiplied by five, by fifteen. Winter is still weeks away but already it gnaws at the days' brittle edges.

He has in a box a stack of photographs he bought for a dollar at a junk sale: blue-black oceans, jagged icebergs, deserts glowing red. When she goes, which he knows she will, he will still be able to look at what he's never seen.

◎ ◎ ◎

At the Last Resort Roy's mother follows a man down the back hallway and out through the fire door while June slips from the bed where Roy lies sleeping. The smooth planked floor is cold under her bare feet but the kitchen is warm, embers still red and snapping in the stove and the blind dog sleeping next to it, curled and breathing on a torn fold of quilt.

She loves the dog, its careful paws and milk-blue eyes, the strawberry nose that is never still. She will miss it.

The man works wrinkled bills from the front pocket of his jeans and Roy's mother shivers, winter at the back of her neck. She knows him by sight but not by name—town is not that small anymore. It has crept, lot by house by mailbox on post, over gully and field; it has clawed up the dirt slopes of the piedmont.

By sight: reddish hair and reddish eyes and sunken in the chest and cheeks, wind-burned there. He comes on Friday nights, mostly alone but sometimes walking slow beside a woman who holds his arm with one hand and the rubber grip of a cane with the other, her drag of bent leg a grappling hook. She doesn't ask where the woman is tonight.

The river twists black. In spring, it swallows the careless.

Roy's mother takes the money with the equanimity of someone who believes she's already earned it. June—of course her name is June but she would answer to any month—pours a glass of water and sinks down to the floor. The dog rests its long muzzle on her bare leg, sighs without waking.

Town is full of dogs less lucky. It is full of buck-shot stop signs and trucks with perforated fenders, bitches chained to the metal beds, teats stretched and bitten raw. Town sees nothing and hears less. It turns its stony face away.

Cannula, hound and hyena, cautery and stitch. Roy sleeps. June hasn't decided which face she will keep. In the alley behind the Last Resort twenty dollars might as well be a million.

In the morning Roy goes to the river, sinks heel-deep into the sucking mud at the steep edge of it and casts his line. The sky hangs gray, ready to split with rain. He can feel the house behind him, warming his back with June's heavy sleep.

He reels in pike and smallmouth, hooks a finger through each set of gills and pulls it through to break the necks, lays the silver bodies across wet rocks.

Show me, she said, the first time he'd brought a fish from the river and laid it on newspapers on the table, and she watched him scale and slit, work his fingers in to drag the guts free, snip the fins. Her eyes were nickel bright.

He's turned both ankles on the stony apron of this mountain, gone blue at the lips and fingers in January water, broken wrists against the needled ground. He's taken fish and rabbit, wild garlic, ramps and fiddlehead, mustard flower.

Let me, she said the next time he brought fish from the river, and he did. The knife loved her hands, their sure and bloody grace. She slipped the blade around the gills and under the spine, lifted the bony column free of the long body while he watched.

Ironic, she said, smiling crooked. I mean—

I know what you mean, he said.

Sometimes he imagines walking her naked into the woods, her wrists in his hand at the base of her spine, that sweet dip where he'd kick just hard enough to send her hands-and-knees to the ground, her sugar-white ass and the muddy soles of her feet to the sky.

Pretty is an accident, Roy thinks. Pretty is the opposite of the spindling trees, the gashed slope and river. It is nothing he is interested in. Her face without scars is not hers. It does not belong to him. It does not belong anywhere.

He tucks the fish into his creel and starts back to the house. He would do anything to keep her.

◎ ◎ ◎

In the morning Roy's mother covers her hair with a paper cap and punches in for her shift at the hospital cafeteria.

Accidents happen, there are no accidents—she has never been able to decide which she believes.

She believes in destiny, not luck; fate, not chance. The first time she saw her son he was covered in her blood, a fallen scrap of meat. Her tongue was a fat dry worm in her mouth, numb as the rest of her. She did not want him. She was fifteen years old: she wanted the stuffed pink pony from her bedroom at home, she wanted to go back to school, she wanted her mother.

Her son in the nurse's arms was cat-sized, swaddled, his face patty-pan flat and dark as a bruise. You have to take him eventually, the nurse said. He needs to eat. And she thought *What does that have to do with me?*

Checks come twice a month: the last Monday from the hospital and the last Friday from the state. That first week after she cashes them is Christmas, is a birthday party, is the Fourth of July. She goes to the grocery store and the liquor store and she takes a bus and a shuttle to the outlets, twenty miles south on the highway. The mall in town is dead. The last store closed in 2010 and now the brick veneers are crumbling away from the cinder-block walls beneath, the walkways chewed through with goldenrod. There's a 3-D theater at the outlet mall, an optometrist and podiatrist and minute clinic. There's a nail spa and hair salon and a Mexican restaurant with five kinds of salsa and eight flavors of margarita. The drinks come in heavy blue glasses with cactus arms sprouting from the thick stems. There's nothing like them in town, and every month she sits at a table by the window, her Dollar General bags in a shiny plastic pile on the chair next to her, and orders a different kind. So far she hasn't liked any of them, not the mango or the kiwi or the other strange flavors—how could fruit be so *sour?*—but she drinks them anyway, looking out over the parking lot to the shuttle stop, her eye on the clock over the door, free chips and salsa slicking the paper-lined basket with grease.

There are the checks and then there's the other money, the tens and twenties on a Tuesday night, creased, used soft; sometimes a fifty but not often. There are things she won't do anymore, and things they can't afford, and if they run short sometimes of cash she'll accept a different currency: drinks are money, and egg rolls from the Chinese place by the gas station. A fresh pack of cigarettes, lottery tickets, a ride home through the wolf-jawed cold.

◎ ◎ ◎

Saturday night and here they are, Roy and his mother and June, the bartender, waitresses, giggling girls and blank-faced men, all of them in a too-loud room strung with smoke-stained paper spiders left from Halloween. Outside the wind hisses and sings; outside bare branches shake.

Inside is a different story. The windows are fogged with drunken laughter and the steam from the glass washer under the bar, and if this place is not exactly safe, it's shelter enough—no one, tonight, will cry or rage or bleed here. That will happen later, when their own doors lock behind them.

Roy and his mother will not see each other. When she shoulders the door open June has Roy's face in her powdery hands, her fingers dusting over his cheeks and lips and eyelids, and his mother, heedless, pushes through the square tables and gouged wooden chairs to the bar, slides sideways onto an empty stool. Between them the air churns, spilled beer and struck matches, and waitresses carry red plastic trays of soft pretzels and french fries above the roil. The older men stare imperturbable into their drinks and the younger ones aim their smiles at the girls who sit in twos and threes, pink cheeks damp and knees jittery, unsteady hands cupped around their lighters' nervous flames.

Roy's mother sorts through the scraps of paper in her purse while she waits for the bartender to mix her drink. Check stubs, receipts, the hospital schedule in color coded triplicate, Powerball scratch-off cards: days and dollars annotated and recorded, incremental, unrelenting. The girls next to her shriek with sudden laughter and grab with oblivious fingers at each other's shoulders, and when the bartender brings Roy's mother's drink they lean across the bar, damp-eyed and gasping, to cry for another round.

June and Roy are side by side in a booth, her legs curled under her and her skirt tucked around them like a blanket, drinks and cigarettes and sticky menu cards on the table. She kisses his neck and tugs her sleeves down over her hands before picking up her glass so that the only skin he can see is her face and fingertips. The rest of her is cocooned in wool, amorphous, indistinct. She is the opposite of naked and his cock is on fire.

Roy pays their tab as his mother starts hers and June slips out of the booth, shoulders her bag and turns for the door. Roy's mother hunches over her glass, steadies the straw with her fingers and sips. He watches June, the pale cloud of her hair swirled and staticky over her shoulders, her skirt hanging uneven and the heels of her boots worn. He would almost recognize her more easily from behind, given how used he is to looking at her back: when she crabs her way up from the river and he follows with rod and fish and creel; when she sits reading at the table while he cooks for her at the stove against the wall. He even fucks her from behind.

Outside it's all he can do to keep from pushing her against the cinder-block wall and shoving her skirt up, his face in her dandelion hair, one hand on her doll-stitched neck and the other between her legs, working them open, her skin glitter and dust, all of her stubborn singularity under his calloused palms.

◎ ◎ ◎

Roy's mother signals the bartender before she's finished her first drink and he nods. She's not a regular here but she may as well be. She'll give it another round, two at most, before moving on. The crowd tonight is young, the girls already getting sloppy and the men—hardly more than boys—already taking notice. There's nothing for her here but more obsolescence.

They used to go shopping, she and her mother and Uncle Al, before he left. The last time was a trip to JCPenney, the cosmetics counter for perfume for her mother and the juniors' department for her, for bell-bottoms with patch pockets and a mother-of-pearl crescent moon on a silver chain. The walls of the store were bubblegum pink, ecstatic with looping neon graffiti. Uncle Al opened his wallet and rifled through credit cards like a magician.

She lifts her chin, presses her tongue to the roof of her mouth to smooth her throat, arranges her face in what she hopes is a serene smile, and waits. Fate: anyone could come in. Destiny: it's just a matter of being ready.

The bartender sets her new drink down and takes her empty glass away. It's an investment, this drink, she thinks; a physical manifestation of her optimism. She has never had a credit card in her life but neither has she ever gone without—electricity, food, a winter coat—she has gone with less, with used, with old, but not without.

You have to think of it as insurance, Uncle Al used to say to her mother. You have to visualize the best possible scenario and then you plan for that. You can't be afraid to borrow against future successes. Do you get me?

Outside the snow begins, not flakes but blowing icy bits, and Roy's mother clasps her hands neatly around her glass. Her fingers are dry and cracked at the knuckles and her nails are chewed but they are warm, her hands, and that's all that will matter when someone ducks in from what's coming.

◎ ◎ ◎

Roy follows June from the truck over the slick of mud and freezing grass. He reaches around her to key the front door open and when he does, she slips through it as though the house has sucked her, frantic, into itself.

He could kick the door off its hinges. Instead he eases it closed behind him, stomps his boots on the towel just inside. She's already dropping layers of clothes where she stands, crouching to stretch her fingers out to the dog who's inching toward her, haunches stiff and shaking, nose quivering at her feet. She looks up to him and smiles, radiant, the scars around her mouth and eyes dimpling, and the thought that one day she won't be here is a barbed hook in his chest.

He can count to twenty in Spanish, French, German. He can name every Tudor king. He knows the difference between simple future and future perfect.

He isn't stupid: he understands how little he knows and how much less it matters.

◎ ◎ ◎

Roy's mother raises a delicate finger to the bartender, who nods and turns toward the register. When he tucks the tab beneath her glass of melting ice she sees he hasn't charged her for one drink, two, four? It's after midnight and she lost track hours ago. He watches her without pretending not to—it's his job, after all. He watches everyone.

She stands, unsteady for only a minute, fishes a five-dollar bill from her purse and that fast he's in front of her, shaggy-haired and broad-shouldered. His collar is ironed and clean. Someone's son. Not hers.

Not so fast, someone's son says to her, eyes crinkling with something close to kindness. He lays his big hand on hers, on the money, on the check. You've had a lot to drink, he says, and it's true so why would she argue? A lot more than it says there—he nods toward her hand under his, squeezes it, and she is neither drunk enough to misunderstand nor sober enough to explain that this was not the transaction she had planned, when she came in earlier; not one she would have agreed to had she been given a choice instead of drink after drink, each more expensive than the last. His hand presses into hers, inexorable as winter.

She sits again, defeated. It's futile to argue with this cold night's economy, which, she understands even now, she was never in a position to determine. None of them are, not the perfumed slurring girls next to her or the men with oil-stained leather wallets in their hip pockets: they are all of them playing the best hand they have. She looks around the room and is filled with compassion, and with rage.

◎ ◎ ◎

Roy fills the dog's bowls and June forks potatoes from the pan on the stove, tears at bits of dried venison with her teeth. He could feed her anything, he thinks sometimes, staghorn sumac and chokeberries, stinging nettle from his fingers. He can picture her stripping bark from the trees with her vampire teeth, digging for grubs with those hands.

The dog snaps and noses the bowl across the floor. Outside the wind pulls the clouds apart and in the distance, town rattles and pants, wakes itself to watch for the coming nothing. June licks her fingers, stretches her arms wide overhead and Roy presses his lips into the skin beneath them, into the raised purple twists along her ribcage.

They gave me fade cream when they discharged me but I lost it, she says, tilting her hips into him, gripping his waist with her knees, and her skirt is ripped at the seams, the boy's undershirt she wears instead of a bra is yellowing along the neckline. He cups her ass in his hands and wonders did she wear clothes like this before him, before here; did she bother to comb her hair, to wash?

She tastes like wet earth and dry leaves, like carnage. The dog whines at her bare feet. It can smell how soon she'll be gone.

She says I think I want to stay here.

She says But I don't think I can.

Venison on her lips and Roy can taste the deer, shot, hoisted and secured then split, hot guts spilling lavish on the ground. The house is different with her in it.

He understands, for the first time since June has been with him, that he will be relieved when she goes, when he will no longer have to wonder when or how it will happen. He understands that her absence will last longer and so become sweeter than her presence, and for a second he almost wants to hurry her toward her leaving, toward the door that will close between *before* and *after*.

Almost.

Her skin is slippery under his hands; it smells of sandalwood, sweat and resin. She hooks her arms around his neck and her legs around his waist for him to carry her to the bedroom, to the unmade bed with the sheets bunched and dirt-smudged at the bottom. He drops her there and turns her facedown, her hair matted and damp on her neck and the soles of her feet dirty as a child's. He kneels over her and catches both wrists above her head with one hand, works at the zipper of his pants with the other and the bed will never be wider than it is right now, the house will never be warmer, town will never be farther away.

Even if I never leave this place someone will know I was here.

◉ ◉ ◉

Simple future: Roy's mother will be found among the vertebral rocks, faceup on the root-split earth, cracked white sky above her.

Future perfect: she will have been there for days.

The sheriff knocks on Roy's door before dawn, before the six a.m. local news, before the papers hit driveways and bushes. Roy answers, shivering in a T-shirt, his hand on the blind dog's collar. He listens. He is alone. He is used to it again. It took no time at all. He leaves the sheriff to wait on the frozen grass while he dresses, thermal shirt then flannel, pants and socks and boots, wool cap on his uncombed hair. He sits in the back seat of the cruiser. It's the first time he's been in one. He was a good boy.

The sheriff drives to the hospital where Roy's mother worked three days a week, where June was made not good as new but good enough, where Roy has never had reason to go since he broke an arm at five. He was a good boy.

The sheriff steps ahead and the automatic door sucks open. Roy follows him through the glassed-in vestibule, past the information desk to the elevator bank. The sheriff hits the Down button. They wait without speaking. When the elevator comes the sheriff hits the Basement button.

They exit into the low-ceilinged hallway and the sheriff pivots to face him.

I'm going to go in with you, he says. I'm going to stay until you make the identification and then I'm going to wait in the hallway until you finish.

Finish what? Roy thinks, but does not ask.

His mother's face is split fruit, bruised; somehow both gaunt and puffy. Her lips are swollen, grayish; blood dried to black at the corners. The skin beneath her eyes is dark and wet-looking; her forehead shines under the lights. The hair is scraped away from it, copper-bright but dark at the roots.

He remembers the eye-burning smell of hair dye, his mother in the bathroom they shared, her hands in clownish plastic gloves and orange rivulets running down her arms and neck, splattering the sink and wallpaper. It was the night before he started first grade and he was waiting for his bath.

Don't you want all your new teachers to think Mommy's pretty? she said, shooing him out of the bathroom with the toe of her socked foot. And that nice Mr. Jaffert in the office? Go on, let me finish.

In the morning she knelt in front of him to tie his shoes and her scalp at the part was the color of a tangerine.

It is not yet eight o'clock when Roy steps out of the hospital. The sun is up and bright, the mountain half in shadow and the moon still just visible, a powdery disc on the blue of the sky. The sheriff is behind him now, and Roy can smell the smoke of the cigarette he's just lit on the cold air.

You want to stop back home first or go into town? he says, and Roy understands that this is not, in fact, a choice; there is work to be done, and it must be done now, and no one will do it but him. Town, he says, and the sheriff nods, flicks his cigarette onto the parking lot and unlocks the car doors.

The sheriff drives slowly under the peacock sky. There's no hurry. Town is patient as a snake and just as cold.

From the back seat Roy watches the frost sparked by sun on the dead fields, the flap and hop of crows on the cold ground, and wonders if it will look different to him once his mother is in it.

In the house that is barely a house Roy wipes the floors down with beeswax and linseed oil, dredges the gutters and recaulks the windows. He puts chains on the tires of his truck and checks the antifreeze and wiper fluid. He removes the screen from the kitchen door, weather-strips the panes and secures the knob to the frame with a bungee cord. In the bedroom he alphabetizes the paperbacks he's collected from the boxes he finds in parking lots, in driveways.

In the pantry he arranges jars of blackberry and rosehip jam, pickled onions and Jerusalem artichokes. By the time he zips his coat on, all that's left of the sun is a crimson lip at the ridgeline, and he flips the floodlights on. They shine directly on the carcass that hangs from the sawtooth behind the bedroom window.

He lays a tarp over the wooden picnic table under the tree, lays out his knife and saw and splitter. He cuts the deer free and heaves her onto the tarp. He breaks her down, shoulders first and velvet neck, ruby loin and haunches. The wind comes in from the west, slow at first and then stronger over the split and silty earth, through the spicebush and rye. He's elbow-deep in her blood. He'll eat the pretty all winter.

A Good Woman

The summer Lizzie was eleven her father left her mother for the most beautiful woman Lizzie had ever seen. Her name was Sheila and her hair was ash-blonde, long and feathery; her nails were perfect peach ovals. Her neck was draped with gauzy scarves and her thin brown arms were stacked with gold bangles. She smelled of Opium and Virginia Slims, and when she hugged Lizzie, Lizzie did not pull away, though she knew she should.

Her mother didn't understand yet that she was no longer someone's wife. She spent her days polishing silver that no one used and making casseroles that no one ate. She organized closets and vacuumed the drapes, sorted Tupperware on the shelf above the refrigerator. She loaded dishes into the new dishwasher and folded clothes Lizzie had outgrown to take to the donation box in the church hall. In the morning she sat at the table in her faded rayon nightgown with a cup of instant coffee and the newspaper folded shut and outside the kitchen door June sprawled, heedless, lush and green.

Days, Lizzie drifted through the spotless rooms, trailing along hallways and staircases in the humming quiet. She lay on the floor in the living room with stacks of library books and listened for her mother's footsteps, the creak of the floorboards overhead, bedroom to bathroom and back. In the books beautiful girls hitchhiked across the country, worked in roadside diners and danced with soft-eyed shirtless boys, fell asleep in wide fields under skies Lizzie had never seen.

She spent weekends with her father and on Friday nights she waited by the front door with a pink nylon duffel and a paper grocery bag of things her mother had packed for her to take: cough drops and shaving cream, new Stafford socks with the tags still on and cellophane-wrapped packs of Pierre Cardin handkerchiefs, shampoo. Lizzie's mother packed these things with a grim dedication, as though she did not believe her husband could find such necessities where he'd gone, as though he lived in a place where peril was everywhere and sustenance was uncertain.

Lizzie watched, waited for the dented Datsun hatchback to make the turn up into their pretty hedged driveway, Sheila behind the wheel and her father in the passenger seat, an arrangement that had never—could never have—happened when he was at home. She shouted goodbye to her mother upstairs but did not wait for a reply before struggling through the door with her bags, out into the warm breath of summer. Sprinklers flicked across lawns and fireflies blinked in the low bushes. Sheila's sunglasses were propped on top of her head and her father's tie was loosened. He opened his door and stepped out, tilted the seat forward and handed her bags into the back of the car before sweeping her into his arms.

Lizzie had never kissed a boy, never even been close. That summer she wore white canvas sneakers and terry-cloth shorts, plastic barrettes and tiny gold starfish in her newly pierced ears. She went for days eating nothing but bread smeared with cream cheese and strawberry jam. She was thin as a blade of grass and her knees were mottled with fresh pink scars where scabs had been and if her father had asked her to come live with him she would have gone in an instant, a heartbeat, the blink of a firefly's light.

◉ ◉ ◉

Elizabeth works in an office down the hall from a room with wall-to-wall carpeting and contract chairs, end tables gouged and water-marked beneath stacks of ragged magazines. This is the room where people—patients—wait. There are other rooms where they go for treatment; still others where they go for news. All these rooms, and the hallways that connect them, are cold. Cold for Elizabeth, and she has a sweater. She has an immune system. She cannot imagine how cold it must feel to the patients, wearing their collapsed veins and paper gowns, their blue lips and fingers.

The news here is different from the news anyplace else. There is less of it, but all of it matters. The treatment is working, or it isn't. There are only so many variations on this theme, so many spots on the continuum where information can fall.

On Wednesdays the staff hours are staggered and she works from six in the morning until two, when she shuts her computer down. She drapes her sweater over the back of her chair and shrugs into her overcoat, takes the back stairway down to the lot behind the building. Her car is fifteen years old. It has never been fashionable. She drives crosstown toward the street where she lives, where she's been living for less than a year in a house she does not think of as home. The street is potholed and oil-stained and crunchy with gravel, lined with midcentury houses, low brick boxes built for GIs returning from Europe, from Japan. There is nothing pretty about them, with their thin lace curtains and wreaths of plastic flowers on the doors, their algae-green birdbaths.

Once inside she strips, leaves her clothes in a pile where they fall. She showers away the smells the day has left behind: antiseptic, wan hope, animal terror. By three o'clock she is in her bed, warm and still damp and slick with jasmine oil. By three-thirty David is there with her.

Elizabeth wraps her warm legs and arms around his dry cold skin, brings his arm to her mouth and presses her lips on the smooth scar there. Outside the sky is gray and heavy with snow that will not fall. Neither speaks; both know better.

She is neither a doctor nor a nurse. She does not heal, or soothe, or comfort. She sits at a computer at a desk and types names into cells on a monthly schedule, numbers into cells on a payroll spreadsheet. She keeps a bottle of hand sanitizer on her desk and is ashamed every time she uses it. She can count on both hands the number of times she's been sick in her life. She has never run a fever over 101 degrees, never had to stay home from school or work for more than a few days. On the rare occasion she feels the hot-eyed fatigue of incipient illness she curls into her bed with tea and vitamins and aspirin and sleeps, wakes every four hours to drink and dose herself, and this is enough.

◎ ◎ ◎

June slid into July and he did not come back. The summer settled over them, deep and green and slow. They drifted through it. Lizzie walked the neighborhood in the seethe of midday heat, kicked through the dust of empty lots that weren't empty. There were prizes: dented toy cars, rotting cardboard, raveled gloves and cigarette butts. Once, a page of loose-leaf covered in a hectic purple scrawl, ragged, still partly legible in spots but blurry as though the letters themselves had wept: *if you don't   I swear   one more time   you promised*   the *you* underlined with a shredding fury. Tangled roots, a damp swollen wallet, a torn pair of nylons. She poked with a brittle stick, pried pink plastic dolls' arms and rusted pull-tabs from the dusty summer earth. Around her the neighborhood shimmered, silent. The houses were locked drum-tight and air conditioners hummed and in the glaring afternoon she was a brave small explorer, intrepid, daring; and in the dark she slid unwashed into bed, her hair a damp snarl at her neck and melon juice sticky on her chin, the day still clinging to her hands and feet.

Lizzie's mother woke up in the morning and made the bed and washed her face with the same constant faith she took with her to Mass, where she went alone on Saturday evenings when Lizzie was with her father, slipping early into the same pew the three of them had sat in for years and fishing her rosary from its brown felt pouch, touching the crucifix forehead-chest-shoulder-shoulder and kissing it. She lowered herself onto the kneeler and the feel of the sticky cracked leather against her skin was familiar, a comfort.

She was home before dark was even close, a slow ghost in an empty house. She checked the doors and windows and flipped off all the lights downstairs but one. In the bedroom she folded the spread down, stepped into her nightgown and out of the bright day. She slipped into bed while the sky was still blue, her prayer book by her side. The window was cracked open: frogs and cicadas, the chit and whirr of August. She closed her eyes and when she slept her sleep was dry and every morning she woke to the day before.

The summer poured over them and he did not come back. On Monday mornings Lizzie imagined herself at the top of a slide, the metal hot on the backs of her legs, mirrored and glaring, angled down; bumpy and sticky and then gaining speed, growing steep; shooting her out to the soft sand of Friday, of the weekend, of trips to the mall to buy throw pillows for the living-room floor and bags of carob-covered raisins and Swedish Fish, amaretto sours for Sheila and her father and a root-beer float for her in a booth at Farrell's when the shopping was done. On Sunday nights she raced up to her room to empty her duffel of what Sheila had sent home with her: pots of flavored lip balm and waxy sticks of perfume, scented eye pads made to look like cucumbers. She tucked them into the back of her dresser and took them out on a Wednesday or Thursday to sample, to practice; to rehearse for the life that was waiting for her.

◎ ◎ ◎

These are the things that Elizabeth knows about David: His parents raised him on organic baby food and handmade toys, all-natural fabrics and public radio. They raised him on universal compassion and benevolent sanctimony. They instilled in him a profound respect for women, for their particular gifts and talents, for the empathy and nurturing energy they brought to the world. By the time he graduated from college he could get a girl out of her clothes with as much effort as it took to slit open an envelope, and by the time he met his wife it was even easier than that.

When he met his wife he liked his girls dark—black hair, black eyes, skin like burnished wood. He liked them wrapped in gauzy skirts, barefoot and off-balance, smelling of musk and roses. He liked them drunk on cheap wine, mouths soft and blurry, cheeks dimpled and damp with laughter. He liked them on their backs.

This was just after college, in that hazy in-betweenness of temporary jobs and temporary roommates, of underfurnished apartments and refrigerators stocked with too much beer and too little food, scattered with packets of soy and duck sauce and cartons of Chinese takeout.

David's wife was tall and blonde and solid, starched and accessorized. She worked for a commercial real estate-development company and carried a briefcase when the rest of David's friends were content to answer phones or wait tables, secure as they all were that something better would be waiting for them when they decided they were ready for it. She had gone to school on scholarships and student loans, and that was a chance she was not willing to take. She drank whiskey on ice with a splash of soda and made pierogi from her grandmother's recipe, browned and dilled and slippery with butter. She had grown up in Wisconsin and was terrified of riptides, which she had read about in magazines. She brought David home the first night they went out and stripped for him in the living room of her apartment, stone-sober, absolute. Her feet were wide, her toenails strawberry pink.

She brought her own comb and brush to the salon, her own manicure set to the spa. She took her tea with milk and honey, she got carded on her thirty-fifth birthday. She got sick, and then better, and then sicker. She could hustle pool. She moved in papery silence through the halls to lay shivering on a table across the hall from where Elizabeth sat at her desk and she knew it would make no difference. She did not lose her hair but her skin darkened then burned then sloughed where the radiation hit and so David covered her with Aquaphor, with kind and desperate lies. She got sicker, and then. Her toenails were sky blue. She was buried in a cashmere dress.

◎ ◎ ◎

When they finish they pull apart, back into their separate skins. They are careful not to touch or speak. There is a cadence to these afternoons, quiet and slow; it begins with the creak of the door opening as he lets himself in, his deliberate steps to the bedroom and the hush of her waiting, then the whisper of skin and sheets, and breath, and stillness. At four-thirty she touches his shoulder, squeezes it. She dresses with her back to him. This is the script. She does not stray.

Are you thirsty? she says, as she does, and waits for him to refuse. Her hair is tangled, still damp from the shower. Her bare feet are chilled, and she remembers the summer feel of soft wood floors beneath them, dust and bits of grass sticking to the soles.

I'm fine, he says. He rubs his face, runs his hands through his hair and glances at his phone. In these weeks he has taken nothing she's offered him, not tea and toast the first time, not whiskey or wine or water since. She is Pluto in worn jeans and a thermal jersey.

He had been standing in the parking lot, in the cold beside his car, watching the back door of the clinic when she came out on a Friday afternoon. She did not recognize him, could not remember having seen him. She had asked if there was anything she could help him with and his laugh was the sound of dead leaves.

I should go, he says, as he does, and she watches him dress, watches his heavy hands, his wide white back. He does not hurry, he does not have to. His freedom is awful and complete.

He folds his tie into a pocket and wraps his scarf around his neck, looks around the room to be sure he's forgetting nothing. And he isn't—he's never left anything behind, these Wednesdays; not a handkerchief or receipt, not a pen or comb. When he leaves he leaves entirely, and this is how she knows the folded bills she finds tucked under her jewelry box or behind her makeup case are not accidents, not oversights; that they have not fallen from a pocket and come magically to rest in small neat packets in places they won't be lost.

When she finds them she slides them into her purse without counting. She unfolds them only on Fridays, when she stops on her way to her parents' apartment at their favorite bakery, an ancient corner shop that smells of burnt sugar and weak coffee and sur-render. She takes her ticket and waits for the sullen girl behind the counter to call her number and when she does she points through the slanted glass at jelly pies and éclairs and turnovers, crullers and strudel, and the girl fills one white box and then another, the tissue in her hand translucent, the pastries gleaming, enough sug-ar to ply the stoniest heart.

◎ ◎ ◎

Elizabeth's parents' church is just a few blocks from the senior housing complex where they live. They can walk the distance eas-ily in good weather, in calm winds and daylight, stepping carefully down curbs and over broken asphalt, squinting up, waiting for the light at the intersection.

Next to the church is the parish hall, its door by the right side of the altar, by the statue of St. Anthony, the rows of candles and the money box. The hall gets use—Wednesday night is bingo, Friday night the middle-school mixer, Sunday afternoon ravioli dinner. It smells of cigarette smoke and burnt popcorn, dry and acrid drugstore talc.

On Sundays after Mass they make their slow way down the steps of the church, her mother gripping the handrail and her father gripping her mother. They stop at the back of the hall, at the long table covered with white paper and set up with tall metal urns of coffee and clear plastic platters of doughnuts and Danish. Once they are safely inside they separate, her father to a table by the television where men are playing cards and her mother across the room with her friends from bingo, the women perfumed and powdered. They cut pastries in halves, in quarters, with plastic knives, and pass the pieces around on napkins. They talk about the visiting priest, the price of lettuce and tomatoes at the market, their children.

Well, you know Lizzie's work is so demanding, her mother says. She says this every week. Working with the cancer patients, she says. Her friends nod their acknowledgement politely. Their daughters are married, with children of their own; they live in enormous houses with vaulted foyers and media rooms. They drive car pools and belong to book clubs. Their husbands are distracted and their children are medicated and their mothers feel sorry for hers, although they would never say as much. They say instead:

Darlene and Jim are taking the kids to Florida next week.

That new principal at Kayla's school thinks he's such a *wheel*.

I don't know how Gail and Bruce are going to manage when that little girl who cleans for them goes to college.

Well, her mother says, I'd better go check on Carl, see if he's ready for some lunch. She stands and the metal chair clatters behind her and the conversation goes on.

You should *see* what Joey got Theresa for their anniversary.

When Sheila left there was no scene, no confrontation or explanation. Elizabeth's father came home to the apartment after work one Friday to find her gone. She'd left an empty pack of cigarettes in the bathroom and a full one in a kitchen drawer, faux-tortoise bangles and a turquoise hair comb on the dresser. Elizabeth's father called her mother, weeping, inconsolable, and her mother waited for him to beg her forgiveness and profess his love, to say how wrong he'd been, to promise he'd make things right. She had been waiting for years. She stood in their kitchen and listened to her husband speaking from the ruins of someone else's.

Barbara, he said, oh God, Barbara—what am I supposed to do without her?

◎ ◎ ◎

On Friday nights Elizabeth's mother cooks linguini with tuna and the three of them eat in the bright kitchen light. They eat their salad from their empty pasta bowls and when they finish Elizabeth clears the table and her mother sets a plate of pastries in the center, sticky dough wrapped around dabs of blueberry or cherry jam, sprinkled with slivered almonds. Her father, who claims he does not like dessert, tears into them. They're not dessert, her father insists, they're left over from breakfast—tell her, he says to his wife.

Your father doesn't eat dessert, she says to Elizabeth, you know that, and Elizabeth knows better than to argue.

She was on her way to see her parents when he stopped her in the parking lot.

You work in there, he'd said, and Elizabeth pulled her coat tight. It was not quite a question. In the clinic, he went on, and she nodded. It was after five and dark already and the cold was sharp, exquisite.

We're finished with appointments for the day, she said. If you need to schedule—

I know that. He opened his hands and held them out: they were empty, harmless. It didn't work, he said. What you did.

And then she understood, she remembered, him and the woman he came with. She'd caught glimpses of them at the reception desk, in the waiting room, when a door swung open or closed, him with a canvas tote bag filled with newspapers, bottles of water; her with a blue scarf wrapped around her neck and shoulders and sunglasses too big for her wasted face.

I'm not a doctor, she said, she could not stop herself from saying, I'm sorry but I didn't—

Listen to me, he said, blinking his dry eyes, nodding as though he were agreeing with something Elizabeth had yet to say, I was going to leave her. Before, I mean—I didn't love her anymore and I made up my mind and then—

He smiled, clasping and unclasping his harmless hands, and even in the dark Elizabeth could see that he was not *there*, not standing in front of her in a freezing emptying parking lot at the edge of a commercial complex, buildings and lots laid out in a grid around them, white lines and divided medians, geometric, inert, immense. He was somewhere she had never been.

◎ ◎ ◎

Friday nights Lizzie played Scrabble with Sheila and her father
while records played, a stack of them balanced over the turntable,
ready to drop. He'd moved into Sheila's apartment, a one-bedroom
on the third floor of a garden complex with a cracked parking lot,
open stairwells and thick metal doors. Inside the rooms were small
and the ceilings were low and there was barely space for her father
and Sheila to sidle past each other, laughing. There were hanging
plants in baskets and a pearly Chinese screen in a corner, a tapestry
thrown over the fold-out couch where Lizzie slept. Sheila heated
frozen French-bread pizzas for dinner, burned at the edges and
cold in the middle, and made salad with green grapes. She brought
the food into the living room and the three of them settled on the
floor around the coffee table to eat. There were candles burning on
the stereo speakers and rough cloth napkins with a fringe, ticklish,
that Lizzie was afraid to use, and white wine from a pretty carafe,
and when Sheila splashed some into Lizzie's grape soda her father
did not stop her.

On Saturday mornings there was always some reason for Sheila
to leave the apartment early, to squeeze past the open couch with
her sunglasses on and her keys jingling—You two go ahead and
have breakfast; I'll grab something out, she'd say, blowing kisses
at Lizzie and her father, but I'll be back for lunch so wait for me!

You understand what she's doing, don't you? her father said,
stirring Ovaltine into her milk, and Lizzie nodded, not understanding at all.

So we can have time alone, he said. She's worried that we
don't have enough time together. He handed her the milk and sat

at the foot of the mattress, set his coffee on the table. She's a good woman, he said, and sighed. Your mother is too. But your mother . . . He rubbed a hand over his unshaven face and squeezed her foot through the sheet. Sometimes, he said, sometimes people who love each other make each other unhappy, even if they don't mean to. Do you understand how that can happen? he said, and Lizzie nodded, eyes wide and eager, ready as any scrabbling dog to agree with him—I know exactly what you mean, she said, and hugged him, her strange new father, thinner and whiskered and smiling, in that apartment that smelled of incense and Jiffy-Pop. She had no idea what he meant and it didn't matter. Her father had been supplanted by a man who was loved by someone new, someone made of silk and clouds, who lived in a world she did not know. And she had taken him with her into that world, shadowy and sweet-smelling and serene. He was not the man her mother had married, not one her mother had ever seen. Lizzie did not need to know what this man *meant*; she knew what he *was*: wanted, desired, coveted. Her father was a man who could be taken, who could leave.

◎ ◎ ◎

Elizabeth's mother says it to everyone she meets, at the first opportunity, or sooner: My daughter works with cancer patients.

But of course she doesn't. She works at a safe distance, as she has throughout her life, each job just on the periphery of real help, real healing; the pre-med undergraduate major dropped for biology and then the biology abandoned for the history of science; the concentric circles growing wider, more diffuse, her orbit farther and farther from the sickness at the center.

But the center is everywhere, in the end.

My daughter works with cancer patients, her mother says, and shivers a bit, flutters her eyelids at the enormity, the immeasurable importance, of it all.

As opposed to what her father says: My daughter works in an office.

Oh, Carl, her mother says, you don't know what you're talking about.

But of course he does. He does not speak often but when he does he is so careful of mistakes. It is late and he is finished making them.

He went home after Sheila left. He was heartbroken but not irrational; he was not going to stay in a shabby apartment in a dilapidated complex where the neighbors tossed empty beer cans from the balconies on weeknights and full ones on weekends, where cars backfired and left fresh oil stains on the crumbling parking lot, where the doorframes and doorknobs were greasy. Not when his house, his wife and daughter were right where he'd left them.

He came home with one small bag, no larger than the ones Elizabeth had taken on the weekends she'd spent with him. He brought nothing back from the life he'd tried, not the suede coat Sheila had given him for their first Christmas or the table lamp with a stained-glass shade he'd let Elizabeth pick out when Sheila's old lamp had broken. He parked his car in the driveway and opened the front door and walked through it. They sat for dinner at the table her mother had set and Elizabeth stared down into a plate of food she could not eat next to a man she could not look at. She was sixteen. She had kissed a boy or ten. She had allowed their hands to stray from her shoulders down her back, around her waist and up, tentative but eager on the cotton of her blouse, on the flesh of her stomach, fingers moving quick and light as tadpoles. She had leaned in, let the blouse fall away from her waist, touched the tip of her tongue to impatient lips.

Aren't you hungry? her father said, her mother's husband again, nothing more than that. Sheila had broken him and he had broken her mother and now they sat in pieces around the table, balanced at the edges of a hole plundered and left gaping.

Let her be, her mother said. She had waited, and won, but the waiting had been unkind: the skin around her eyes was puffy, her cheeks were powdery leaf. Let her go, she said, and Elizabeth slid from her seat, disappeared up the stairs to polish herself into something delicious. She twined her wrists with silver and wound her neck with beads and her hair smelled of green apples, of pouring rain. She slipped from the house while the sky was still silver blue and pricked with birds, hurtled across the lawn and into a waiting car, into a boozy tangle of bare arms and legs, a different car every night but the same pulsing joy inside, the same cheap beer and cheap weed and keening guitar and so much yearning it spilled like molten candy from the windows.

Of course she was hungry. Her legs were long and brown and entirely hers and she wrapped them around boys who were dim and sweet and grateful, safe as shallow water. She crawled the stairs past midnight smelling of sweet wine and smoke, her knees scraped and caked with dirt, her mascara smeared and hair matted, shoulders kissed and bruised and bitten.

◎ ◎ ◎

This is what David knows about Elizabeth: that she left home as soon as she could after her father returned, to a college far enough away that trips back were infrequent and polite and brief enough for her to carry just another duffel, no bigger than the one she'd used on weekends as a child. During this time her father aged with the same alacrity as her mother had while he was gone until one Christmas Elizabeth saw that they had reached a kind of symmetry, both of their faces pulled flat and smooth, both of their bodies torpid.

She drifted restless through her twenties. She found a job as a receptionist at a walk-in clinic in the country and moved in with a man who'd brought his father in for heatstroke. He'd sat in a molded plastic chair in the glass-fronted waiting room with listless children and gray-faced women in housecoats and slippers and the warm gold of his skin was an affront, an insult she could not refuse. His house was sprawling and primitive, one room built onto the next over damp green hills, briar rose and blackberry climbing the edges of rough wooden decks. It was peaceful and he was kind and she stayed just long enough to recognize that kindness and peace meant nothing more to her than a glass of iced tea on a hot day or a cool pillowcase at night: pleasant enough but inessential, replaceable.

When she left she did so gently. She packed in the bright morning and he watched her, sitting at the wide wooden table with a cup of coffee growing cold. He followed her outside, gave her a paper bag of ham biscuits and peaches and cucumbers his father had packed. She took it and set it on the passenger seat of her car and he told her to drive carefully, to be happy, to come back.

She hopscotched her way through jobs and towns until her mother called to tell her they had decided to sell the house, that the stairs were too steep and the lawn too wide and the rooms too full of remorse. It's time, her mother said. Your father and I are ready.

She went back and saw how time had worn them, how they had worn each other. She stayed. She took the job at the treatment center and rented a house and made herself necessary, cleaning and sorting and packing chipped dishes and folded clothes, greeting cards and photographs ordered and dated, everything her mother had treasured and her father had suffered. When she finished she stacked the boxes of her parents' lives in neat small piles against the walls in the dining room, the den, and when she saw how few there were she looked away, ashamed.

◎ ◎ ◎

Outside the ground is frozen, the grass brown and brittle. The sky will not move. Inside Elizabeth lies in bed with David next to her, with David so far away his skin beneath her fingers is already a memory. There is no reason for this to end: no wife will call, no husband will accuse, no children will sob in confusion. They have stolen nothing from anyone.

Were you a good husband? she says. He looks at her with something close to hate, and she is pleased. She wants to make it easy for him to end this—it is all she can give him, it is his barest need. He has refused everything else she's offered him.

Not good enough, he says. He stares out the small high window at the piece of winter sky. There is no room in this house where he loves her, no corner of this world where he could.

But you stayed, she says. What matters is that you stayed.

Bread, wine, expiation: he has accepted none of it. The afternoon is so gray and small.

I wouldn't have, he says. *If she had lived,* he doesn't say. But Elizabeth hears. She thinks of her mother, her life small and tidy enough to fit in a dresser drawer. She imagines pulling it out and shaking it open, made beds and washed dishes and half-answered prayers flying free and coming to rest again in perfect order.

David slides from the bed and begins to dress. She checks the clock; it's time. She has no idea where he goes after he is finished with her because she's never asked. When he leaves she stands at the open door, watches as he disappears into the raw dark, into whatever cold relief waits there for him. She does not wonder or worry; there is nothing she can do for him once he's gone.

Her life so far is smooth and clean as a new shroud and her heart is calm and ready.

Then stay now, she says, and David turns, his shirt still open, his wallet already in his hands. This is what he pays for, the chance to leave and leave and leave and know that she's still breathing. He would no sooner stay than he would rake and scrabble the icy dirt on his wife's grave.

◎ ◎ ◎

On Friday night Elizabeth pushes their cart through the fashionable new grocery store by her parents' apartment. Her father waits napping in the car and her mother ranges just ahead of her, lost among the shelves of vitamin supplements and gluten-free snacks, the aggressive displays of organic exotic fruit. At the end of an aisle she stops, reaches out for the edge of the cart and steadies herself.

What are we looking for, Ma? Elizabeth says. It's bright inside and crowded with men and women in tailored overcoats and smart shoes angling their baskets past one another, half of them balancing cell phones on their shoulders and the other half staring glazed and blank into the middle distance. Among them her mother is small and faded and Elizabeth wants nothing more than to hurry her back into the safety of the early dark.

Milk, for your father's cereal tomorrow, she says. And a few grapefruits. And I wanted to get some of that marinated chicken for tonight.

I could've gotten all that for you, Ma—you didn't need to come in, she says. But her mother is moving again, still holding onto the cart, pulling it behind her.

And if they have those nice pecan buns, she says, as though she has not heard Elizabeth, and it's possible she hasn't, Those buns your father likes but from the other place . . . She pulls the cart after her and stops short at the wall of dairy, of soy and almond milk and tubs of flavored vegan cheese. She lifts a thin hand toward a row of cartons and hesitates and her skin itself is pale as milk, tissue-thin, translucent.

Here, Ma, Elizabeth says, reaching over her from behind, The two-percent?

Your father is worried sick about you, she says, and Elizabeth sees she is fighting back tears, there in the bright hum of the dairy display. You have no idea—*no idea*, Lizzie—he's beside himself. What's she doing, he keeps asking me, she's throwing her life away, she's going to end up alone, *with no one*, and what can I tell him? She's almost gasping, her narrow shoulders heaving in the overcoat that's too big, that's swallowing her mother whole.

Ma, come on, she says, It's late. Here—take the car keys, I'll get all this.

Lizzie, honey—her mother lays her hand over Elizabeth's on the cart and it is so cold and dry, You two are just alike, she says. You know that? Stubborn and impossible.

This is ridiculous, Elizabeth says. There's nothing to worry about—I'm happy this way, all right? Tell him not to worry—tell him I'm fine, and I'm happy. She yanks the cart backward and swivels it to face the front of the store, the parking lot and car where her father is sleeping, is dreaming.

Oh Lizzie, her mother says, *No one's* happy alone.

◉ ◉ ◉

After dinner Elizabeth measures decaffeinated coffee into the maker and sets out a bowl of oranges.

What about those pecan things? her father says, and her mother puts one on a saucer, tears off a paper towel to set beneath. She sits down across from him and takes one of the oranges, works at the navel with a crooked thumb.

Here, Ma, Elizabeth says, and her mother hands the fruit to her, grateful. She watches her father as she peels, his clumsy fingers, the soft dough pulled between them. The smells of orange and coffee fill the quiet kitchen.

Is that good, Dad? she says, and he nods.

Not as good as the ones from last week, he says. He presses a finger to the saucer to collect fallen shards of icing. They had a chocolate glaze. Your mother got them. He taps the bits of icing back onto the last bite of pastry before he eats it.

Okay then, Elizabeth says. She hands the peeled orange back to her mother, bends to kiss her. I should go, she says, today was a long one, and her mother clucks, smooths her hair.

You do so much, honey, she says. Carl, next week let's take Lizzie out for dinner, someplace nice—won't that be nice, for a change?

Her father wipes his hands and face with the paper towel, leans back in his chair and closes his eyes and says Whatever you want to do is fine with me, and Elizabeth sees how easy it is for him to say this, and mean it, because he was finished with wanting years ago, and because he is too exhausted to lie. Her mother pries an orange segment free and places it on his saucer and her fingers are chapped and stiff and his are rough and swollen at the knuckles. He must be so tired of so much forgiveness, Elizabeth thinks, of so much mercy.

◎ ◎ ◎

Elizabeth has no idea what happened to Sheila—where she went, to whom she ran—after she left. Her father might—if he did he would not have told her—but she doubts it. For some time she did not know whether she was terrified to see her or desperate to: out to dinner with her parents on a Saturday night after church and she'd scan the dining room, looking for Sheila's red hair and flashing earrings at every table, her heart racing and sick with desire and dread. But she was not there, she was never there, and eventually Elizabeth's heart calmed, and she realized she was no longer looking.

Because what was there to find? Sheila was kind. She worked for a commercial flooring company, drove to an office in a strip mall in a rusting Datsun hatchback. She smoked Virginia Slims and gave herself a manicure every Sunday night and ate rocky-road ice cream from a rainbow-striped bowl. She was generous to a stranger's daughter, a stranger's husband. She was all of these things, and more, and none of them mattered. She disappeared back into the world and there was nothing extraordinary about her.

Elizabeth steers the car off the highway and onto a surface street, slows down even though there is no traffic. It's nine o'clock on a Friday night—the people who are home are home already and the ones who are out are out for as long as hope will last. The houses are locked boxes, curtains drawn, shades down, windows wide blind eyes. She turns onto her street and the houses march themselves backwards past her moving car, square and still, their foyers and kitchenettes and master bedrooms dark. But when they were new those houses must have glowed with importance, with promise. Inside they would have smelled of White Shoulders and Old Spice, cigarette smoke and roasting meat, while nervous brides waited, manicured and powdered and cinched, for their husbands to come home, to mix the drinks and light the fire and flip the radio on; and their husbands slipped their shined shoes off at the door, hardly more than boys, hollow-cheeked and gangly, proud and spent and ready for the happiness they'd been promised to begin.

Elizabeth pulls into her shallow drive and kills the ignition. On the passenger seat is a bag filled with the pecan buns—You take them, her mother had said, I'll get the kind your father likes better tomorrow.

Make me disappear, David said to her that first white afternoon, Make me well. He had asked for nothing else.

Her mother's life fell away from her in ribbons and she wove it up again, imperfect and inviolable. Her hands are worn and graceless now but invincible. They will be the last to touch her husband before he dies.

Elizabeth turns the key in the lock and shoulders the front door open and the house is silent, filled with waiting dark, with ghosts that are not hers—those boys and their brides, with a war behind them and their lives before them. They drift through the rooms like snow, like love.

Ambivalence

On Wednesday mornings the father hoists someone else's daughter onto his naked lap
  bends someone else's daughter over the pressboard motel desk
  flips someone else's daughter onto her skinny back
  does not think about his own
  will not think about his own.
  His own is younger than this one
  but not by much
  not by enough.

His own is a junior at an all-girls prep school, an honor-roll student, a varsity field hockey player. He should be so proud. He should tell this one how proud.

This one likes banana daiquiris and smoking meth off of shiny foil squares and giving head. She has lavender-painted toenails and skin that tastes like watermelon candy, sticky lips and straight white teeth. When he looks at them he can think of nothing but what they feel like on his nipples.

He lifts her onto his lap and she hooks her legs around his waist, flips her crackling hair over her shoulders and sets to unbuttoning his shirt. With dexterity, with aplomb, with great industriousness.

Her name is Samantha and she likes to be called Sammy and he does not give a fuck. He feels somewhat aggrieved that he knows her name at all. She lowers her head to his chest. Those teeth. It's eleven in the morning.

Wednesday is made of the hours between ten-thirty and noon, or sometimes one, if he is lucky. Wednesday is furnished with two queen-size beds covered in rough blankets and sheets that smell of bleach. It is a comforting smell, the white nasal pinch of it. When he was a young man he worked in a commercial laundry and bleach to him still smells of possibility, of a vast and numbing freedom.

There are paintings of harbor scenes on Wednesday's walls, piers and skiffs, gulls screaming in this motel room one hour into Pennsylvania.

His belt buckle jingles. Samantha's busy hands are at it. They are soft, lotioned. Her nails are uniformly long and shiny and filed into perfect ovals.

His daughter's nails are chewed and ragged; her knuckles bruised and palms calloused. Samantha lowers her face and her giggling breath is hot, unbearable, and of course he would never tell this one *anything* about his daughter, his little girl, his pumpkin, of whom he should be, remember, so proud.

He finds he has a fistful of Samantha's hair, doll's hair, pale and plasticky. He finds he *has* no daughter on Wednesdays. He yanks and this one's head jerks back, her throat pulses.

No daughter, no five-bedroom house, no three-car garage. He stands, ridiculous, shirt open and pants sagging at his hips, shuffles to the closer bed with Samantha still clinging to him. Wednesday is too small to hold anything beyond this tired room. He drops her backwards onto the bedspread, his belly soft above her. It quivers with his breathing.

No tennis club membership, no Saturday tee time, and he lowers himself onto her. On the nightstand: a clock radio, a plastic stand with brochures for buggy rides and quilting demonstrations, her purse. No airport-lounge priority pass and no NFL season tickets. Her purse is canvas trimmed in narrow strips of leather; her shirt stretchy and thin, an oversaturated purple. The fabric looks spotlit. He shoves it toward her armpits and she squirms helpfully, works one shoulder out and then the other. Seagrass and sand dunes and lighthouses on the wall behind her and her clothes in a cheap rayon pile on the rug and somewhere outside the Wednesday door the Amish are plowing and scything and tilling, he thinks, aren't they, isn't that what they do, when they're not dealing methamphetamine to some other father's daughter?

One hour into Pennsylvania and this one is on her hands and knees with a boardwalk hanging over her head, what looks like a boardwalk, what could be a plank. If he backhanded her she would go flying off the bed like a doll, but it's only eleven-fifteen. Plus, those teeth.

◎ ◎ ◎

Herewith, a partial accounting of things the father doesn't know:

That his daughter's boyfriend is a preening dolt, Lacoste shirt and khakis and deck shoes notwithstanding. He gives her hickeys in spots her clothes cover and fingers her in movie theaters. The father, having never seen the hickeys nor been to the movies with him, likes the dolt a great deal.

The daughter doesn't. Sometimes she actively dislikes him, but he's got the manners and the car and the haircut. He goes to a Catholic boys' school across town and when he comes to pick her up on Friday nights he doesn't just pull into the driveway and honk, he rings the doorbell and shakes the father's hand while the daughter collects her purse. This gets her an extra half-hour on her curfew, which she wishes she didn't have to spend with him. He keeps a flask of Jack Daniel's in his glove box and wedges it between his legs when he drives. He sucks on it at stoplights, slouching low behind the steering wheel.

Even so, the boyfriend is not as stupid as it suits him to appear—the daughter knows this; she can tell by the sneaky glint in his eye when he says or does something particularly idiotic, which happens only when they are with other couples.

Juggling raw eggs blindfolded, for instance, or trying to steer a car with his feet.

When they're alone he is quieter, less foolish, nastier. More handsome, somehow, though she hates admitting this, even to herself. His eyes go hooded and snaky and when he looks like that her face heats up, and her belly, and she thinks maybe he isn't so bad, maybe she shouldn't be so hard on him even in the privacy of her own head, maybe her father sees something in him that she's missing.

He likes to shotgun beer. He likes lacrosse and breaking shit and paying the pizza delivery guy with hundred-dollar bills. He likes to slide his hand up under her blouse in the parking lot by the upper school playing field in the minutes between the red sun going down and the fluorescent lights coming on. He likes the way her breath hitches when his fingers find the nipple—she can tell by the way *his* breath hitches.

Her father doesn't know how much she likes *that*, or how much she likes to see the wet tip of the boyfriend's tongue caught between his teeth, or the way his warm hand trembles, just barely, on her skin. She likes how his eyes widen before he blinks them closed as though he can't bear to look at her and she likes to imagine what he sees when he does.

She's smart—her father knows that much—but sometimes smart is useless. She's too young to understand this yet. Her father has no such excuse.

◎ ◎ ◎

When they're finished Samantha climbs over the father's legs to get to the bathroom, where she urinates without closing the door. He can see most of her in the mirror, leaning over to examine a toenail while she sits on the toilet. Her hair brushes the floor.

Who *raised* her, he thinks, a prissy twist to his mouth, who didn't even bother to teach her to close the door?

Long legs splayed, lilac flash of toes on the tile, she hugs her knees, rests a cheek on her naked lap to smile at him.

I'm hungry, she says. Droplets hit water and she reaches for the toilet paper. Do you have time to maybe have lunch? I can shower quick.

Lunch, for God's sake, he thinks, and again his face contorts, enough that she notices, that he can see her notice: her sunny smile falters, the fastest cloud. There are truck stops along the highway and, farther down the two-lane roads, buffet restaurants with names like the Bird-in-Hand or the Plain 'n' Fancy, restaurants with wide parking lots and reserved areas for hitching horse-drawn wagons, restaurants that serve friendship soup and shoofly pie but no alcohol.

She stands and flushes the toilet, dampens one of the hand towels with hot water from the sink tap and presses it to her face and she is nothing but a body, solid and symmetrical and crowned with that pale spill, shrouded and silent and perfect.

There's a vending machine in the lobby, he says. He can't look away from the pinkish hands holding the white towel, the flushed belly and thighs. He pictures that body dressed again in the bright cheap clothes it walked in wearing. He imagines following it into the Dutch-Way Smorgasbord and sitting down with it at a table set with spindled wooden chairs and paper napkins.

Plastic tablecloths, plastic flowers. A small wooden triangle pegged with brightly colored golf tees meant to keep children busy. When she was three his daughter had a wooden box with basic shapes cut out of it, circles and triangles and X's, each piece small enough for her hands but too big to shove into her teething mouth.

Aren't all children here busy, aren't they kept so, from the time they're old enough to milk cows

bale hay

knead dough?

Too big to choke on.

Samantha rehangs the damp towel carefully on the rack. It's like checkers, the game with the triangle and the golf tees. Her cheeks are shiny, clean of makeup. He can't remember if she was wearing any when she arrived because he hadn't looked at her face.

Busy tilling fields shelling peas mending clothes?

He tries, these Wednesdays, not to look at her body after he's finished with it. He tries to tell himself: her flesh is nothing to him once he's no longer inside it.

Things his daughter put in her mouth: towels, shirtsleeves, keys on the ring. The edge of seat cushions on kitchen chairs, cork coasters. The end of his leather belt, of his backup plans and hedged bets.

His stomach rumbles. What would it be like, to follow that body into a place that smells of gravy and yeast rolls and sawdust?

Her mouth like an opening flower, a depthless pit. Her flesh the context for his, nothing more.

Then I'm going to push on, Samantha says. She steps into her underwear, a scrap of hot pink, the brightest thing in the room by far. How many Wednesdays has Pennsylvania swallowed?

Enough, too many, a few. Over the underwear, pants of some flimsy material made to look like denim. She works her way into them.

To sit at a table in a room that smells of coffee and leather and virtuous sweat across from that hair, those wet white teeth?

The sleeves of her shirt are too short; she tugs at the cuffs but they come only to midforearm.

Next Wednesday, she says, I'm taking my grandma out for her birthday. Her wrists are thin as skim milk. His hand is big enough to circle both of them, to squeeze till the birdy-bones grind. So I won't be able to make it, okay?

He could yank her arms clean out of the sockets without even trying; he could dislocate her shoulders.

Which raises the question: what could he do if he tried?

◎ ◎ ◎

The father pulls out of the motel lot onto the state road that will take him to the interstate that will take him to the beltway.

Following, a selection of places the beltway will not take him:

To the upscale retirement community where he installed his parents, believing they would partake of movie nights and Scrabble tournaments, day trips to casinos and outlet malls, but where instead his father had immediately fallen on the slippery indoor pool deck and his mother had flooded both their apartment and the one below when she left the kitchen faucet running overnight. Stitches, antibiotics, insurance claims and mold remediation.

To his daughter's school, all twenty-six grassy acres and $32,000 per year of it, every trimmed hedge and power-washed brick of it.

To the church where he was married, the office where he first practiced law, the bar with French movie posters and carriage lights where he'd ordered dry martinis with the partners in his firm and laughed at every one of their vulgar and tasteless jokes, where he wanted to drink himself blind and deaf so that he would not have to see or hear them, where he first began to understand how familiar he would become with the juniper chill of regret.

To the laundry and his body as it worked there, strong enough to move sixty wet pounds of fabric from one end of the steaming floor to the other and back, not stopping for hours on end, agile and steady in rubber-soled shoes.

To the hospital where his daughter was born prematurely, unexpectedly, and the apartment of the paralegal he'd been fucking while the infant was transferred, purplish and gourd-sized, to the NICU.

To the partially subsidized duplex where Samantha lives with her sister, her sister's boyfriend and the boyfriend's cousin and the cousin's—nephew? uncle? He has no idea because he stopped listening to Samantha's cheerful recitation of her housemates once he realized that she would not be upset if he failed to respond, that she did not in fact expect a response, that she was happy enough to talk to him in much the way she must have once talked to her dolls. He realized this on their first Wednesday. If he hadn't, there would not have been a second.

If, if, if.

If he had known his parents would be so indifferent to the activities listed on brightly laminated calendars in the hallways of their building he would not have bothered paying for such an overscheduled facility. If he had known his daughter's birth was imminent he would certainly not have been fucking the paralegal.

The beltway smells of hot asphalt, honeysuckle and wastewater and exhaust. It is congested and too sunny and it will also not take him to his wife, or if it would he has no idea how, because his wife's location is yet another thing he does not know.

If he did know, how would that knowledge change this day? Would he be more or less likely to speed, to tailgate, to change lanes without signaling? Or would it make no difference at all?

He knows that she is not at home, that she has not been home for three years. He knows that three years is enough time to disappear from whatever place a person has come to hate, or possibly only to no longer love enough. It is enough time for many other things to transpire concurrently.

It is enough time, for example, to find oneself at fifty giving motel change for candy bars to a girl who is *youngenoughtobehisdaughter* but who is nothing like his daughter, who might as well be a different species entirely from his daughter and his daughter's kind, who was made to be consumed without thought or guilt, and who is lucky that he is the one doing the consuming.

Sunlight bounces from chrome and mirrors and he is hot, he is hungry, he is going to be late for a meeting with the affordable-housing associates, most of whom are under thirty-five and optimistically committed to securing HUD financing and low-income tax credits for similarly idealistic corporate clients, and none of whom yet understand that contradiction in terms.

It is enough time to recognize how few decisions make a mattering difference, to consider that Samantha's dolls most likely had hair the same color as hers, to realize that he has no idea what his own daughter's dolls looked like.

He has found himself at fifty marveling at how his wife has managed to remain so perversely *present*—she is in the slight cleft of his daughter's chin and the length of her slender ring fingers, the unconscious throat-clearing when she is nervous or impatient. She is in the way his daughter lately has of closing herself off to his attempts at what he hopes is appropriate fatherly intimacy, of dismissing his lukewarm overtures with an offhand amusement. She is in her absolute self-possession and her uncanny ability to inhabit an unreachable galaxy when they are in the same room. This is neither insulting nor hurtful to him. It is absolution.

What do fathers *do*, with the daughters who belong to them? It is the arterial pulse of his life, it seems to him, sitting in traffic on this bright Wednesday, how little he knows, but if if if he did.

◎ ◎ ◎

The daughter is spending her lunch period smoking weed in her new best friend's Prius. The new best friend's name is Rachel, and she has greenish hair and a pierced septum and a plush ass the daughter would kill for. She has a perfect GPA and a bubblegum smile and she finds organized sports and the daughter's boyfriend ridiculous in equal measure.

The daughter tells herself that Rachel doesn't think *she's* ridiculous, and sometimes she even believes it.

The father doesn't know there's a new best friend, or that the old one has been demoted. The old one didn't know she had been demoted until she overheard a senior dishing eleventh-grade gossip in the bathroom.

The daughter pinches the joint out carefully and tucks it back into the repurposed sea-salt container on the dash. She checks her watch and Rachel rolls her pretty eyes at this, which are watery and bloodshot and more vividly green than her hair.

Don't start, the daughter says.

Slave to the dick, Rachel says, and the daughter laughs, although it is not funny, although it is true. It's not funny *because* it's true. She doesn't want to keep him waiting.

A bunch of people were thinking about going to Chase's after the game on Friday, she says. His parents are out of town but his sister's home for break so she'll buy.

Rachel shrugs, slides the salt tin into her backpack and frees a hairbrush and a bottle of perfume. I have a Habitat meeting at seven, she says. She sprays the bristles and runs the brush through her hair. Maybe after, if it doesn't run too late.

Cool, the daughter says. She digs through her own pack for her makeup bag. Can I tell my dad I'm spending the night at your place?

Tell him whatever you want. As long as he doesn't call my mom to check.

The daughter flips down the visor and angles the mirror, dabs on lip gloss that the boyfriend will immediately tell her to wipe off. She checks her watch again, surreptitious this time. She has study hall after this, fifty minutes where she could be in any library on campus. Honor system for honor students: the school prides itself on its liberality. It'll only take her ten of those fifty to walk down the delivery road behind the cafeteria to the back entrance of campus, where he'll be waiting. The interior of his Volvo smells like old beer and dollar-store air freshener and sometimes, now, her. Her father approves of the safety rating.

He won't even ask for a phone number, she says.

◎ ◎ ◎

His daughter's kind is expensive. Dermatologists, sports therapists, tutors. Manicurists and psychologists. Coaches for field hockey and standardized test prep, for public speaking and college interviews. Four hundred dollars and four hours in a hair-salon chair and when she's finished he can't even tell what's been done.

His own office chair is deep, soft leather, silent casters and shining chrome. It's after one o'clock and he's eaten nothing and the ozone smell of commercial-grade odor neutralizer is still in his nostrils. He considers the briefs on his desk and the inbox filled with emails he has to force himself to read. He considers the fact that, if asked under oath, he would have to say it: he would rather be with an undereducated tweaker who likes sucking cock than his own daughter.

Of course he would. Any man would, and any man who'd claim otherwise would be torn apart on the stand.

◎ ◎ ◎

The truth is that could have looked harder for his wife. He knows this, on some level, on the level he keeps sealed, drum-tight, barely lit. The level he prefers not to visit.

He had the resources and the money and the connections, and the further truth is that if he'd wanted to he could have had her dragged back from whatever inadequate hiding place she'd tucked herself into, she'd imagined would be sufficient.

What he did, instead: made a few phone calls—to her sister in New York, her friend from college she spent one weekend a year with, her personal trainer—and accepted whatever bullshit story they told him. Calmly, resignedly. Chastened. I'm so sorry to have bothered you, he'd said, can you think of anywhere she might be? Would you call me if you hear from her? I can't thank you enough. Sorry. So sorry.

His voice drifting into the dark while he sat with the cordless on the back deck of the house, his daughter's bedroom window glowing above him, a tumbler of single malt on the weather-sealed picnic table. A June night, honeysuckle and cut grass, the gold wink of fireflies in the soft sky and a bass line thumping from his daughter's open window, her sobs beneath it. Warm enough to switch out the Scotch for gin.

So that he could say he'd done it, so that he could say he'd tried.

Even three years on, he thinks, he could find her, could haul her resisting or not from her brother-in-law's place upstate or an ashram or a convent or an apartment complex in Albuquerque made of Flexicore and vinyl cladding. Or the mixed-use development right behind his office, for all he knows.

But instead he will leave her untouched in the sheets folded at the back of the closet shelf, the serrated blade in the kitchen drawer, the sleeping pills in the medicine cabinet. It is the one remaining kindness he has left to show her.

◎ ◎ ◎

Friday afternoon and the daughter is working her phone at the kitchen counter, legs crossed and one shoe dangling from a toe. Brown moc, white sock, a leg that needs shaving. Both legs actually, armpits too. He doesn't want to notice but how can he help it, especially when she comes home in the hockey uniform she couldn't be bothered to change out of, no longer sweaty but still flushed in the cheeks and at the base of her throat? She has her mother's testy skin.

As she gets older he finds it increasingly difficult to look at her.

Except the truth is that he's never found it easy to look at her. She was too fragile as an infant and too noisy as a toddler and too easy to ignore in grade school, always huddled over notebooks or textbooks or a stack of creased and wrinkled paperbacks from the public library.

He tells her he loves her every morning before she leaves for school and every night before she goes to bed. He does not think of her in the intervening hours, and he is grateful to her for this.

Do you mind if I spend the night at Rachel's? she says, not looking up from her phone. Her hair at the roots is slightly matted, still damp from practice. Her cleats are in a pile on the floor. He has no idea who won.

That's fine, he says, and pours another gin and tonic. Will Rachel's parents be home? The name means nothing to him.

His daughter nods, drops her phone on the counter with the air of a frustrated CEO. She huffs a breath out and loose strands of hair flutter at her forehead.

Her mom, yeah. It's for a school thing. I'll be back probably early tomorrow morning. She slides off the stool and yawns, stretches; stubbled armpits and bruised thighs and a scrape below one dirty knee.

The teachers at parent-teacher night last Thursday told him how motivated his daughter is and the mothers told him how well-rounded she is and the other fathers told him how ruthless on the field she is and he nodded and smiled and thought of what he had done to someone else's daughter the day before during Urbanization and Progressivism or Concepts of the Utopian Movement or General Chemistry or whatever useless subject was on the docket for juniors in the eleven o'clock hour.

Showering, then heading out, his own says, brushing past him up the carpeted stairs. She carries the smell of her tribe: sweat and wintergreen salve, orange wedges, Gatorade, wood-fire smoke above the bleachers. He can picture the sidelines, open duffels under benches, shin guards and mouth guards and damp piled towels, younger students cheering. In the lowering dark boys in khakis watch girls in ponytails running the length of whatever field, legs pumping, hair flying, clots of dirt and grass the only sacrifice. Sweat cooling on necks. Offsides, obstruction, the referee's whistle. He doesn't have to be there to know those girls are running faster than they'll ever have to run again, if they're lucky. And his daughter's kind is nothing if not lucky.

◎ ◎ ◎

Samantha twists her hair up and secures it in a stretchy flounce of elastic. She turns the shower on and lines up the stingy plastic bottles—shampoo, lotion—on the lip of the tub. She empties the shampoo onto the washcloth and scours until her skin is blotched red. When she towels off she hums. She squeezes the lotion into a damp palm and slathers, slopping viscous white onto the floor. She blots it with the bath mat.

I don't think it smells bad at all, she says, as though he's asked her. He asks her so little. Wednesdays are too short for questions.

He watches her from the bed. Of course she's *youngenoughtobehisdaughter*. That's the fucking point. The hard mattress is the point, and the thin white sheets and thin white walls, the harness-jangle and hoof-clop and dust outside the motel windows. Her clean skin is the point and her body when he is inside it.

Her body when he is not inside it is irrelevant.

Also irrelevant: whether she understands how unnecessary she is, or how quickly the damage accrues.

◉ ◉ ◉

Check this out, the boyfriend says, and angles his phone so the daughter can see. It's a video of a living room filled with naked women licking and grinding on each other while men pour beer on them and cheer. She can see pimples and razor burn on the men's necks, sweaty layers of slap and spackle the women have covered their faces with. Beer foams over expensive-looking upholstered chairs and a coffee table—this is disgusting, and it's happening in someone's *house*, the daughter thinks. Who has to clean this *up*?

She pushes his hand with the phone away and straightens her skirt. I need to get back, she says. They're in the front seat of his car, parked in the overflow lot behind the auxiliary gym. If I'm late for lab I'm toast.

The boyfriend slides the phone into his pocket and draws back, looks her long in the face and here in his car under the cold red leaves and flicker of sun there is nothing foolish about him; nothing *dismissible*, and she forgets the stupid video because he's moving in to kiss her, because the tip of his tongue is so salty, because smart only matters so much.

What matters more is everything she doesn't know: that he doesn't kiss the women he orders from a website, or let them into his car without spreading the faded beach towel he keeps in the trunk over the seat. She doesn't know that he keeps that towel for exactly that reason. She doesn't know that sometimes, when he's finished with them, he pulls off onto a side street and shoves them out onto the shoulder, or that he laughs when he crumples twenty-dollar bills to stuff into their cheap spike-heeled booties before throwing the shoes out after them.

◎ ◎ ◎

Outside, the motel parking lot is cracked and dry, the striping faded, barely white. The sides of the road are strewn with beer cans and plastic soda bottles, candy wrappers and oil-stained rags.

The father is waiting for Samantha. He's sitting at the flimsy desk, his briefcase propped against the wall by the door. He won't leave anything in the car.

She hadn't understood that. These people around here wouldn't *steal*, she'd said, earnest, wide-eyed—they're *religious*.

Fast-food bags and shoes worn through. A bleach bottle by the entrance to the parking lot. He'd laughed at her when she said that.

Her car pulls in, a bit of rust on the side panels and a dented rear bumper, a plastic lei hanging from the rearview, long enough to obstruct visibility. If he cared just a little bit more than he does he would tell her to be careful—of cops, for starters. Of her dealer, of whoever cooks the shit she knows better than to smoke in front of him.

She parks in the last row. In the cornfield the husks are dry, crushed down and broken.

He doesn't know that just as he opened this Wednesday door his daughter was running from a Volvo where she let a feckless twat hike her skirt above her waist and do things that girls like her are not supposed to want but do

but do

but do.

If he knew he would care, but only a little. His daughter is smart, his daughter is careful, his daughter is close to gone herself.

Just not close enough.

Plastic straws and paper bags, horseshoes and hypodermics, the cold wind visible in a ground-spin of dust. Samantha picks her way across the asphalt in what looks, from where he sits, like a flimsy pair of bright pink sandals, and his heart, mutinous, clenches. Her feet are small and bare in them and he closes his eyes and they disappear. He can just hear the clatter and pock of blown gravel against the window, and he thinks, listening to it, that he should tell her to be careful of people like him. She's someone's daughter, after all.

Acknowledgments

These stories were written in a second-floor room overlooking a magnolia tree in Nashville and a fourth-floor room overlooking power lines and an alley lined with garages in Baltimore. They were written in hotel rooms in Paris and Las Vegas and Amsterdam, and on Southwest flights to and from St. Louis. They were written in what was, I think now, an unusual lack of ambient professional noise: at no time during this period was I affiliated with any academic institution as either a student or an instructor; I didn't have an agent or publishing house or editor, and I didn't participate in any workshops or attend any residencies. No one saw drafts of these stories before they went out into the world. This admission is meant as neither a boast nor an excuse, but an explanation: if these acknowledgments seem wanting or insufficient or otherwise ungracious, it's not because I'm thankless. It's because I somehow settled on a way of working that was solitary in the extreme. This wasn't deliberate. It was circumstance turned habit turned requisite.

My profound thanks to the editors of the magazines and journals in which versions of the following stories originally appeared:

"You Are Here" and "The Anniversary Trip" in *The Gettysburg Review*, "Ambivalence" in *The Idaho Review*, "Accident, Design" in *Egress*,

"Like We Did" and "As Though I Have A Right To" in *Agni*, "A Little Mercy" in *The Sycamore Review*, "Dinosaurs" in *Michigan Quarterly Review*, "Undertow" in *The Massachusetts Review*, "Other People's Children" in *Alaska Quarterly Review*, "So Happy" in *Hayden's Ferry Review*,

"A Good Woman" in *The Idaho Review*, "Whatever Happens" in *The Missouri Review*, "Better" in *The Cincinnati Review*, "Everything is Fine" in *The Antioch Review*. Sincere thanks also to Heidi Pitlor of *The Best American Short Stories* and Bill Henderson of the Pushcart Prize for reprinting "The Anniversary Trip" and "Ambivalence," respectively.

And finally, immeasurably, endlessly—thanks to S., who first told me to lay off the adverbs in 1996. I forgave his pesky opinionating then, he's forgiven my Calabrese stubbornness many times since, and here we are.